To _____

Love always,
Kate !
xo

A HARSH
AND
PRIVATE
BEAUTY

A NOVEL

KATE KELLY

Inanna Poetry & Fiction Series

INANNA PUBLICATIONS & EDUCATION INC.
TORONTO, CANADA

Canada Council for the Arts Conseil des Arts du Canada

We gratefully acknowledge the support of the Canada Council for the Arts and the Ontario Arts Council for our publishing program. We also acknowledge the financial support of the Government of Canada.

Cover design: Val Fullard

A Harsh and Private Beauty is a work of fiction. All the characters portrayed in this book are fictitious and any resemblance to persons living or dead, is purely coincidental.

Library and Archives Canada Cataloguing in Publication

Title: A harsh and private beauty : a novel / Kate Kelly.
Names: Kelly, Kate, 1960– author.
Series: Inanna poetry & fiction series.
Description: Series statement: Inanna poetry & fiction series
Identifiers: Canadiana (print) 20190197609 | Canadiana (ebook) 20190197617 | ISBN 9781771336611 (softcover) | ISBN 9781771336628 (epub) | ISBN 9781771336635 (Kindle) | ISBN 9781771336642 (pdf)
Classification: LCC PS8621.E5595 H37 2019 | DDC C813/.6—dc23

Printed and bound in Canada

 MIX
Paper from responsible sources
FSC
www.fsc.org FSC® C004071

Inanna Publications and Education Inc.
210 Founders College, York University
4700 Keele Street, Toronto, Ontario, Canada M3J 1P3
Telephone: (416) 736-5356 Fax: (416) 736-5765
Email: inanna.publications@inanna.ca Website: www.inanna.ca

For Fay Galloway Campbell,
who saw me before I saw myself

And he rewrote the piece, pasted it up with bold fingers, went out and got drunk. To quell the pain of the irksome canker sores. How could they know he swallowed glassful after glassful to comprehend a harsh and private beauty.

—E. Annie Proulx, *The Shipping News*

1.

EVERYTHING BEGINS IN LARCENY AND CHAOS, and then history legitimizes it all. Funny how Leland's words come to me like this after all these years, after all these lives I've seemed to live. It all begins in larceny and chaos, and we invent the rest as we invent ourselves, as the world was invented, as the country was invented. Civilization and manners—these are nothing but the shining veneer that covers our darkest beginnings. Leland, you were right. In your joking way you always saw the truth, clearer than any philosopher, laughing over subjects, but always landing heavily on the mark. I miss that the most. I miss you the most. Would you recognize me now, Leland? Your Ruby Grace, actress and night-club singer, aware of entrances and performances, unpredictable and unconventional, is now old and frail and very civilized. My larceny and chaos is far behind me, buried beneath years of good manners. But you knew me. Just like the truths you were always uncovering, you grew to understand and to know me—insomuch as it is possible to know another person. Sometimes I think that we can't even know ourselves; we can only know of ourselves. It was through you that I found myself. You made me laugh, Leland, at myself, at the world, at the larceny that was my heritage, buried as it was under layers of upper-middle-class morality. I am my father's daughter. Daniel Kenny is very much part of who I am. Was that what you saw in me? Was that who you saw in me, your Ruby Grace? Oh Leland,

I miss you, sitting here waiting for death, living every day a little less in the present. I can feel it slipping away. It's hard on the children, but I can't help it. I don't know when looking back became more interesting than looking forward. It wasn't when you died—God knows I was too young to pack it all in, as they say—although your absence was like a stone in my chest that never lifted, even with Jack and our years together. Was it when Jack died that I began to find comfort in the past? I began to retreat into it, like a favourite blanket pulled out from the drawers of memory and laid across my mind for warmth. Comfortable old blankets, softened with age, taken out to be shaken and refolded one after another, a reassurance of a life lived. Maxwell said that the storyteller tries to make life acceptable, but that in talking about the past we lie with every breath we draw. Oh well, you see, Leland: we begin in larceny and end in larceny, stealing and debauching the truth, bending belief to our own ends. You would like that, my love, the joke in the end, our histories retold in lies.

"MOM. MOM." His voice is gentle but insistent, pushing into his mother's reverie. "Mom?" It's a question now. She is vaguely aware of a presence, but the subtle moving shadows undulating across the table are engrossing. Ruby Grace follows the shifting light, her thoughts as fluid as the movement. "Ruby." He tries again. Ah, recognition—her eyes refocus and she finds herself seated in a room she does not quickly recognize, in a time she cannot place. Snapping back to the vividness of the light, she is reluctant to let go of her reverie. "Mom. Mom, it's me, Gary, your son." Unable to hide his concern, his voice rises on the last word.

She smiles to reassure her son as well as herself—the self she had been watching as it slipped by on the smooth reflection of the table—and adjusts herself slightly in the chair. She is hoping to appear perceptive and coherent, but the effort itself leaves her feeling somehow empty. "I know it's you, Gary. Don't worry,

I'm here." She nods and clears her throat, watching the light playing across the table. "I know you are." Laughing with relief, he moves to her across a distance that spans a lifetime. "Did you remember about today, Mom?"

"Remember about today." She repeats, not quite a question. She looks down at her hands in her lap holding her cane. They are old hands, she thinks. *Can they be mine?* "We are going somewhere today." She answers, not quite a question.

"Yes, Mom. A dedication. Your picture at Centennial Place. It's been painted by Jason Murray and they're unveiling it today. It will hang in the theatre for years to come. Remember, we spoke about this during the week and again last night?" Gary is patient, a learning experience. "The Centennial Theatre."

She smiles, nodding. "Yes, the theatre. I've always loved the theatre! There is always something wonderful about the ability to suspend reality. Don't you think, Gary?"

"Yeah, I think suspending reality is always a good thing to be able to do." Smiling, Gary continues. "We are headed to the theatre now, Mom, because the unveiling is today."

"Unveiling? My God, it sounds like a Middle Eastern wedding. The unveiling. It's just a painting of me, an old woman. Ha! I don't know why we need all the pomp and circumstance." She shakes her head, enjoying the indignant sound of her own voice.

"They want to honour you, Mom, and all the years you gave to the theatre. You were the biggest star who ever performed there, and they're proud of that and of you." Moving toward her, he continues. "Come on. We don't want to be late." He extends his hand. He is strong and competent, solid, this son who stands before her, past his youth, age moving in and taking up residence around his eyes, making its presence known.

"Do you think they are going to present me with flowers at this 'unveiling,' Gary? Because if they do, I hope you told them about my aversion to roses. Just can't abide the smell of those flowers." She shakes her head for emphasis. "It just makes me plain gag. Ha!"

"Yes, Mom, I think I may have mentioned the fact that you suffer from a unique aversion to the common rose." Gary smiles indulgently, his brown eyes alive with humour as he looks at Ruby.

"Well, I don't know about it being unique." She fires back. "Maybe it is, although I have never minded being different. In fact, you could say I have a strong aversion to conformity as well." She nods, looking at her son, her gaze level. "I like to think outside the box."

"Mom, you are so outside the box you wouldn't recognize one if you saw one!" Gary laughs.

"No, Gary, that's not true. I know what the box looks like. I even know what it feels like. But the next box I'll ever be in will be my coffin! Ha!" She bangs her hand on the table for emphasis.

"Mom!"

Ruby holds up her hand, warding off his objection. "I know, I know. Don't worry, son, it's only black humour." She takes his hand again. "Well, if you're finished with all this chit chat, we should get a move on. We don't want to be late. Although, I imagine they'll hold the 'unveiling' for me. I'm an old woman—I move slowly." Pulling on her son's hand, she eases herself up from the chair. "I'll never live to be as old as I feel, Gary."

"Mom, you've been saying that for the past twenty years."

"Well, it's true. Just wait for the day you wake up and your body doesn't feel like your own! Then you'll know what I'm talking about."

"Actually old lady, I think I do."

She looks at her son, at the handsome structure of his face softened now with the years. "You look like your father, Gary. You look like him and you sound like him. You're a good boy, a good son. You always have been, but I don't think I've ever really told you that, have I?"

Gary, taken aback by Ruby's sudden intensity, smiles awkwardly. When he speaks, his voice contains a forced joviality.

"Well, thanks. It's nice to know I'm appreciated."

"Yes, yes, you are, appreciated that is, and it's important for you to know that. Life is just too busy sometimes, and we forget to tell our children the things they need to hear. Important things. I'll have to have a good talk with Phoebe and Francis. I wish your brothers and sisters didn't live so far away, but at least you're here." She pats his hand and looks up into his eyes, taking in his features, his hair, slowly receding to reveal his broad forehead. "We repeat ourselves in our children don't we, son?"

"Yes, we do," Gary answers, looking at his mother, this woman who has always been an enigma to him, so familiar and yet so unknown.

"Speaking of children, is Lisa with you? And where is Bernadette?" Ruby asks sharply, looking around. Her abruptness changing the mood of a moment ago.

"Berny couldn't get away from the school. Department meetings and Principal meetings—you name it and she's got to be there."

"That's right, Bernadette is the new principal. Good for her! I like to see a woman in charge. Ha! In my day there were no women principals, only men. Bernadette deserves it; she's worked hard all these years.

"Yes, she has." Gary smiles as he thinks about his wife last September, setting off for her first day of school as the new principal. She hadn't slept a wink the night before, and in the morning as she stood before the hall mirror scrutinizing herself one last time, Gary could see the little girl she must have been on her first day of Kindergarten. "Don't worry, honey, you look great. You're going to make the most wonderful principal. You've worked so hard for this, and no one deserves it more than you." Standing behind her and watching her worried expression turn to an impish smile, he wrapped his arms around her and, leaning forward, placed his head next to hers. "If I was a teenage boy again, I'd get into trouble just to sit in your office."

"Well that's because it's been so long since you were a teenage boy—you don't know what you're talking about." Bernadette laughed, breaking out of his embrace. "But if you keep this up I'll be late for work and then you will be in trouble."

"I can only hope." Gary smiled wickedly.

"Well, I'm glad to see that you're feeling like your old self." Laying her palm against Gary's unshaven face, she asks, "What time is your MRI today?"

Rousing himself from the memory, Gary continues, aware that his mother is watching and waiting.

"Berny will meet us later today at the reception, but Lisa's with me. We also picked up Jacklyn on the way—she didn't want to miss today. Even though Phoebe won't be there, her daughter will. So, both of your granddaughters are waiting in the car. Lisa pulled up in front of the doors so I could just pop in and grab you."

"Well, if you were hoping to make a quick getaway, you should know that at my age, nothing moves quickly."

"Yes, I can see that." Holding up a black-and-gold handbag, he asks, "Did you want to take your purse?"

"Oh, yes. I'll need that. I had to learn to use a purse when I was young and now, I'm paralyzed without it. I don't even know what the hell I have in it anymore. Check and see that I have some money in my wallet will you, Gary? I'll want to give the girls some money."

"Mom, you don't have to do that. Lisa and Jacklyn are both working, and they have their own money."

"Just check, Gary. I don't need your permission to do what I want with my money." Under her breath she adds, "I always give my grandchildren money—that's what I do."

Gary looks through the wallet, shaking his head. "All right, all right. Yes, you have wads of money in your wallet."

"Good. That's just the way I like it."

"Can we go now, Mom?" He hands her the purse and guides her toward the door.

"Yes, of course. I don't know why we're standing here talking like this while my public awaits."

Shaking his head and smiling again, Gary moves his mother through the opulent lobby, past the front desk, and outside to the waiting car.

"Have fun, Mrs. Grace!" The nurse at the desk calls after them, her smile warm and genuine.

"Thank you, lovey," Ruby calls over her shoulder and then says to Gary, "I wonder what she considers fun at my age, what do you think?"

"I don't know—getting out and socializing?"

"Oh, I've done enough socializing to last me a lifetime. I just hope they'll have some sort of spirits there. I could do with a good drink—it always makes these things go better. What's that saying, 'candy's dandy but liquor is quicker'? Ha!" Ruby laughs, a dry and deep rumble.

"That's the saying all right. Alcohol is a social lubricant, there's no doubt about that."

Raising his hand to the waiting car as they exit the front doors, Gary continues. "I'll see what I can do for you—I'm sure there will be some quicker liquor there." He opens the car door and helps her in, taking her cane for a moment before handing it back to her.

"Hi, Nan. Everything all right back there?" Lisa asks, pushing her dark hair over her shoulder as she turns to look at Ruby from the driver's seat.

"Couldn't be better, honey." Leaning forward, she touches Lisa's shoulder. "Your dad was just reminding me of the occasion, but I hadn't forgotten."

"Hi, Nan." Jacklyn smiles and reaches over to help her grandmother settle herself in the seat, the scent of Ruby's perfume evoking a lifetime of memories.

"Hello, honey." Taking Jacklyn's hand, Ruby asks, "How are the boys? I haven't seen them in a while, have I?"

"No, Nan, it's been a little while since you've seen them.

They're getting big. Jeremy starts junior kindergarten this September and Alex will be in grade one."

"Where does the time go, I wonder? It feels like it was only yesterday that Phoebe was starting school, holding on to Francis for dear life as I watched them from the porch. Gary was just a baby on my hip, biting his fist to help cut his teeth, ha!" Ruby looks at her son and sighs before continuing. "Well, it's nice to have my two darling girls with me today for this 'unveiling.' You see, Gary, I haven't forgotten." Ruby raises her voice and her eyebrows at her son.

"Well, good. I'm glad to hear that." Gary buckles up and looks at Lisa. "Okay, let's go. Did you buckle up, Mom?"

"Yes, Gary, I did," Ruby answers as she pulls the shoulder strap down and toward the buckle. "Well, I'm trying. These darn things can be difficult."

"Here, I'll…" Jacklyn begins, leaning toward Ruby.

"No. No, I got it." Ruby snaps the buckle into place with a sigh and a shake of her head, grey curls dancing in the sunlight. "Praise the Lord for small miracles." She pulls at the strap across her shoulder, readjusting it. "I didn't hear from your mother, Jacklyn." Turning to her son, she asks, "Will your sister be there, Gary?"

Gary, catching Lisa's eye, turns to Ruby. When he answers, his voice is noncommittal. "No, Mom, Phoebe couldn't make it, remember? She's in Chicago right now at a convention. Remember, she lives in Vancouver and it's always difficult for her to get back to Ontario, but she couldn't have made it anyway." There is an extended silence; Gary and the girls wait expectantly.

"Didn't Mom call you, Nan? She told me she spoke to you about it." Jacklyn's voice, edged with concern, breaks the silence.

"Yes, yes, she told me. That's right—I remember now. She's in Chicago." Looking out the window, Ruby continues. "I was born there, you know."

"Yes, Mom, I do," Gary answers patiently.

"Not that I can remember it," Ruby continues, as if Gary had not spoken. "Your granddad was from Chicago. Yes, that's right—Daniel Kenny, first born American citizen of Irish stock! Ha! Met and married my mother, Jeanie, in Montreal and took her back to the States to live. Then suddenly, in '24, they returned with me to Montreal."

Ruby's words are measured and metered; this is a story she knows by rote.

"Why did they return, Nan?" This part of the story has always fascinated Lisa.

Ruby shakes her head. "I'm not sure, lovey." Falling silent, she retreats into her seat, her thoughts spinning around old familiar questions, family mysteries, impressions that are always just beyond her grasp. Gazing out the window at a landscape she really can't place, she leans forward to watch the sky, white vaporous clouds against a blue vastness. The same light that played across her tabletop now moves across her shoulder and upturned face, its beauty catching her breath, her thoughts. She would like to drift away, to lose herself to her thoughts, to Leland and her memories. They are growing more vivid each day while everything around her recedes as though of its own accord. But Lisa is talking to her now. Ruby recognizes the question in the tone of her voice. She is being pulled back into her body. Begrudgingly, she thinks, *not yet, not when I'm on the cusp of a memory, more than a memory, something visceral, a touching, my name being spoken. Not Jack, no.* "Leland?"

"No, Mom. It's me, Gary. And Jacklyn and Lisa."

"Gary? Oh, I thought you were someone else."

Lisa looks furtively at her father and then back to the traffic. "Do you remember where we're going, Nan?"

"Do I remember where we're going?" Ruby takes stock of things—something she is used to doing these days. It will come to her, and if it doesn't, someone will tell her, or not. It seems not to matter. "Where we're going..."

"Mom..."

Holding her hand up to silence him, she asks, "What is the date today?"

"May third. Mom..."

"May third." Ruby smiles. Not allowing Gary to finish his thought, she says, "It's my mother's birthday."

There is silence in the car. Gary and the girls are fearful—Jacklyn for her grandmother, Lisa for her father, and Gary for his mother. She has always been in control, quick witted and present. These episodes—a stupid word to explain the slipping away of a mind—leave him feeling frightened and helpless. Ruby is silent, as she works to bring her thoughts into the present, struggling like a fish on the end of a line, then, with an effort, splashing into the vividness of the moment.

"What's the date, Gary?"

"May third, Mom."

"May third? It's my mother's birthday."

"That's right, Nan." Lisa nods, watching Ruby in the rear-view mirror. Reaching for her father's hand, she squeezes it, trying to impart what little confidence and comfort she can.

"We're going to the 'unveiling' at Centennial Theatre, I believe."

"That's right, Mom!"

"Ha! Don't sound so relieved, Gary. It's irritating." Ruby shrugs her shoulders and winks over at Jacklyn.

The girl's laughter fills the car. Smiling, Gary looks around at his mother, who is sitting small and defiant in the back seat. "Sorry. I'm just relieved that we're on our way and not running behind."

"Or that your behind's not running! Ha!"

Lisa, laughing, catches a glimpse of her grandmother's impish face in the rear-view mirror. Ruby's eyes are still so blue and engaging at eighty-nine that she wonders what they were like when Ruby was young, when her face was unmarked by the years, when her mouth was full and smooth and her body lithe and agile. She had been beautiful. When Lisa looks in the mirror, she often finds herself trying to catch a flash of Ruby Grace in her own reflection. Lisa watches her grandmother looking out the window. She recognizes in the expression and the slight tilt of her head that Ruby is gone from the present moment, pulled into a past that seems to call to her more and more....

"RUBY? RUBY GRACE?" Reacting to the sound of her name, Ruby turns from the small group of friends and acquaintances who frequent the Golden Cockerel nightclub in Toronto. Singing here for the last four months has given Ruby a freedom she thought she had lost forever. She has finally found an outlet for her artistic energies. She realizes that she is happy for the first time in a long while.

"Ruby?"

She doesn't recognize him. His face is a little too broad to be classically handsome, but his dark eyes capture her attention. He extends his hand, and she automatically takes it in a handshake.

"You were wonderful tonight." He says, leaning forward to be heard.

"Thank you...?" There is a question in her voice.

"Oh, sorry, I'm Leland James. I've heard you before, but tonight when you sang, "I'll Be Seeing You," I decided I wanted to meet you. So I could thank you in person." They are still holding hands. He watches her eyes, dark irises exploding like universes into the blue liquid surrounding them. She extracts her hand, awkwardly but reluctantly.

"Well, you're welcome, Leland James." Not quite sure what else to say, she looks around to break the connection. The night club is busy; the small tables are crammed with drinks, ashtrays, and laughter, the excitement of life buzzing through the thick blue smoke that circles up like morning mist, smudging all lines. Turning back to Leland, Ruby searches for something to say. Finally, she asks, "Are you here by yourself?"

"No. I brought along some friends. Well, business associates really." His mouth is close to her ear, his breath warm and sweet with liquor. "We were working late and needed a diversion so I suggested The Cockerel and luckily you were here."

"Well, I'm glad to be a diversion." Ruby smiles, nodding. Then, almost as an afterthought, she adds, "That's what music should be, an escape from the pressures of life." A moment passes. They stand in awkward silence until Sarah Vaughan's voice floats around them, distinct and lyrical, a recording Ruby recognizes. Tilting her head slightly, drawn to the sound that pulls at her soul, listening with her whole body, she is lost. *"I don't know why/ but I'm feeling so sad/ I long to try something/ I've never had."*

"Sarah Vaughan." Leland nods, captivated by the music as well as the woman before him. "'Lover Man,'" he says slowly and evenly, "one of my favourite songs. You sound a little like her, you know. I think it's those low notes, the way she hits them, very sweet, very compelling." He watches her, his dark eyes bright with mischief and invitation.

"I'll take that as a great compliment. I love the sound of her voice—deep and sad and yet so full of beauty at the same time—but I don't think I'm quite that sultry." Ruby's mind floods with thoughts of her father: his love for the blues and his passion for jazz. Music had been such a part of him that she can't think of one without the other. "Blues is about the heart, Ruby, and jazz is about the head. But they are both the sound of the soul."

Listening, she aches with the memories that are evoked by every nuance of the music; every note holds something of him. Closing her eyes, she sighs, lost in the feeling of the music. The memory of her father swims closer to the surface of her mind. Floating up to her, he is as tangible as the smoke in the room. Only music can do this, she thinks, transport one back in time and place, to memories and emotions. She can hear her father regaling her with stories about jazz clubs and speakeasies, and the sounds of Billie Holiday, Jelly Roll Morton, Louis Armstrong, and Bessie Smith filling her childhood home. The sound of the music, of blues and jazz—the crazy, moody, heart-wrenching beauty, developing out of everything and nothing, out of the physical and the intellectual, out of passion and pain—always brings her back.

"Just listen to that, Ruby." She is five years old and listening to the gramophone with her father. Rather, he is listening while she is whirling around to the music. It is a recording of "The Mojo Boogie" by J.B. Lenior, whose voice is full of fearlessness and hope, always hope. "This is the sound of every man's soul, Ruby. It's the music of a people, the uneven, gritty flavour of the world." Her father laughed. "Isn't it great!"

"You have a beautiful smile, Ruby Grace." Leland's voice so close, his breath on her hair, brings her back to the night club and the simmering excitement in the room.

"Thank you." She pushes her hair from her face, unsure what else to say.

"You're welcome," Leland answers, his intensity drawing her in with a curious force.

They are silent for a moment as Ruby returns his gaze. Then, "It was a pleasure to meet you ... Leland." Almost dismissively, Ruby turns back to the small group of friends. Feeling off balance and distracted, it takes a moment for her to insert herself back into the conversation and the buzz of the nightclub.

Amused, Leland moves through the low hum of conversation and chemistry that hovers in the air with the smoke, back to his table, to his associates and his scotch. He returns almost every evening that Ruby performs. At first, she is annoyed with him, with his self-assured countenance and constant smiling, but soon she begins to look for him. On the evenings he is not there she finds the night club and the singing unfulfilling. It is disconcerting that so much of her time is being taken up wondering about and hoping to see Leland James. *What am I doing? I'm a married woman with two small children, day-*

dreaming like a schoolgirl about a man I hardly know.

It is 1950, and Ruby and John Grace have been married for seven years. Last year John took the transfer from Montreal to Toronto that Deca records had offered him, moving his wife and young family from Outremont to Yorkville. Oh, how she had fought that move, even while she recognized it as John's attempt to start fresh, to save the marriage.

"But, John, I don't want to move to Toronto. My life is here; my parents are here. Who will help with the kids when you're on the road and I have an engagement? It's just too far away from everything! Except for Bob and Sophie Brant, I don't know anyone there." Ruby's voice raised in pitch on her last few words, her eyes smarting with frustration and impotence.

"You'll meet new people; you'll make new friends. I'm sure LeLiberté can give you a letter of introduction or something. Didn't you study in Toronto for a while? It'll be fine. You'll find opportunities." John, turning back to his small desk, dismissed Ruby and any further discussion.

"No, John. It's not the same. I don't want to go." But her words fell on deaf ears. She knew the move was imminent, and, truthfully, if she moved aside her fear, she was excited. The opportunity for change in her life was one she can't ignore. Over the years, unhappiness had settled gradually onto her shoulders like a shroud. She would try anything to shake it. The birth of her son Francis did little to change the dread she felt, seeping into and around her. The miscarriage and then Phoebe's birth four years later seemed only to heighten these feelings. Little did she know that it would take the move to Toronto and the reintroduction to jazz, blues, and Leland James to enable her to once again feel the light of hope, the exhilaration of longing.

THE SONG IS GEORGE GERSHWIN'S "Summertime," first performed as a lullaby by Abbie Mitchell in the opera, *Porgy and Bess,* in 1935. She is lost in the runs, the notes forming in her head like colours, some bright and sharp, others muted and dissipating. It is a song of atmosphere, a spiritual in the style of the African-American folk music of the era, sung slowly and easily, leaning more to blues than jazz, evoking the Deep South, the languid humidity, the sultry heat. But more than this, the song brings back, sharp and immediate, the memory of hearing it sung for the first time at the Colonial Theatre in Boston.

"Jeanie, Boston is only a few hours from here. Let's take the kids and see the performance. It's important, this music. It's something they will always remember."

It is 1935 and Ruby is almost fourteen when her father, mother, and younger brother, Edward make the trip from their summer home in Maine to Boston Massachusetts, "the city on the hill," to hear the first American folk opera. It's late September, but the heat of summer clings to the days with a force that seems unreal; only the evenings, cooling quickly with the setting sun, bring a respite to the heat. Pulling her favourite lavender sweater around her shoulders, Ruby settles in beside her father. "This theatre is so beautiful isn't it, Dad?" Ruby says, looking around and taking in the deep red curtains, the vaulted ceiling, the gilded columns.

"Yes, it is, honey," Daniel says, his voice edged with excitement. He is unable to sit without fidgeting while they wait for the lights to dim. He has read about the opera, which has received excellent reviews. He's anxious to experience one of his favourite novels, Dubose Heyward's *Porgy*, on the stage and set to music.

While his decision to take the family to this musical was spontaneous and out of character, his love for the music is something Ruby recognized and appreciated. The following year, Billie Holiday recorded "Summertime," and it rocketed to twelfth on the charts. It is this recording that Daniel played over and over again through the years. Although it eventually became one of jazz's most famous songs of all time—covered by

Miles Davis, Ella Fitzgerald, Louis Armstrong, and the like—
Ruby has always associated the song with the Billie Holiday
recording. Its influence can be heard in her rendition tonight.

The jazz clubs are keeping her busy. Jazz is fun to sing, but it
is the sound of the blues that resonates with Ruby. The blues is
sultry and sad and painful, but it keeps moving, finding beauty
in the harsh struggle of life. It is the sound of the soul that
cannot be defeated, the voice of the voiceless. The older she
gets, the more meaningful the music becomes. Holding on to
the note just long enough to find the pain, Ruby slips through
the music in spectral grace.

The tables are full—small candles flickering, smoke hanging
in the air like vapour. Ruby is living in the moment, her body
following the undulating rhythms, her mind flowing around
the notes like liquid. She is aware of the nuances of her voice,
the colour of the music, her movement, all that is around her.
She is at the centre of it all and, at the same time, observing
it from a quiet corner of her mind. And through it all, she is
wondering and hoping that Leland will be there.

The song ends, the applause begins, and Ruby smiles graciously as she thanks the crowd. She is in her element, feeling
alive and aware. She is totally herself, and yet not herself; she
is somehow larger, a small part of something greater.

With the second set over, she lifts the hem of her evening
gown and steps from the stage, scanning the room.

"You waiting for somebody, Ruby?" Phil Manning, her
pianist asks, helping her down and sensing her anticipation.
"Is John coming by tonight?"

"No, just some friends said they might pop by." Her lie
sizzles the air around her. *Damn, what is happening to me?*
she wonders.

She considers compounding her lie with another, but suddenly she is saved by the sight of Leland James. "Good set,
Phil. You are really on tonight, lovey." Patting his shoulder
in dismissal, she moves away before he notices the flush

staining her cheeks. Making her way through the crowd, her emotions cramping in her stomach, she considers, not for the first time and not without bemusement, what she is headed for. She has a husband and two small children—her son Francis is six, and her daughter Phoebe is eighteen months—but their presence, their needs are not as pressing as the need she feels to be with this man. But to what end? Tucking a strand of hair around her ear, she pushes these thoughts from her mind. Allowing only the present to matter, she continues toward Leland, stealing what time she can to be with him.

Leland, watching her approach, smiles. He recognizes her. She has the kind of beauty that speaks to him of truth, of meaning, that reassures him. But he is never sure exactly what it is about her. Is it the line of her movements, the unconscious lift of her hand while she talks, the corner of her mouth, the scent of her skin, rising up to meet him in the heat of the club? This is the reason men and women exist, he thinks, feeling the lure of her body like a planet caught in a gravitational pull. He is captivated by her movements, her laughter, her voice, and behind her eyes there is a soul that he knows, that he yearns for. Who could have known that it would be her, that Ruby Grace would be the woman to fill his head, that her presence would be the only thing to quiet his heart and centre him in his mind, in his own life?

"My, aren't we a bit serious tonight, Leland James? What happened, a bad day at the office?" She chides him, recognizing the gravity behind his eyes and wishing to break the tension.

"I'm thinking serious things tonight, Ruby," he says, looking directly at her and nodding.

"Things like hard work and ambition or things like love and chemistry?"

"Things like love and chemistry, although I never really gave them much thought ... until now," Leland says, dropping his voice on the last few syllables, awkward and unsure of his footing.

Ruby waits for him to continue, the silence between them becomes deafening while he watches her in his quietly unaffected way. Finally, she can stand it no longer—she laughs and asks him, "So what do you think about love now, Leland James?"

"I never believed in it. I never believed in chemistry or love. I have always believed in hard work and ambition, as you suggested." He smiles, searching her eyes before he continues. "And in laughter and longing. But never love." He feels foolish, but allows the emotion to remain, experiencing it with a degree of ironic amusement. He is after all, a realist, even though he feels like he has walked into a dream. Extending his hand, he takes Ruby's, lifting it to his lips. "So, beautiful lady, can I buy you a drink?"

Ruby's laughter releases the emotion of a moment ago. "Goodness, you are corny, Leland James."

"Isn't that what you find so charming about me?" His flashing look draws her toward him against her will, and she shrugs in an attempt to free herself.

"In a word—no. It is a mystery what I find so charming about you. Or, if I find you charming at all," she answers chidingly.

He looks up from her hand still held in his, dark eyes alive with mischief. "Don't you?" The question like a dropped stone ripples in the quiet pond around them. "Now, about that drink?" Leland graciously breaks the tension.

"I'll have a ginger ale."

"Ruby Grace." Leland laughs hard and loud. "Prohibition is over. Let's not snub our noses at those who risked life and limb in order to imbibe."

Laughing again, enjoying this banter, Ruby replies, "Prohibition was never big in Canada, although being American by birth perhaps I will have a drink in salute to those brave souls."

"That's my girl. What would you like? I'll get you anything, Ruby Grace."

Ruby laughs again, feeling a rush of happiness bubbling up with the sound. "Anything?"

Looking squarely into her eyes, Leland is suddenly serious. "Yes," he replies. "Anything."

So it goes, this love growing between them. Their words become caresses as their eyes lock each other in place. Their connection is like a drug, an addiction that neither one of them can control, a selfish, driving need that grows stronger with each encounter.

They both feel a palpable heat, frightening and exciting at the same time. She wants to hold him, to smell him, to be overwhelmed by him in every way. Only when she is physically away from him does she allow herself to feel any guilt. She has begun to lead a double life. During the long days at home—the work of a wife and mother never done—she yearns to be in the company of another man. She is constantly moving between two realities, stealing from one to be with the other. The songs she sings are for him, are about him: "*I'll be loving you always / with a love that's true always; your eyes so blue / your kisses so true; Ain't misbehaving / I'm saving my love for you.*" He fills her head the way only the music can fill it, completely and without compromise. Living without Leland would be like living without music.

"MOM. MOM, WE'RE HERE." Gary's voice, gently disturbing, breaks into her dream. Ruby opens her eyes; the overpowering light of the late afternoon sun blinds her momentarily. A shadow pulls her focus; her son holds the car door, his hand extended to take hers.

"Sorry, Gary, I must have dozed off." She sounds confused, even to herself. She has lived both of these moments. They are separated only by time, and that separation, the border in her mind that holds them apart, is growing thinner with every minute.

"Well, that's understandable. It was a long afternoon." he says, taking her hand in his.

"Yes, it was." Extracting herself with surprising agility

from the back seat, Ruby looks around, allowing her mind to catch up with the present. "The mayor was lovely, wasn't he? Although his speech was a bit too long, don't you think? I began looking around and wondering who the hell he could be talking about. But that's politicians for you. They can make a silk purse out of a sow's ear, ha!"

"Nan!" Lisa says, feigning shock, as she closes the car door and hands Ruby her cane. "I thought what he said about you, all of it, was excellent and true. You're a pioneer; you were out there doing things that not too many women were doing. Really, Nan, it's something to be proud of. Not too many people accomplish what you have in your life, especially at a time when women didn't really have the freedom to pursue such things. Don't you think?"

"I don't know. It wasn't such an effort—it was what I had to do. I was following my passion, I suppose. Yes, I did accomplish things, it's just that the speech sounded too much like a eulogy to me. I'm not dead yet, you know. Ha!"

"And from the look of you, you won't be for a while," Gary says, smiling down at his mother and then at Lisa and Jacklyn.

"Thank you, son, that's reassuring."

Stopping, she places her hand on Gary's arm, and he turns toward her quizzically. "Gary, I've been thinking, ha! —I know it's not like me—but I'd like to take a trip to Chicago to meet up with your sister, Phoebe."

Startled, Gary laughs. "This is a bit sudden don't you think, Mom? How do you propose to get there? Did you want me to drive you? It's quite a distance from here."

"No, I was thinking more along the lines of taking the train. The train is so much more civilized. It's the way we travelled when I was young."

Straightening her shoulders, she continues. "I thought I'd call your sister, and then she could meet me at the other end. I've never been to Chicago in all these years, and I'd like to have a look. And I would like to spend some time with Phoebe. Maybe

I could even go from there to California and visit Francis. You know if Mohamed won't come to the mountain. Ha!"

Staring at his mother, Gary is at a loss for words. Typically, she sees the adventure and he, the enormity of what she is proposing.

"Gary, close your mouth. You look like you're catching flies."

"Mom, you are not a young woman anymore." Gary cajoles. "Chicago is a long trip. Why don't you wait until Phoebe comes back and have her come visit you here? She'll have no trouble catching a cheap flight from Vancouver to Toronto. Then you can call Francis, and maybe he can come for a visit too. Classes are finished for the year. He'll have time."

"No, that would defeat the purpose. I want to go to Chicago, and I want to see Phoebe there."

"But, Mom, I don't think it's a very good idea. It's not the smartest thing. You're in a retirement home with twenty-four-hour supervision—there's a reason for that." Gary shrugs.

"I know, I know. It's twenty-four-hour supervision, and I feel like an exhibit in a cage, what with the feeding times and bed times, only getting out for special occasions, ha!" She laughs, but there is sadness behind it.

"Yes, because you can't be by yourself anymore. How do you expect to travel to Chicago on a train?"

"Like everyone else does. With a ticket! Really, Gary, unless you want to crate me and send me in the shipping car. Ha!" She laughs, patting him on the shoulder reassuringly. "It would only be half a day. What's the worst that could happen? I would nod off and miss my stop? I'm sure someone would wake me."

Gary's head is swarming with thoughts as he stands before his mother, her usual determination emanating from her. "It's more than just a few hours, and you don't have ... you can't ... we couldn't..."

"Dad," Lisa's voice is level, almost soothing as she taps his hand. "I can go with her. I have some time off—I'll go with her." She pushes her dark hair from her face and drops her hand to encircle her father's fingers with her own.

Gary's face reflects the trepidation he is feeling, but before he can formulate an argument, Lisa continues. "We can see about going this weekend—maybe leave Saturday and return Monday or something. It would be fun, Nan and me on a trip, meeting up with Aunt Phoebe. She'd love it too. I don't think the California thing is doable, but Chicago is." She turns to Jacklyn. "Could you make it this weekend, Jackie? It would be fun. All the Grace girls having a weekend together—your mom would love it."

Ruby smiles at her granddaughter's enthusiasm. "Good, it's settled. We can try and make it this weekend, Lisa, you're right—God knows I'm not getting any younger. Will you make the arrangements, honey?" She takes Lisa's hand.

"Not a problem, Nan." She turns to her cousin, a look of excited encouragement on her face. "Jackie?"

"Well, it sounds like an adventure, that's for sure, but it's pretty sudden. I'll talk to Greg and see if I can swing it. I can't promise anything, but I'll see."

"Good, that's my girls! It's settled—we will all go to Chicago. Phoebe will be so surprised." Heading for the door of Hill and Dale Retirement Home, Ruby turns back to the others. "Maybe the following weekend we'll go see Francis. Now let's get in—it's bloody cold out here for May."

2.

FOR MORE THAN FIFTY YEARS, thousands of steamships sailed into the New York City harbour. One by one they came, moving slowly through the muddy waters of the Hudson, carrying millions of immigrants. They passed under the iconic gaze of the Statue of Liberty. A generous gift from the French in 1884, it stands as a beacon to the world, then as now, heralding in the huddled masses of Hungarian, Czechoslovakian, Albanian, Dutch, German, French, Macedonian, Irish, English, Italian, Scandinavian, Russian, and Polish immigrants. Between 1846 and 1915, millions of men, women, and children came to America. By 1915, fifteen percent of America's total population were newcomers, fleeing prosecution and poverty. In 1846 and 1847, crop failures and mortgage foreclosures in Europe forced tens of thousands of the dispossessed to travel to the new world. In that same year, Irish people of all classes emigrated as a result of the potato famine. In 1882, thousands of Jews fled anti-Semitism in Russia. Between 1894 and 1896, Armenian Christians emigrated to escape Moslem massacres; they were all fleeing prosecution, persecution, poverty, segregation, and degradation. They were all seeking to make their way in "the land of milk and honey," a land where "the streets are lined in gold." When they descended the gangplanks of the ships—*Bretta, Saxon, Santiago, Freeman, Rhine Mara, City of Paris, City of New Orleans*—they imagined themselves to be stepping through the doorway of opportunity. They arrived in the United States, where the dream of America becomes the American dream. They entered in droves into the chaotic madness of Ellis Island, where twelve million newcomers were inspected and processed, and where the U.S. bureau of immigration enforced order in haphazard, accidental ways. It was a chaotic kind of order—like the universe itself—where the heap of humanity became society. Where sweating, swearing, clammy bodies crushed against bags, boxes, suitcases, section boards, and other bodies, their odour thick and pungent, inhaled like the breath of hope, translated through the masses in hundreds of different dialects, murmuring through barrel-vaulted ceilings, ringing through the air like discordant music, hesitant, tired, confused, but with the promise of life—the voice of the new world.

And from Ellis Island to where? Between 1861 and 1865, many young men went straight to the Union Army, shipped to a hostile frontier to die in a war they knew nothing about, a civil war, the worst of wars. Later, new immigrants were sent by subsidized rail to northern and western cities in order to populate a country in need of physical labour. New York, Boston, Buffalo, Philadelphia, Chicago. New people bringing new ways, new stories, new languages, new religions. The overheated, dizzying mix of the melting pot, lumpy, congealed, confused; life screaming for meaning, crying, laughing, singing, puking, chaotic. Life, messy and tumultuous, making its way toward civility.

JOSEPH AND ANNIE KENNY and their five-year-old son Michael are part of the squalling mass. They are a tired, huddled family overwhelmed by the crowds of people and connected through shared grief. Katie-Rose, their two-year-old daughter, is among the thousands who die in the hospital facilities on what was known as "The Island of Tears." The burial is quick, the sorrow deep.

After two harrowing weeks, they depart Ellis Island, unsure of their direction and clinging to each other for sanity. For Annie, death has stolen the light from the future, leaving her stunned and hollow, blind to the world. The rail trip to Chicago, the days of adjusting, of surviving, the confusion, the cold, the night, the day, all are eclipsed by grief. Even the quickening of life within her cannot shake the sorrow from her heart.

Joseph watches Annie as she stares out the train window at a landscape that is harsh and unfamiliar. He reaches to take her hand. As he leans forward, the movement of the train rippling through his upper body, Michael, asleep on his lap, groans at the disturbance. "Are you well, Annie?" Joseph asks, his pain evident in his weak smile.

"Aye, Joseph. I'm well," she answers, but does not turn from the window. The countryside slipping past means nothing to her; her eyes are unable to focus on anything past the image of Katie-Rose, her face pale and beautiful, her body limp and solid in Annie's arms. Unconsciously Annie pulls her arms across her chest, expecting, hoping to find her child there. But it is a daydream, she knows, a painful yearning that she cannot let go.

Joseph tries again, anxious to have any interaction with his wife. "It won't be long now. Soon enough, we'll be arriving in a new city, in a new country, and with a new beginning."

Annie turns, a weak smile on her face, and takes in her husband. His face hardly recognizable as the young man she married, but she recognizes his efforts as his form of love. Her eyes soften, but when she answers, her voice, holds no conviction. "A new beginning, Jo Jo."

The train jostles them, and they move as one with the rest of the passengers, squeezed in shoulder to shoulder, children held on laps or on the floor, leaning against legs. It is uncomfortable; the air is stale and ripe, the odour of unwashed bodies and broken spirits, an atmosphere of sour hope. Annie has come to associate this odour with the new world, but she knows there is no going back. She takes Joseph's hand and leans more solidly against his body.

"Sure. We will be all right, Annie," he whispers to her, encircling her with his arm and kissing the top of her head.

WHEN DANIEL JOSEPH KENNY is born on April 1894, it is a new era. It has been five months since his parents and brother were nationalized, and six months since twenty-seven million people visited the Chicago world's fair—where they saw new sights, new inventions, glimpsed the future, romanticized the past. Thousands of these visitors, recent immigrants—mostly single young men and newly emancipated women—decided to settle in Chicago, increasing the land value and forcing developers to make room by moving in the only feasible direction: up. At the time of Daniel's birth, tenement living is becoming a way of life for the working class of Chicago's north side. The steerage passengers of Ellis Island find themselves on the lowest rung of society; the American dream, held in their collective unconscious like an overfilled balloon, has deflated in degradation and squalor.

Joseph Kenny has no trouble finding employment in the growing city. He works long days in the rail yards, where a thousand trains a day enter and leave Chicago with insatiable momentum. He enjoys the work, hard and dangerous but steady and honest.

"I'm away to move the world," Joseph jokes each morning, kissing Michael, Annie, and the new baby. "He's a fine looking one, is he not, Annie?" Touching Daniel's fingers, that curl around his own, Joseph smiles at the new life.

Michael has found adventure and a new way of life on the Chicago streets. Taking to them like the proverbial fish to water, he runs wild in a world without rules. His mother's efforts to restrain him are feeble at best.

"I want you straight home from school today, Michael. No Hurley in the streets."

"It's not Hurley, Ma. I told you—it's stick ball." Michael's young voice is edged with impatience.

"And don't you be using that tone of voice with me, young man. Or I'll stick ball you all right." Annie playfully cuffs the top of his head.

Michael smiles. "All right, Ma, I'll come straight home. But after I set the fire can I go back out?"

"We'll see."

Annie has no road map in this new world, no tethering post to steady herself; at times it's as if she is stumbling through darkness toward something too undefined to realize. She understands the baby—his immediacy, his dependency, his existence, so tied to her own. She holds him close, along with her fears and her faith, focused on this new life. He is clever, this youngest son of hers, the first born of this land, and like the young country he is full of promise. Annie pins her hopes on him with unabashed enthusiasm that can't help but spread to Joseph and Michael. Daniel is the one to lift Annie back from the darkness.

Katie-Rose's death stopped Annie cold; she moved as if she were living in the depths of the Atlantic, unable to feel, unable to care. There was no comfort in Joseph's body or in Michael's laughter. She could feel only the need, the hollow, empty pining for her daughter, her baby, whose absence filled her to distraction, obliterating the days as they passed. Joseph found himself adrift in a land without family, with a wife absent with despair, and a son confused and frightened by his unfamiliar surroundings, unfamiliar emotions.

For those first months, Joseph's life is a narrow band of worry. He is forced to leave Annie and Michael in the morning with the porridge he made and push through the work day at the rail yard, his need to return to Annie, all consuming.

"Try and eat something, Annie-girl." Joseph's voice, soft in her ear as he places the plate of mince before her.

"I can't. I've no appetite, Jo Jo." She is quiet and tired, with a weakness that nests in her bones and clouds her mind. With a start, as if waking from a dream, she says, "And tell me what it is we are doing here? A new life, a new life. It's all I ever heard from you and look," she lifts her arm to indicate the shabbiness of the room, "this is the new life. And my Katie-Rose ... left..." Her voice breaks, her throat constricting with the pain in her heart.

Joseph can do nothing; her sorrow excludes him. Placing his arm tentatively around her shoulder, he continues in a voice that sounds as absent as he feels. "Eat something for the new baby. Keep your strength to tell Michael and the new wee one all about Katie-Rose."

Sitting next to her, he takes her in his arms, the contact of their bodies the only comfort he can offer. Rocking her, she weeps for life—its endings and beginnings, confusing and unfair. Grieving for one child and worried for the one to come. Would she love this next child? Could she allow herself to love this next child? Thoughts she can hardly form, words she will never say, lie like weights on a drowning soul.

Daniel's birth changes all this. Holding his small, warm body, Annie responds to his demand for life, feels the waters around her recede. The pained look of loss is replaced by the smiles the new baby begins to pull from her reluctant heart.

Growing up, Daniel is quick with numbers. At six, he can work out the odds for his father at the local betting house. Annie has no worries about tucking a list and money into his pocket for the butchers. "Now remember, Danny, the best of corn beef Mr. Marlow has and four pieces of gammon. And check your change before you're leaving the store."

"Yes, Ma, I know. I'm not an imbecile!"

"And if you come across Michael, send him home, the toe-rag. I don't know what I'll be doing with that brother of yours."

"There's nothing you can do about him, Ma. He's a one of a kind who emerged from a broken mold!"

Annie laughs and ruffles Danny's hair, "You're a dandy. What would I be doing without you?"

Daniel has inherited his father's love of words and his tenacious sense of humour, and his mother's striking blue eyes and black hair. He adores his big brother, who accepts the hero worship as an older brother's right. Michael is twelve, loose in his skin like a lanky horse and bursting toward the future with the enthusiasm that comes with a new country, anxious to test himself, anxious to scratch the maddening itch of ambition that has settled on him like an affliction.

Daniel trails after Michael his pursuit relentless, when he can find him that is.

"And take your brother with you!" This is Annie's constant war cry; the worst thing Michael can hear. "At least he knows better than to be getting into trouble."

Michael slips from the house like a ghost, hoping that his mother—busy at the sink, or the stove, or the sewing—won't lift her head at the last moment, calling after him. It's a sixth sense she has. Shaking his head at the door, his freedom in sight, Michael sighs. His father is right—she's got eyes in the back of her head! "Do I have to take him, Ma? He'll only be in the way and I can't be watching out for him."

"You'll take your brother and you'll watch him or, Jesus, Mary, and Joseph, you'll be getting the back of my hand."

"Oh, come on then, Danny." Michael waves, his body tight with frustration. "And if you're causing any problems, I'll skin ya' alive."

Daniel runs after his brother, pretending not to notice the resignation in Michael's eyes. "I'll be so good you won't even notice I'm with you, Michael."

MOST MORNINGS, Michael leaves for school with Daniel, but he seldom makes it as far as the school grounds. The lure of the street and his best friend Vincent Ducci—who at thirteen has all the makings of a gangster—are too enticing for Michael to ignore.

Pulling off his school tie and ramming it into his back pocket, Michael turns to Daniel. "All right boy-o, I'll see you at home." Scanning the street for Vincent, Michael has already forgotten his brother's existence. It takes him a few minutes to realize that Daniel is following him back toward the tenement. "Danny, get going!" Michael points toward the school. "You'll be late."

Daniel stands his ground. "But I don't want to go to school. I want to stay with you." Rushing to make his case, he continues: "I can help you find Vincent. There are too many streets in Chicago for one person."

Michael, laughing, ruffles his brother's hair. "No, Danny. You can't come with me. You're too small. Little boys need to be in school."

"But I don't want to go to school." Danny repeats what he's already said, but this time with a whine, kicking at the ground in frustration.

"Danny, I'm not going to tell you again. If you don't get going, I'll march right back home and tell Ma that you're playing hooky."

"But you're playing hooky too. How can you tell Mammy on me? You'd be telling on yourself! Besides, I hate school."

"No, you don't." Michael grunts. "You love school. You're good at it. You get all your sums right—you're the shining star of St. Pat's. I was never good at sums. I can read and write as good as anyone and that's all I need."

"Michael!"

Turning, Michael waves at Vincent Ducci, who is coming down the alleyway. Vincent is big and dark, moving toward the boys and brimming with the mischief of his age. He has taught Michael all the swear words in Italian and how to toss for pennies. Michael can't help smiling at his approaching friend. Then he looks back at his brother, whose eyes are swimming with disappointment. "Get going now, Danny," he says impatiently, pushing him in the direction of the school. "You'll have to run now to make it on time." He pushes him again. "Now get going. If I hear you're late I'll tan you black and blue."

Daniel shrugs and turns slowly, moving in the direction of St. Patrick's.

"Get going now!" Michael calls again, prodding his brother into a slow jog. "And Danny?" Daniel turns, his satchel swinging against his legs. "If you get all your sums right, I'll take you to the White Sox game on Saturday. You can look through the fence with Vinny and me!"

Daniel smiles, the disappointment of a moment ago forgotten with the promise of the White Sox.

"Your brother's gonna be late for school." Vincent Drucci says, sidling up to Michael and watching Daniel weaving through the early morning pedestrians.

"It's nothing new. He won't catch too much for it though. He's St. Pat's prize pupil."

"So, he don't take after you?" Vincent asks, smiling.

"No, he don't and he better not or I'll kill him."

The boys watch like worried parents until Daniel is lost to the street. "Come on, Mick. Enough babysitting." From his thin jacket, Vincent pulls a warm bun, rips it apart, and holds out the small half to Michael. "I grabbed this from O'Malley's on the way by." He shoves the bread in his mouth and continues, talking around it. "Let's get going, I told Hymie we'd be at Holy Name by nine."

Making their way through the streets of Kilgubbin, the Irish area of Chicago's North Side, Michael and Vincent experience a sense of pride, of ownership almost. They know these streets as well as they know the faces of their families. Weaving along the sidewalks, jumping garbage cans and crates left on curbs, sometimes moving into the street to run alongside horses and carts, they make their way with naïve confidence to Holy Name Cathedral. Earl "Hymie" Weiss is already there, watching their approach, smoking a cigarette swiped from his old man.

Chicago is a brooding, dirty, exciting city on the southwestern edge of Lake Michigan. It is a break bulk point, with waterways and railways bringing commerce and influence to a growing population of immigrants. It is chaotic with growth and the inevitable problems that arise with too many newcomers and too few accommodations. Max Weber likened the city to "a human being with his skin removed"—pulsing reality exposed, grotesque and wonderful in its harsh beauty, a place all too readily available as a testing ground for three young boys on the precipice of manhood.

"You guys are late. I been here fifteen minutes already." Hymie spits at them, flicking his butt to the ground for emphasis.

"Micky was kissing his brother goodbye. Besides, I didn't know ya' could tell time, Hymie. Whadya do, steal a watch?"

"It's more than you can do, Ducci, you dumb wop," Hymie fires back not without humour.

"Boys, boys! Enough!" Michael extends his arms for emphasis. "We're waistin' time. Settle down and tell me: where do we wanna go this fine morning?"

"Let's go over to Ragen's. They got a new ring set up," Hymie suggests eagerly.

"Yeah, and you two can climb in and blow off some steam." Michael laughs.

"I'll be Jim Jeffries," Hymie says, throwing punches, bobbing and weaving, looking more like a dancer than a fighter.

"You'd be the last choice for the great white hope, Hymie." Vincent laughs.

"At least I'm whiter than you," Hymie answers.

"I'll be Jeffries," Michael says, weighing in on the argument, "and I'll take ya both on one at a time. Youse are both so slow you'll never lay a glove on me!"

THE RAGEN'S ATHLETIC and Benevolent Association is an athletic club on Chicago's south side. For years, it has been attracting men and boys from the neighbourhood who, looking for a feeling of belonging, pour their angst and misery into organized sport and rivalry. The boys who move through the early morning streets on their way to Ragen's are familiar with every nuance of the city: pilfering fruit from the store fronts, stealthily feeling through pockets, laughing at their antics. They are relaxed within the stream of city life the way their fathers and grandfathers only a few short years ago were relaxed within the rural life of the country. By the time they reach Ragen's, their colour and spirits are high.

Vincent stops abruptly, his hand on Michael's chest, nodding toward the front door. "Hey, Mick. Ain't that the little gimp Dean O'Banion from our close?"

Michael follows Vincent's gaze. "Yeah, that's Deanny. Lives in the next tenement and sings in the choir at Holy Name. What's the little bugger doing here? He should be at St. Pat's with the rest of the babies."

"Let's go give 'im what for." Hymie smiles at the prospect.

"What for?" Michael asks for fun.

"Shut up will ya and let's just do it," Hymie answers with little amusement, pushing through the door and grabbing Dean O'Banion by the scruff of the neck. "What ya doing here, gimpy?"

Dean, struggling from Hymie's grip, turns and, with the momentum, plows Hymie in the side of the jaw with his fist. As Hymie staggers back, Dean dives head first into him, shouting through clenched teeth, "I ain't no gimp you lousy, smelly kike."

"Hey, hey!" Hymie shouts, his voice pitched to a squeal.

The men in Ragen's turn in unison to watch the two boys, now rolling and flailing, a cyclone of legs and arms.

"Shit, that kid's wild," Vincent says. He turns toward Michael, but his eyes never leave the two boys locked in mortal combat, their grunting and swearing punctuated by cheers of encouragement from the onlookers. It's Frank Ragen himself, roused from his office by the commotion, who wades in to separate them. Frank is big and brawny, and he parts the boys with ease, holding each one by the scruff of the neck. The boys are panting hard, their eyes locked on each other with unabashed aggression.

"Ya' little beggars! Ya' won't be disrupting this place, do ya hear!" Frank shouts. Dragging them to the door, he pushes it open with his foot and tosses them out onto the street. "You keep your street brawling where it belongs and not in an establishment like this. And don't ya' dream of coming back, or so help me god your mammies won't recognize you." Frank turns from the door, the smile on his face slipping when he notices Vincent and Michael standing there. "And you two—get the hell out of here! We don't need Ities and North Side scum the likes of you in here."

Stunned, Michael and Vincent stare.

"I said, get the bejeezes hell out of here! Or will ya be needing my help?"

"No. No, Frank. See, we're gone," Vincent says, grabbing Michael and propelling him toward the door.

"And it's Mr. Ragen to you lot!"

Michael and Vincent make it to the door, followed by the jeering and laughter of Ragen and his friends. The Ragen Athletic and Benevolent Association will eventually evolve into a gang that, by 1910, will begin to finance the careers of hundreds of Chicago officials, aldermen, police chiefs, and city treasurers. Frank Ragen himself will become a Chicago police commissioner.

"Good work, Frank!" one of the men calls from the ring. "Those little buggers don't need to be coming round here."

"Yeah, well see to it that I'm not disturbed by them again, or else I'll be flailing the skin off every man here!"

Frank Ragen and the Ragen gang will contribute to the Chicago Race Riot of 1919 by pitting black against white in the South Side neighbourhoods. The violence will last for four days, resulting in the looting and destruction of homes and businesses, injury to more than one thousand, and the deaths of thirty-four people. Some of the Ragen gang members eventually split off and form the NFL football team, the Chicago Maroons, later the Chicago Cardinals. But for now, they are happy with the expulsion of the boys.

Outside, Hymie and Dean pull themselves together. Hymie, still on the ground, checks out the rip in his pants, the scrape on his knee visible. "My ma's gonna be some mad."

"I hope you two fools are happy wid yourselfs. We've all bin thrown out." Vincent seats himself on the curb, spitting to emphasize his displeasure.

"It was that little gimp's fault." Hymie nods toward Dean.

"Let's not be starting anything again," Michael jumps in.

"Who needs them anyway? We can start our own club," Dean says, his voice earnest and sincere.

"Aren't you a little young to be telling us what to do?" Vincent asks.

"What does age got to do wid it? 'Sides, I'm almost the same age as Michael and twice as smart."

"Well, that wouldn't be hard," Vincent quips.

"Shut up Vinchenzo." Michael hits the back of Vincent's head and takes a seat beside him on the curb.

Dean O'Banion sits down on the other side of Vincent and continues as if he had never been interrupted. "We can get the money together and make our own place, our own club."

Hymie joins them on the curb. "How do we get the money, smarty-pants? It ain't growin' on trees."

Dean looks at Hymie and then at Vincent and Michael. "I got a few ideas."

So begins the Market Street Gang. Dean O'Banion, although the youngest of the boys, is by far the most imaginative and a born leader with a gift for oration. His skill with language and his fearless attitude lends itself to the developing underworld of Chicago, where moral absence is a reflection of a people dispossessed and disillusioned, struggling to find meaning in a developing, industrial, city.

Starting small, the boys begin to steal for the black market, finding numerous fences anxious for whatever they can produce. Another friend from the neighbourhood, George "Bugs" Moran, joins the gang. Although Daniel intends to join and run with the Market Street Gang when he gets older, Michael will always keep him at arm's length, allowing him to hang out with the guys but never letting him take part in any activities. He will remain an observer, a bench warmer, watching but never participating. Daniel will experience his own war, overseas and catastrophic, the war to end all wars. He will return with new eyes, aged with suffering. Back in the familiar streets of his own city, he will continue to watch people die as petty larceny, violence, and gangs begin to organize themselves into deadly syndications. The systemic growth will span countries and continents, slowly making its way into the fabric of America.

WHEN DANIEL IS TEN, Dean and Michael are working as waiters at McGovern's Liberty Inn. It is a busy three-storey inn with a bar and restaurant on the main floor. Catering to travellers and regulars alike, it is a smoky, pulsing place, eager for entertainment and novelty. On busy evenings, Dean sings to a crowd captivated by his melodic Irish tenor voice. While the patrons are carried by the gentle, heartfelt ballads back to the emerald Isle, Hymie, Vincent, and Bugs move through the crowd lifting wallets and bill clips. The singing is like a drug, appealing to the need for what is good and pure in humanity, a connection that is beyond the physical, beyond the demands and harshness of life.

Michael can't help but feel bad for the poor suckers as Dean soothes their weary souls, caressing them with memories and dreams with the voice of an angel, stealing from them while offering hope and beauty. And afterwards in the back room of their club house, Daniel counts and sorts the money, keeping a ledger full of his precise notations and exact accountings.

He keeps a running tally in his head; the books are for Dean, who has become the undisputed leader. Daniel's ability with numbers serves the club well, and they nickname him "Strings" for purse strings, since all the money flows through him. Daniel has the combination to the small safe; his youth and innocence ensure his trustworthiness. He is being paid for his services; the gang agreed that he is an essential asset to any well-run organization.

"So, what was the take last night, Strings?" Hymie asks, watching Daniel finish with the money and the ledger.

Daniel smiles. "Eleven dollars and twenty-seven cents."

"Oh, Deanie boy, they love your sweet voice, don't they?" Hymie jibes, looking over at Michael and nodding.

"Don't they just." Michael jumps in, ready for some good ribbing. "You've a voice of an angel, sure and you have, Dean O'Banion." Michael slips into the brogue, pinching Dean's cheek.

"The voice of an angel and the heart of a devil." Vincent laughs.

"Youse are just jealous of my talents." Dean smiles out of the corner of his mouth. "God bestowed the voice and the brains—it's up to me to use them to their best advantage."

"You mean use them to take advantage." Daniel adds, seating himself beside his brother.

"Am I taking advantage, Danny boy, or given 'em a respite in their journey, singing of the 'aul sod,' given 'em what they wants."

"Yeah, while we takes what we want!" Michael cracks and they all laugh.

"We're living in new times," Dean goes on when the laughter subsides. "We can own the world if we want, mark my words."

MICHAEL WORKING as a waiter and running with the gang brings in good money. Joseph is well established at the rail yard, and the Kenny family can feel the fulfillment of the American dream pushing in around them "with the strength of a Liffey current" as Annie would say.

It is Wednesday afternoon in late March; the promise of spring is on every breeze. Daniel sits at the kitchen table, his homework spread out before him, listening to the street noises wafting up from below: streetcars, dogs barking, kids shouting, and his friends being called in for supper. He can sense their reluctance to go inside now that the days are longer and stick ball and scooters clog the street. His pencil dangling from his fingers, Daniel dreams about the scooter he wants for his eleventh birthday the coming week. Annie, fixing supper at the stove, calls over her shoulder, rousing her son from his daydreams. "Danny, go ask your brother if he'll be wanting some tea before he goes to work."

"No, Ma. I'm running late." Michael answers, coming from the bedroom, his seventeen-year-old frame filling the doorway, his white shirt starched and bright in the late afternoon light. "I'll eat something at the tavern. There's always..." He is interrupted by a knock at the door, hesitant but immediate, its rapped rhythm foreboding in its insistence. Daniel will always remember this scene, a tableau etched in his mind: his brother frozen in the doorway, the pencil in his own hand dangling from his fingers, and the look on his mother's face in that moment. She must have known, must have felt the knowledge hammer through her with each rap of the door. Michael moves to the door, and Annie's right hand, still holding the dishcloth, moves to her chest, her eyes wide with precognition.

Opening the door, Michael finds an unfamiliar man on the doorstep. His face is flushed with effort, his eyes hooded with discomfort. "Is this the Kenny home?"

"Yes," Michael answers, confused by the strong emotion emanating from the stranger.

Annie moves to the door, placing her hand on her son's arm, gently moving him aside. She, not her son, will take this news. "This is the Kenny home, and I'm Mrs. Kenny."

The man pulls his cap from his head and crushes it in his hands, the information he has run all this way to impart frozen on his tongue. His eyes dart from Annie's level look.

"Speak up, man."

Nothing. The silence lengthens, extrapolates; Daniel's heart quickens with every moment.

"Where is Joseph?" Annie asks, the question a command that he can finally respond to. "He's on his way, Mam. That is, they're bringing him, Mrs. Kenny."

"They're bringing him?" Annie repeats, knowing but not wanting to hear what is coming.

The man looks at her, beseeching her to forgive him for his part in this tragedy, then speaks to his shoes. "They're bringing his body, Mam."

Annie turns, moves to the kitchen table, and stumbles into a chair, the dishcloth still clutched in her fist. The man, his hand extending toward her, follows her into the small room, unable to stop the torrent of words now loosened from his mouth. "There was an accident." He clears his throat. "The shunting of the rail car it ... it happens sometimes, you know. Well, it happens too often really. We was filling the car, the crates were being loaded...."

Annie hears his voice, the undulations, the hesitations, the running on of his story, but her mind is blank, preparing itself. She knows the lifeless body of her husband is being carried through the streets and home to her.

"I ran ahead to let you know. You'll want to be getting the priest."

"Ma?" Michael moves toward his mother, wondering if this is just a bad joke, unable to process the information.

Annie turns her attention to the man standing awkwardly in their kitchen, his despair as obvious as the day's grime covering his face. "I'm grateful to you Mr...."

"O'Sullivan. Gerald O'Sullivan." He bows his head.

"I'm grateful to you, Mr. O'Sullivan. Go on home to your

family. They'll be waiting on you. We know what to do."
Standing, she accompanies him to the door. "And thank you
again for your kindness." Closing the door quietly, she takes
a moment before turning to her boys. "Michael, son, go and
fetch the priest and tell McGovern's that you won't be in tonight. Danny, get the bucket from the back closet and fill it
with warm water. I'll need some linen as well...." She continues
speaking, moving to the bedroom. The room is small but neat,
full of the familiar smell of bodies and talcum powder. Moving
with purpose, she takes her best linen from the bottom drawer;
it was carried all the way from Ireland, a wedding gift from
her Aunt Biddy. The finest of Irish linen, she thinks, feeling its
texture against her arm as she carries it back to the kitchen. It
was meant for a prosperous home, and now it would be used
to bury her husband.

By the time Joseph's body arrives—carried in an improvised
litter by four men, dirty and tired from their day's work but still
compassionate in their cumbersome yet valiant way—Annie
has cleared the kitchen table, lit lamps, and found as many
candles as she can. The kitchen glows in a perversely welcoming
way, and Daniel thinks it looks more like a celebration than
a place to lay his father's unnaturally still body. Annie, in her
preparations, seems to have forgotten Daniel, but as he stands
against the door frame, half hidden by the darkness of the back
room, she turns to him.

"Come see your father, son." She holds out her hand toward
him, a bridge between the living and the dead. "Come, Danny.
He's still your Da. He's with the angels now. Don't be afraid,
there's naught here to be frightened of. Come and say goodbye
and bless him on his journey."

Taking his mother's hand, Daniel steps into the light, studying his father's body for any sign of movement. Annie holds
her son by both shoulders, her body warm and comforting
against his back. Leaning forward, she pushes the hair from
Joseph's forehead, gently, as if he were sleeping and she afraid

to wake him. Daniel can see the sweat and dirt of the day on his father's face, the lines like fine cracks emanating from the corners of his eyes. Breathing in, he closes his eyes, holding the scent of his father, memories toppling like falling buildings. It is overwhelming. Letting out his breath he realizes that he is crying, the insulating effect of shock withdrawing to make room for sorrow.

He is reeling, dizzy and frightened standing before his father, his mind desperate to escape. It is the feel of his mother's hand stroking his head, just as she had his father's a moment ago, that holds him in place, the familiarity of her voice breaking the last of the barriers. "It's all right to cry, Danny. Crying heals the heart." She lets him cry, turns him to her, kisses the top of his head. He can feel her arms around him and the wetness of her tears, the trembling of her body. His eyes closed, his head against her chest, he can hear her heartbeat and feel the darkness of her despair tightening around his own. But no moment can last forever. She moves to part them, but he is afraid to let go, to move on. Holding him at arm's length now, she says, "Look at me, Daniel." Reluctantly, unsure of what this new world will look like, he finds her eyes. Her look is fierce, defiant. "We'll keep each other strong. Won't we, Danny?" She nods her head, her eyes hard on his own until he nods as well. Pushing the tears from his eyes with the back of his hand, he lets out his breath.

"Now, can you go to my top drawer beside my bed and find the fine soap I have there? I want to wash your Daddy with the soap he bought me for my birthday."

The moving and the doing, as Annie knows, helps them to focus—"keeping the banshees at bay." She talks to Daniel, reassuring him, already telling stories about the man his father was.

When Michael returns, he finds his mother gently washing his father's body. With Daniel's help, she has stripped him down and laid the linen across him. Joseph's arm is resting on her shoulder. She wipes him with gentle caresses, singing and humming under her breath. His face is clean and pale, his hair pushed back to reveal his high forehead, his small ears. Michael stares. His father, so vulnerable, looks like a child whose mother is readying him for mass on Sunday. He is no longer the worn, over-worked man Michael sees when he thinks of his father. Stepping closer, his eyes never leaving Joseph's face, he reaches out to touch the still, pale cheek and then stops.

"Yes, Michael." He hears his mother's voice coming to him from far away. "It's all right. Give your father a pat on the cheek. He loves you. Let him know you love him too."

His father's cheek is cool and smooth; the stubble of new growth below the cheek bone catches at the back of Michael's fingers. "I can't believe he's gone. I can't believe he's gone." It is all he can find to say and then, "Ma?" The questions in that one word. Annie shakes her head, knowing what he means but not knowing how to answer, not knowing what the future will hold for them all.

Placing Joseph's arm on the table, she runs her hand along its length. She studies Joseph's face, unimaginably motionless and pale, but still the face of her husband. "What did the priest say?"

Michael pushes his words out, his throat constricted with grief. "He's coming. I couldn't find him right away." Still looking at Joseph, he continues. "He was making calls in the neighbourhood. He'll get his things at the rectory and be here directly."

Annie nods and continues her humming. Occasionally she sings songs from her youth, and finally, when the songs are not enough, she breaks into speech. "Joseph Michael Kenny, what have you gone and done?" she scolds him in a playful manner. The washing and preparing of the body have been a soothing comfort, these last interactions with her husband, an intimacy she will never again know.

There is little or no noise outside the apartment; the neighbours are all too aware of the presence of death and are paying respect in the only way they can, with their silence. Later they will do so with food, and finally with words.

"Michael."

"Ma?"

"Take Daniel and yourself to Mrs. O'Neil's. Tell her what has happened. She'll feed you, and she'll want to come and sit watch."

Michael doesn't move. Annie turns, her voice soft. "Go now, son. You'll be needing your strength for the days ahead."

Nodding, Michael reaches for Daniel and they move to the door.

"Ask Mrs. O'Neil to bring more candles."

"I will, Ma." Looking back at her from the doorway, he adds, "The priest should be here any minute."

"There's no rush." Annie answers. "Your father has made his peace with his maker, and he was never too keen on Father Donavan anyhow. What was it that he called him?"

"Father Do again." Daniel answers, smiling at his father's joke, trying to remember the man he was, not the one lying on the kitchen table, so lifelessly unreal.

Annie laughs. "That's right, Father Do again. If ever there was a perfect name for a bumbling priest."

DANIEL FINDS IT DIFFICULT to remember anything about his father's wake and funeral. It is all a blur: the apartment, always busy, the women crying and then cooking, the men drinking and then crying. McGovern's sends a keg of brew, or so Dean and Vincent say, bringing it over and tapping it with expertise. Neighbours and friends who are quiet and confined at first, slowly grow to fill the room with hesitant laughter, with stories of Joseph and the things he said, the things he did. Then, his favourite songs fill the apartment, sung with such feeling, ringing with such life, a celebration—death in the midst of life. Or is it life in the midst of death? Daniel can't decide which, but either way it makes him angry; if feels like an affront. The confusion Daniel feels frightens him, unmoors him. Here is death stealing his father's life, taking everything and leaving nothing, nothing but loneliness, nothing but Daniel's own self. Here is death, taking one soul and injuring another.

Annie treats death like a visitor in their home. Not a welcome visitor, but still worthy of the deferential treatment a visitor is due: never invited, but begrudgingly respected. and while death dwelt—courageous. There is nothing else for it, Annie knows, but to find strength in dignity, to put the dead to rest as peacefully as possible. Life goes on no matter what. Her mother and father, her young brother, her daughter and now her husband have all passed on; this life is truly a vale of tears. So, she sings, in the face of death, the songs Joseph loved. She tells stories of their life, their young love in the hills of Wicklow, of a young Joseph, no older than his own son, who courted a young Annie Marlow after seeing her at the county fair, following her home, determined to make her his own.

Daniel listens as he falls asleep, immersed in the stories. This is how Daniel comes to know his father, as he comes to know death: through his mother. He will continue to face death like this, automatically falling into the rhythm and tempo of his mother's dignity. In the streets of Chicago, where death comes to men in mills, in shipyards, in rail yards, to people on the street hit by carts, trams, vehicles. In the fields of France, where men die in unimaginable ways, bleeding to death, drowning in ditches, choking on gas. Later, in his own home, where babies die in childbirth, and children from disease. Annie teaches him how to go on, how to steal back from death, to move forward, taking one step after another until moving and living and continuing become natural, and the dead are at rest.

3.

"NAN, HERE, LET ME HELP you with that." Lisa takes the oversized purse from Ruby and continues, "Why did you bring such a big purse?"

"I'm an old lady, Lisa. I can't travel light anymore—between bottles of pills, spectacles, tissue, and well, you know, 'old lady candies,' I need the room."

Lisa smiles at the joke. Her grandmother has always carried candies in her purse. When she and Jacklyn were young, Nan would produce them like magic, scrounging in the bottom of her purse, a wizard with a bag of tricks. Humbugs were the typical offering, but sometimes lemon drops or mints made an appearance. But Lisa and Jacklyn agreed that humbugs were the best, and they always called them "old lady candies."

"Before you put that away, honey, can you take out my book and glasses?"

"Sure, Nan. The bus will get us to Union Station in about an hour and a half, so make yourself comfortable."

"Well, that would be quite a trick at my age! I can't remember the last time I felt comfortable."

Ruby moves out of the aisle and takes the window seat, placing her cane against the arm rest. She smiles at Lisa as she slides into the seat beside her. "You know, I really don't need this cane. Sometimes it just feels like more of a nuisance then anything. And that's not vanity talking either; God knows I'm too old for that."

"I know. I have to say, for your age you're pretty spry. I hope I inherit your genes." Taking her grandmother's hand, Lisa continues: "But don't you think it's reassuring to have it, since the stroke and everything, just in case you get dizzy or something?"

"It was only a small stroke, nothing to worry about!" Ruby shrugs her shoulders and settles into her seat before turning back to Lisa and continuing. "Well, it does help when I'm feeling tired I suppose, and that seems to be happening a little more often these days. When I was your age, my energy seemed boundless. And now? Well the spirit is willing but the body is weak. I guess that just happens. Youth slips away." Looking out the window and smiling to herself, she adds, "Much like the years."

The doors close and the bus begins to back up slowly, the gears and engine groaning like an old man complaining of his stiffness. Ruby closes her eyes, and the sounds and smells take her back to some of those lost years, to her youth in Montreal. When she studied vocal training under LeLiberté, she would travel by bus and train to Toronto once every month to study at the Conservatory of Music. How many times she felt the same feelings, heard the same sounds. The bus feels different somehow, brighter with more metal and chrome, more modern, less opulent. That's how most things feel these days, she thinks. Even the seat, as she readjusts herself, feels harder, less inviting, less roomy. She was hardly aware of her surroundings back then, straining forward as she was toward the future, her career, the excitement life had to offer. Her father took her to the bus station every month, and every time she was excited to be heading to Toronto, toward opportunities yet to be realized.

"Have a good time, Jewely. I'll pick you up tomorrow night," Daniel says, kissing Ruby on the top of the head. "Say hi to Bob and Sophie for us, and tell them your mom and I will be down soon for a visit." Daniel raises his voice over the slight distance between them as his daughter rushes with youthful enthusiasm up the stairs. Feeling pulled between worry and pride, he follows her progress into the bus and along the aisle until she finds a seat by the window and waves to him. Bob is a long-time friend of both Daniel and Jeanie. He knows his daughter is in good hands, but sometimes when he looks at Ruby, he can't help seeing the child she once was. "I'll pick you up tomorrow night!" he calls, hands cupping his mouth. I must be getting old, I'm repeating myself like an old man, he thinks.

As the bus pulls away, Ruby watches her father and the other people at the station recede into the distance. Daniel keeps waving even after the bus disappears around a corner. Ruby looks at the money her father has slipped into her hand—a ten-dollar bill. He is always so generous, willing to give her anything. Her thoughts stay with her father for a while, lingering on the invisible bond they share. And yet, as close as they are, there always seems to be another Daniel Kenny, a man she can never know. He has always been a loving father with her and her brother, a good husband, and a successful business man, and yet she has caught him sitting, when he thinks no one is around, lost in thoughts that seem too deep for such a joyous man. She remembers vividly as a little girl of five or six, finding him for the first time in his study, sitting at his desk, papers strewn around. He was sitting perfectly still, his eyes focused on something she couldn't see. The stillness around him somehow evoked a fear that she rushed to extinguish.

"Daddy, what's wrong?"

"Ruby, where did you come from?" Startled out of his reverie, Daniel is almost curt with her. "I mean, I was daydreaming and I didn't know you were there."

"What were you daydreaming about? You seemed so sad." Taking her father's hand, she asks again, "What were you daydreaming about?"

"Nothing, sweetheart." Cupping her chin in his hand for a moment, his smile moves from his mouth to his eyes.

"Is it the war?" she asks, eyes trained on her father's, determined to pull the sadness from him, to bring him into the lightness of her youth.

"Yes," he answers with a slow shrug. "It's the war."

"But it's over now, and you're here with Mommy and Edward and me."

"That's true, it's over...." His thoughts hang in the air. Ruby thinks that if she can just pierce those thoughts, she could let the sadness slip from her father like a lanced boil. Still holding his hand, she watches his face for any hint, any insight.

"You're right, sweetheart. The war is over and in the past." Daniel's voice is low, his words coming from a place of regret that has nothing to do with the present, with his small daughter whose eager face lights up the room. She is too young to understand, but he continues anyway. "But the things we do—the decisions we make, right or wrong, in times of distress or whenever—are forever a part of us."

"Is that what makes you sad, the things you had to do in the war?"

"The things I've had to do don't really make me sad, honey, just responsible. And responsibility is a sobering thing." Daniel is silent for a moment, lost again to his thoughts, almost forgetting Ruby standing anxiously at his side, her face fearful and confused. Finally, Daniel rouses himself, he continues, his voice bright with forced effort. "But this isn't for you to worry about, my little Jewel. Now, go ask Mommy when supper will be ready. I'm so hungry I could eat a horse!"

WATCHING HER FATHER'S FIGURE retreating in the distance, Ruby thinks about the mystery that is Daniel Kenny. He is her hero, her greatest fan, her anchor in this world, and yet she perceives something else in him, a pain, a vulnerability that she can never understand. He is getting smaller as the bus moves around and out of the station, his hat raised in his hand to her. And then she begins to relax in the comfort and calm of the bus as it shunts and moves, eventually smoothing out with greater speed into the flowing traffic. She is looking forward to her lesson with LeLiberté, her anticipation picking up speed with the bus itself, leaving the past and heading toward the future. Smiling, she thinks of the aria she will sing. It is always a good idea to run it over in her head, and the hours on the bus provide her with the perfect opportunity. The sheet music is in her purse somewhere. Looking around for it, she is suddenly perplexed. *I know it's here. Did I leave it at home?*

"You okay, Nan?" Lisa watches Ruby searching either side of her seat. "Nan, what is it? Did you lose something?"

"My sheet music. I'm sure I brought it with me. I just want to run over it in my head, but I can't find my purse."

"I put it under the seat here. Don't you remember? I can get it for you if you like, but I don't think there's any sheet music in it."

There is a long pause, both women waiting for clarification. Then Ruby continues, "No, no, there is no sheet music." Slightly confused and saddened, she nods her head and takes in the moment.

"Are you okay, Nan?" Lisa takes her grandmother's hand, searching her face for some sort of reassurance.

"Yes, I'm okay, honey. Not to worry." Ruby smiles and looks over her glasses into her granddaughter's concerned face. "It's just these old bones, always complaining about something. Either I'm moving too much or sitting too long."

Pulling out of the station, they move from shadow to sunlight. The bus manoeuvres in and out of traffic, stopping and starting and turning until it finally reaches the ramp leading to the highway, picks up speed, and falls into a smooth rhythm heading south. Half an hour later, as they merge into the traffic on the 401, Lake Ontario opens up to them like a silver disc and follows them all the way east to Toronto, the spring sky pale and fragile against the darker depths of the water.

"Dad thinks this is a crazy idea, you know, Nan," Lisa jokes, shrugging out of her sweater and making herself comfortable, her green eyes paling in the sunlight.

"You mean going to Chicago to visit Phoebe?" Ruby asks, her words ringing with satisfaction.

"Yeah, he thinks you should wait until Aunt Phoebe comes home. Then she can make the trip from Vancouver to visit you instead of you having to endure the bus ride and then the train."

"Honey, I've endured more than a ten-hour journey in my life! Besides, I'm tired of being at the retirement home. I can't tell one day from the next when I'm there. It feels like a holding cell. Which I imagine it actually is! And all the 'activities,' as they call them—ha! Damn, I really don't like them. I've participated in life all I want to. Now I just want to sit. I just want to be still. My whole life I've felt like a full-time participant, and now I just want to sit on the side lines." She turns to Lisa. "You won't understand what I mean, not at your age."

"Actually, I think I do." There is a seriousness to Lisa's tone.

Ruby, taking in her granddaughter's attitude, continues, "I think maybe you do, honey, but I don't know if that's a good thing, or a bad thing."

Smiling, both women look out the window at the landscape moving past to the rhythm of the bus. After a moment, Lisa continues, "I was listening to one of your albums with a friend the other night."

Ruby laughs, the sound musical and soft like wind chimes. "Really? I haven't heard one of my albums in years. I think the last time was when Jack was alive."

"It never ceases to amaze me, Nan, every time I hear you. My favourite is 'I'll Be Seeing You.'"

"I remember recording that. It was Leland's favourite too. I don't think you remember Leland, do you, honey?"

"Vaguely. When I see pictures of him, I seem to get an impression that I know him. He seems so familiar. But it might just be that I knew of him from Dad and you."

"Yes, your Dad and Leland got along well. Leland was really the only father the kids knew. After John and I divorced, he had less and less to do with them. His job didn't help, with all the travelling, but mostly I think he was embarrassed." Ruby nods softly.

"Embarrassed? Why would he be embarrassed?" Lisa asks, intrigued.

"Embarrassed by the divorce," Ruby answers flatly.

"You think Grandpa Grace was embarrassed by a divorce, Nan?" Lisa's voice is louder than she intends.

"Well, I don't think it, lovey. I know it."

"But I don't understand. Why would someone be embarrassed because they were divorced?" Lisa looks squarely at Ruby, her eyes tight with confusion.

"Oh, Lisa." Ruby almost chuckles. "It was a different time—it feels like it was a different place. People back then, well, they just didn't divorce. It was quite scandalous really. They called it the *D* word, the same way they called cancer the *C* word. People just didn't do it. It was a black mark. I think John felt that, felt the loss, felt the failure."

"And what about you, Nan? Did you think it was a black mark? A failure?"

After a moment, Ruby replies, "Yes, honey, I'd have to say I did. That was the thinking of the time and it's hard to go against that."

"Then how did you have the, the..." Lisa searches for the word. Strength? Bravery? Fortitude?

"Nerve? Ha!" Ruby finishes for her.

"Well actually, I wasn't going to say that."

"But that's what it came down to, child. Plain nerve." Ruby shakes her head, proud of her choice. For years, she has pushed it away into the recesses of her mind, but here—sequestered in their own time and place, the world outside moving by without them, her life's memories pulsing and insinuating themselves into every moment—there seems to be no reason to deny it, or to make it something it was not. It feels good to say it, to admit it. She says it again.

"Nerve. Yes, plain and simple. My mother believed it was a selfish decision." Ruby smiles in recollection before continuing. "Nobody I knew was divorced. It just didn't happen—well, not to middle-class working people. It happened to big stars or singers, but not to the everyday Catholics who went to church. Back then, people stayed married. Women stayed married. I call it nerve, other people call it selfishness, but I could never come to terms with being somewhere that felt hopeless, even if that somewhere was a marriage."

There is a silence, both women lost in thought, and then Lisa wonders out loud: "It must have been difficult for women in the forties and fifties. There were so few options. What could women really do if they were unhappy in their marriage?"

"Not much, let me tell you! Women got married and stayed married. That was their lot in life. I always thought it was funny, you know, that in the Bible Lot's wife turned to a pillar of salt. That was her lot, Lot's wife." Ruby falls silent for a moment. She watches the countryside pass by, but without really seeing it. "How many women turned to pillars of salt?" she continues, her voice quiet, thoughtful. "In my day, women got married and had children. And if your marriage wasn't a good one, what could you do? Who even knew what a good marriage was? And women rarely worked out of the home. Without a husband, how could they support themselves and their children?" Ruby shakes her head. "Nope, divorce just didn't happen in good families."

"And yours was a good family?"

"One of the best." Ruby laughs. "Yes, one of the best."

"So how did you find the nerve?" Lisa watches her grandmother as she gazes out the window, lost in a past that Lisa herself can only ever glimpse vicariously.

"Yes, how did I find the nerve?" Ruby repeats. "I guess I had to find it. There was no other way." Turning, Ruby studies her granddaughter's intent face. "I suppose I was quite independent for the time. I had something of a career in music, as small as it was. I wasn't on the world stage or anything, but I was singing in nightclubs and working at the radio station—they called it *The Nabob Hour*. This was in Toronto, just before your father was born. Radio was big back then, and I was lucky to get the job."

Ruby remembers clearly the small booth, the large condenser microphone, and the nervous feeling clawing at her stomach while she waited for the light to flash on, the one that told her she was live. Reaching all those people at one time. It never ceased to amaze her how, standing in one place, she could be in so many other places. Singing to an audience she couldn't see. The radio was exciting and new, bringing new hopes and dreams to a career she had thought lost.

"OKAY, RUBY, YOU'RE ON IN TEN. Studio B. The boys have already set up. You want to go warm up and get ready?" Graham Fraser, program director for CKLM, sticks his head into the ready room and spots Ruby seated in the far corner, a coffee mug in her hand. She is staring gloomily at the oily residue as it circles on top of the brown liquid, turning her tender stomach.

"Sure, Graham, just give me a minute," Ruby responds with a weak smile, unsuccessfully covering the wave of nausea flushing over her face.

"You all right?" he asks, stepping into the room to get a better look.

"Yes, it's nothing, just a little indigestion. I was rushing to get here. You know, work, the kids, dinner, streetcars. Next week I won't eat beforehand."

"Yeah, life can get pretty hectic at times. Your little guys must be getting bigger, eh?"

"Francis is almost eight and Phoebe is two and a half now."

"Yup, busy times for you. How's John doing?"

"Great, thanks. He's not back until Tuesday, so I'm running the show."

"Well, if anyone is capable it's you!" He glances at his watch. "Okay, you better get to the studio. We'll be counting you in in less than eight now."

Ruby rises, putting down her untouched coffee. The nausea has receded somewhat, and she can almost imagine that it was just indigestion caused by the frantic rush to feed the kids, gulp down a bite, and settle the babysitter all in an hour and a half. The children crying as she left didn't upset her as much as frustrate her. They are well taken care of. Audrey is wonderful with them; she is a god-send to Ruby. Audrey lives two doors down, a widow who loves children and has made a career as a homemaker. Now with her own children grown, Audrey fills her days with the care of Francis and Phoebe, affording Ruby the luxury of unencumbered time to pursue her burgeoning aspirations, one of which has become Leland James.

He fills her thoughts in the same way that music fills her soul, lighting every corner of her being, bringing her into the beauty of the present more deeply with every breath she takes. He is like a drug. She, who hardly drinks, who up until recently couldn't understand the biting necessity of need, now finds herself an addict, stealing moments, ignoring her guilt, turning life upside down, risking everything to secure her ecstasy. His voice, his laughter, his thoughts, his touch, all pull at her with a force she's never known.

She will be meeting him after the radio show, and the anticipation helps her forget, helps her blur everything else into insipid shades.

"When will you be back?" Audrey asked earlier that evening as Ruby was gathering up her things, running her check list through her head with practised agility.

"I'm not sure. Can you stay the night?" Tucking her sheet music into her carry bag, Ruby rushed on, her lie staining her cheeks, hindering her ability to meet Audrey's naïve goodness face on. "I'll be going to the Lounge right after I leave the radio station, so it'll be quite late."

"Mommy, Mommy," Phoebe sang, hanging onto Ruby's purse and swinging back and forth, her baby weight tugging at Ruby's arm.

"Let go, Phoebe!" Ruby's voice was harsh with impatience and stress. Then she added, more tenderly, "Mommy has to go to work. You stay here with Audrey and Francis and be a good girl." Untangling Phoebe from the purse and, after a quick kiss, moving her toward Audrey, Ruby looked at Francis. "Francis, you be a big boy now and watch your sister and help Audrey, okay?"

Audrey smiled, lifting Phoebe into her arms. "She'll be fine. As soon as you leave, we're going to play Old Maid and then have a bath. It will be lots of fun, right Phoebe?" Audrey kissed the little girl's dark hair. Phoebe nodded, buried tight against Audrey's sweater, tears gathering in her eyes.

Francis came in from the hallway, taking up a silent stance of independence beside Audrey as the three of them watched Ruby run down the steps toward the street. Turning, Ruby raised her hand, the sense of freedom soothing her anxiety like a salve and spreading across her face in a moment of genuine happiness. Audrey returned her wave and smiled, hiking Phoebe's small body up against her. Then she closed the door, happy to be needed.

READYING HERSELF before the microphone, focused on the music she is about to sing, Ruby feels a sense of calm come over her. More and more she is appreciating what she is singing—blues and jazz, her father's favourite music. He loved the melancholy of the blues, the excitement of jazz. "Jazz is a sensual thing, Ruby, full of physical passion and creativity. But you couldn't have jazz without blues; there is no joy without pain. They come from the very deepest part of the individual, and there is nothing else like them."

She is pleasantly surprised to find her father's enthusiasm seeping into her understanding of the music. Ruby relates to the blues; it is sultry, sad, and painful, yet it keeps moving, finding beauty in the harsh struggle of life. It is the sound of the soul that will not be defeated, and her voice hangs on the notes with the pain of her own struggle. *"Love will make you drink and gamble/ make you stay out all night long/ Love will make you do things/ you know is wrong."*

She knows that loving Leland is wrong, but there is no escaping it. She needs him; she wants him, as she has wanted nothing else.

"NAN. NAN?" Lisa touches Ruby's hand. "Nan?"

Startled, Ruby turns. "Phoebe, honey. Where are we?"

Gently, Lisa replies, "Nan, it's me, Lisa. We're on the bus."

"Lisa." Ruby's expression has not changed. "Lisa, Gary's daughter."

"Yes, Nan. I'm your granddaughter. I'm your son Gary's daughter."

"Yes, Lisa, Gary's daughter." Nodding her head then looking down at her hands, Ruby continues, "Francis never had children. Two marriages and no children." There is a long silence. Ruby's mind tumbling along with the movement of the bus, unable to land on any one thought, consumed by a sense of fault, of confusion. Lisa cannot help. Holding Ruby's hand, she can only wait, a comfort in companionship. When she continues, Ruby's voice is strained with effort. "And Phoebe has a daughter."

"Yes, she does." Lisa smiles. "Do you remember her name, Nan?"

"Phoebe's daughter is Jacklyn."

"Yes, that's right."

"I never knew where Phoebe got that name from. Jacklyn. At first, I wasn't so sure about it really—ha! But now I like the name very much, and I wonder at my own hesitation. I suppose children grow into their names, don't they?"

"Yes, I imagine they do," Lisa answers with a smile. "Jacklyn has two children of her own now. Do you remember their names?"

"Jeremy and Alex," Ruby answers with a proud nod. "I'm a great-grandmother."

"That's right." Lisa smiles again. Pushing her hair from her forehead, she looks out the window. Her reflection and that of her grandmother are side by side on the glass, vague ghosts against the landscape.

"You don't have children do you, Lisa?" Ruby asks, her voice husky with confusion.

"No. I don't." Lisa turns from the window and continues patiently, "I'm not married."

"Well, honey, you don't have to be married to have children. Those days are long gone!" Ruby says with such enthusiasm that Lisa laughs with genuine amusement, dissolving the fear and worry of a moment ago.

"You're right, Nan. Those days are long gone. I don't have any children. Yet."

"And don't have them until you're good and ready. Don't even have them at all if you don't want them, Lisa. That's my advice to you, honey."

Although she doesn't add that she speaks from experience, the implication is there. Age has given her a freedom, an ability to stand in the harsh light of truth and not turn from it. Her dark secrets, kept hidden in the corners of her subconscious, have begun to float to the surface of her mind like driftwood, tempered by the years and becoming buoyant over time. They seem separate from her, drifting of their own accord through the passage of memory. They are no longer the heavy weights that held her down; they are simply part of her reality, a reality that moves and shifts so quickly that it is best just to embrace it all. She should never have had children. They were simply a by-product of sex, she thinks, a harsh and private thought.

But if she hadn't had children, she would not now be in the company of this lovely young woman, her companion, her grandchild, herself.

The irony of life, Ruby thinks, is coming to realize the truth too late. *But there can be no regrets, life is what it is.* "Maybe I was given children at the wrong time in life," Ruby continues, unaware that she is speaking out loud, the thoughts tumbling out with a life of their own. "I loved my children, but I could not help feeling that they were a hindrance. Francis and Phoebe, and then Gary, all before I knew that there could be a choice not to have children. In my time, women got married, and married women had children."

"Nan?" Lisa looks at Ruby and touches her hand, bringing her back to the present. "I didn't know you never wanted to have children."

Ruby turns, confusion edging her voice and lending a hollow sound to her words. "My children?"

"Yes, Nan. You were just talking about your kids. You said that you felt they were a hindrance, and that you never knew you had a choice not to have them."

"Yes. That's right! I did say that," Ruby replies after a moment. "Don't look so shocked, Lisa."

"I'm not shocked. Well, maybe a little surprised. I guess I never really considered..." Lisa trails off, her look of surprise replaced with one of confusion.

Ruby, taking up Lisa's hand, looks at her and smiles. "I know most women want children. Biologically and socially, we as women are programmed that way. There is no getting away from that. But in the moments that I can stare truth in the face and not look away, I can see that I never wanted children. It made me different." Ruby nods to herself, Lisa momentarily forgotten. "I felt the difference in me, and it seemed to alienate me from other women. I simply did not and could not share their passion about children."

Lisa nods with this new understanding, her own thoughts

racing with bewilderment. Minutes pass as she struggles to find the words to reply, and the silence somehow seems to amplify Ruby's confession. When Ruby continues, it is as if Lisa were not present, and she is thankful for the anonymity. "I wasn't running headlong into marriage in order to have children. For a middle-class Christian woman in the forties, marriage was the only way to experience sex. When I met John Grace, I was twenty-three and more than a little anxious for the experience. I don't know how other women felt. Mine was a time before the sexual revolution, before Oprah and self-help books began to examine the female psyche and sexual propensities. Ha! I simply knew that I was interested in knowing about sex. I wanted to know what it would feel like to be overpowered by a man, to have him, his physical presence above me, to be with him to the exclusion of everything else...." Ruby falls silent as she drifts off, becoming lost in thought.

She had felt the need, the curiosity, in the childish daydreams of her youth and later in the more informed desires of her late teens and early twenties. But to marry simply to experience that area of adulthood—barred as it was to single women—brought with it feelings of guilt and indecision. She couldn't explain this to her mother, who married at eighteen, never knowing the frustration of spinsterhood, of forced virginity. Marriage could end that.

She remembered the old house alive with light and activity the night before the wedding, full of excited voices punctuated with laughter. Her father was in his study, leaving the living room—or parlour, as mother had called it—free for the women to finish her dress. Aunt Lucy was there, Mrs. Worthing, the seamstress, Catherine Lowery, her maid of honour, and her mother. They were flushed, energized by the preparations. She was standing on the old burgundy ottoman while Mrs. Worthing hemmed her wedding dress, and she had felt like an observer, an interloper, so separated from the excitement she could feel all around her.

"What is it, darling? You look so worried." Her mother's voice jarred her from her thoughts. How could she have explained what she was feeling? That she was stealing the life of a man by this marriage in order to satisfy her own curiosity, and her own cravings. She was being dishonest. She felt sure that she should have other reasons for marrying John Grace. But perhaps, she told herself, there were no other feelings; maybe there was only the feeling that she wanted to know more, to take the next step in adulthood, to marry and to have children.

LISA'S HAND IS ON RUBY'S ARM as she watches her grandmother's fragile eyelids flickering with the movement of her dreams, so present and so removed. "Nan, wake up. We're pulling into the station."

Startled, Ruby looks around, her dreams receding slowly, disorientation in their wake.

"Are you okay?" Concern pulls at the corner of her voice.

"Lisa." It's almost a question.

"Yes, Nan. It's me, Lisa." She takes her grandmother's hand.

"My God, I was dreaming it was the night before my wedding. I was in my mother's parlour. I could even smell the room, wood polish and cold ash, and my mother, so young and alive."

"Are you okay, Nan?"

"Yes. Yes, I am, honey. It was beautiful, really, being there again in the house I was raised in. Seeing my mother and Catherine Lowery—I haven't thought of her in years. We were best friends until John and I moved to Toronto, and then slowly we lost touch." Ruby stops, her mind still in the past, reluctant to let go.

"Well, Nan, we're pulling into Union Station. We'll get off the bus now and onto the train, but first let's find a nice place and have a cup of tea, okay?"

Ruby shakes off the past and focuses on the present. "Never mind the tea, honey, I think I need a good stiff drink."

Lisa laughs, always amazed by this woman. "All right, a drink it is. A toast to old friends."

"Yes. A toast to old friends."

It feels good to disembark. Ruby is stiff and slow geting off the bus and following the crowd along the walkway and into the station. The energy and the grandeur of Toronto's Union Station and its Great Hall reinvigorating them.

Within minutes, they find a small crowded bar with tables and chairs spilling out onto a gated patio. The Great Hall is spacious, with four-storey-high vaulted ceilings of Guastavino tiles, the walls faced with Zumbro stone from Missouri, the floors made from Tennessee marble, the light natural and diffused from over-storey windows. The furniture is wrought iron and the patio is polished flag stone. Large double doors open onto the patio, exposing the darker recesses of the inside of the bar.

"You know, I sang in places that looked very much like this," Ruby comments as she sits, nodding toward the bar.

"You have had an extraordinary life, Nan. Was it as exciting as it seems?"

"It certainly was. It had its bumps, but I was blessed right from the beginning. My parents, your great-grandparents, were very well off and they doted on me. I was well educated for a woman of my day, you know. My father insisted on that. I was in training for years with LeLiberté."

"LeLiberté? Yes, Dad has mentioned him. He was quite famous in his day, wasn't he?"

"Yes, he was. I was being classically trained in voice. He was the renowned master of the time. Originally from Europe, he had a wide influence, you know."

"But I thought you sang blues and jazz?"

Ruby laughs. "Yes, I did that, too."

"Can I take your order, ladies?" A busy young waitress sidles up to the table, empty glasses on her tray, a practised look of boredom on her face.

"Yes, I'd like a vodka gimlet," Ruby says, happy with her choice.

"I don't think we have those, Ma'am." The waitress replies, shifting her tray in impatience.

"Do you want something with vodka, Nan?" Lisa asks, leaning over to her grandmother.

"Yes, I do. That's why I ordered the vodka gimlet." Turning to the waitress, she continues, "You do have a full bar here don't you, dear?"

"We do, but I've never heard of the drink you asked for."

"Well, perhaps your bartender has. Take my granddaughter's order and mine, and if the bartender doesn't know how to make a vodka gimlet, I can give him the ingredients. Would that be too much to ask for an old lady?"

The waitress turns to Lisa, unsure whether or not she has been somehow reprimanded, and Lisa smiles with a look of commiseration. "I'll have a white zinfandel, thank you."

"Well, I hope they can make my drink. I'm feeling quite nostalgic. Now if only they were playing some Billie Holiday or Nina Simone."

"You know, I've started to really listen to jazz. Dad has always loved it, and so I know about Billie Holiday and Nina Simone."

"Yes, two of my all-time favourites, along with Ella Fitzgerald and Sarah Vaughan. I was even told once that I sounded very much like Sarah, and, truth be told, I used to try and imitate her style." Ruby, nodding with pleasure, continues, "She was a contralto or mezzo soprano, and her songs were easy for me to sing. That music, it's the beginning of everything when everything was beginning. I still hear it in some of the new singers today."

"Yes, you're right about that. Like Norah Jones and Diana Krall. Have you heard Duffy? I have one of her CDs. 'Mercy' is one of my favourite songs, but now I'm listening more and more to the older stuff, like Etta James and Lena Horne. I guess I have you and Dad to thank for my taste in music."

"And I have my father to thank for my love of the same music." Ruby smiles. "He got to hear many of the original players. Our home was full of the music he loved, and I think it just seeped into my bones. All my memories play out around that sound."

"The soundtrack of your life. It's a great one to have, Nan." Leaning back from the table, Lisa makes room for the waitress.

"Your drinks, ladies." The waitress, almost smiling, places their drinks on small square napkins .

"Thank you, dear. And is this a vodka gimlet?" Ruby asks, leaning over and peering into her drink.

"Yes. I don't know what's in it—the bartender had to look it up in the book behind the bar. Enjoy."

Not waiting for the waitress to leave, Ruby barks, "Thank God for the book behind the bar. Ha!" She sips tentatively at the drink. "Not bad," she pronounces. "You know, I've always liked being in a night club, or bar, as you young ones call them nowadays. I think it's in my blood. My father and mother enjoyed it too. Well, perhaps my father more than my mother. I think she just went along with him, but my father loved it. Did you know he took me to my first night club in Montreal?" Her question is rhetorical.

After a sip from the cool, wet glass, Ruby continues with her story. "I was eighteen, and in Montreal jazz was big"—she learns forward to emphasize her point—"and bad! Well, most of my friends' parents frowned on it, believing it to be an inferior type of music. They believed it 'put the sin in syncopation,' as they say, with its evil influence. Ha!" Ruby laughs, her wide grin dimpling her face.

"That's the same thing they said about rock 'n' roll when it first came out." Lisa nods, enjoying the thread of this conversation.

"Yes, exactly! But my father was different. He loved the wildness, the improvisation of the music, the fact that it was made up as it went along." Ruby smiles, remembering her father's words. "He always said that there were two kinds of jazz back then, the white jazz and the real jazz."

"Real jazz?"

"Yes, the hard-driving, high-energy music with ragged rhythms and complex melodies. This was the jazz my father craved, and he knew all the best places to find it, although they weren't always run by the best people."

Lisa looks quizzically over her glass at Ruby.

"Well, Montreal was ripe with organized crime, and a few of the 'families' ran some of the best clubs." Ruby takes a long satisfying drink before continuing. "It was just the times. My father knew some of the men, I think. Well, I got that impression anyway. He could always get us in anywhere, anytime. But the place he liked the best was the corner." Ruby's voice drops as she thinks of Daniel Kenny, her father, and the mystery he remains to this day.

"The corner?" Lisa gently prods after a moment. "Was that a night club?"

"What's that, lovey?" Ruby asks, roused from her thoughts.

"You said your dad took you to the corner. Was that a night club?"

"No, no." Ruby laughs. "The corner was where St. Antoine meets Mountain street in Montreal and there are, or were, two clubs there: Rockhead's Paradise and Café St. Michel. The Rockhead was a three-floor show bar where the best of the best played. The owner was a good-looking man, a black East Indian named Rufus Rockhead. He'd stand by the door of the club, dressed in a beautifully tailored suit, allowing only the people he knew and the best musicians to get in. He knew my father all right! Ha!" Shaking her head in wonder, Ruby sighs, her mind alive with the hustle and excitement of those evenings. She savours the feel of her memories—smooth beads begging to be handled—before returning to the present and continuing her story. "The Café was where Louis Metcalfe, the famous American trumpeter had his band. He played there for years. Both clubs would swing, let me tell you, with the best jazz, the best musicians. But it was a time when things were still segregated, and often we were the only white people there."

"Weren't there any clubs for white people?"

"Oh yes, uptown had some great clubs too, but my father preferred the sounds on the corner. He said they were authentic. He liked the free-spirited, rebellious rhythms and melodies, and they attracted all the greatest players. He was right of course. I first saw Oscar Peterson there. He was a few years my junior, maybe fifteen or sixteen years old, and playing boogie woogie like a man twice his age! Everyone in the place danced to his music. I wasn't formally introduced to him until years later when I was working at the radio station in Toronto. But even as a kid, he was something!" Ruby says, slapping the table top for emphasis.

"Montreal must have been something during those years, Nan. What an exciting city to live in."

"Yes, it really was. It was an exciting time that passed too quickly." Ruby nods, her voice dropping with a note of nostalgia. "But Montreal changed. By the sixties, there weren't any more after-hours clubs. Rock 'n' roll took over. I suppose they were trying to clean up the city and its reputation, but I think they just plain lost something. My father never did like Jean Drapeau as mayor. His campaign to clean up the city's reputation ended up ruining its extraordinary night life. Clubs shut down, and places like the corner just faded away. Eventually the area was pulled down to make room for an expressway and blocks of social housing. It's a sad statement about progress, let me tell you. But that's the way life goes. I guess we never know what it is we have at the time we are in it, at the time we are living it. Everything is always clearer in retrospect. It's the same with our own personal history as it is with a city's or a country's history. There is no plan, no road map; there is just doing what you think is best and then trying to make the choices acceptable in the retelling." Ruby sighs, staring down at the table. She studies her hand around the glass; it's a hand she can hardly recognize, dark with liver spots and thick with veins.

"Would you ladies like another drink?" the same young waitress asks, her eyes on the table and Ruby's empty glass.

"Yes, I believe that would be in order. Wouldn't you say, Lisa?" Ruby asks, looking from the waitress to Lisa.

"No, thank you. I'm still working on mine, but you go ahead and have another one. We're on holiday."

"Well yes, dear, I think I will!" Ruby says. "I'll have another vodka gimlet. Thank you." Watching the waitress retreat, Ruby continues, "I think in light of the story, a few drinks are called for. Prohibition is over, you know. Ha!"

"So, how did you go from singing in the night clubs to community theatre and then to the movies?" Lisa asks, enjoying the conversation and hoping to coax her grandmother into revealing more about her long and interesting life.

"Well, I left Toronto. It was expensive, and at the time I was supporting the kids on my own. The work I had with the singing wasn't what you would call reliable and I needed something I could count on. I can't remember how I decided on Peterborough, but I did and it worked out well. I found a steady job and a great place to live. But provincial Ontario can be pretty insipid after the excitement and flavour of a big city, as you can imagine." Ruby looks directly into Lisa's eyes, her seriousness bringing a smile to her granddaughter's face. "Thankfully, I met Robert Davies. He was the editor of the *Peterborough Examiner* and a drama enthusiast, not to mention a writer—one of Canada's greatest! He and his wife, Patricia, befriended me, and it just grew from there. Oh, we spent so many evenings together, reading over a play Robert was working on. He'd say, 'Ruby, you were born for the stage,' in that deep, resonant voice of his, and I believed him.

"That was a wonderful time, and Robert and Patricial became our best friends. The stories I could tell about those years!"

"Were you married to Leland James then?" Lisa asks. She has always been curious about her grandmother's love affair with Leland.

"Yes. Leland followed me to Peterborough, and eventually we married. Leland would come to the readings; he would even read some of the parts, and he was good. He had a keen sense of humour, and that sharp wit was always there behind the words." Ruby says, smiling in recollection before lapsing into an introspective silence. Minutes pass, and Lisa worries if these memories may be too much for her grandmother. But then Ruby continues abruptly, speaking mostly to herself before turning back to Lisa. "But he had no desire for the stage. He encouraged me, though, and he loved watching me on stage. He was at every performance and all the closing parties afterwards, of course. They were some wild times, let me tell you! Ha! You'd never think it now, but we were so young, so full of life." Fingering the side of her glass, her gaze turned inward again, she thinks for a moment before continuing. "Youth, which is forgiven everything, forgives itself nothing; age, which forgives itself everything, is forgiven nothing."

"That's quite profound," Lisa says, her voice flat, her mind still lost in the past with Ruby and Leland.

"It's not me, honey. It's George Bernard Shaw," Ruby says, smiling. "I heard it when I was young. Now I think I understand it. When I was a young woman, I was too impatient to figure it out. You really wouldn't have recognized me..." she says and looks over her glass and directly into Lisa's eyes, "... and my wilder side."

"No, Nan. I think I can," Lisa says. Looking at Ruby, she glimpses, not for the first time, the vibrant woman her grandmother had been. "I often imagine how you would have been when you were young, when you and Leland were together. I wish I could have been there, been part of that whole story. You were forging new roads, going new places, and having great parties, by the sounds of it."

"Yes, we were that! The evenings after performances were always wild, when everyone's adrenaline was pumping, emotions soaring—we didn't want it to end. Everyone would end up back at someone's place, sometimes ours, and the kids would be woken up by the noise, the music, the singing, going all night. The birds would be calling to the morning, and Leland and I would just be going to bed, still feeling too alive to sleep."

The scene comes to her, vibrant and real: their bedroom, washed in the ghost of morning light, the feel of Leland's body, warm and solid against her, the sweet smell of liquor on his breath as he kisses her lips, her ear, her neck. His broad hand running the length of her body, pulling her against him, and the sheer exhilaration of wanting him, of wanting to open herself up to him, kissing his chest and inhaling the scent of him, then pulling his face to her lips as he enters her slow and hard and present.

"Are you thinking about Leland?" Lisa leans forward and touches Ruby's hand, her grandmother's skin smooth and dry against her own.

"What?" Startled, Ruby looks up from her glass, the condensation capturing prisms of light like crystals.

"Were you thinking about Leland James? I can always tell when you are."

"Yes, lovey, I was." Ruby smiles to herself. "I was thinking of Leland James."

"Well, I think we better drink up. I'll go pay our waitress," Lisa says, looking at her watch and rising from the table. "We have to find the train that goes to Chicago, although we do know the track number."

"Yes, time waits for no man!" Ruby says playfully. "You go pay, and I will get myself moving after I finish this drink. The pleasures in life are too few to waste when you get to my age. Ha!"

As she waits for the bill, Lisa watches Ruby, her white hair so distinctive, her movements so familiar as she raises the glass to her lips, savouring the last drops and nodding to the couple at the next table. Lisa can't hear what she is saying, but the couple laugh in reply and Ruby joins them in their laughter. Then for a moment and without warning, Lisa feels a cold knot tighten in the pit of her stomach. Looking at her grandmother and watching the interplay between them, the nuances of Ruby's movements, Ruby's laughter alive in her ears, Lisa knows she will never again have this, this moment, this epiphanous understanding of the woman who is her grandmother. What is happening to me? Lisa wonders, reproaching herself and wiping the tears from her cheek. This is ridiculous, she thinks. Her emotions seem to push against her with physical force.

"Did you want to pay cash or debit?" the waitress asks, breaking into Lisa's thoughts and releasing her from the moment.

"Cash, thank you," Lisa says, forcing a smile as she regains control of her emotions. The transaction gives her a focus, freeing her mind from her fears and allowing her thoughts to race ahead to the train and the journey, to her aunt Phoebe and the excitement of Chicago.

4.

"I THOUGHT I'D FIND YOU HERE, Danny boy," Michael says, moving in along the bar. He places his hand on his brother's shoulder, feeling the muscular warmth beneath his shirt. Daniel nods in recognition but doesn't take his eyes from the stage, where Clara Smith is improvising with staccato vocals around the piano notes in the smoky, charged atmosphere of the North Side Chicago night club.

"Do you want another?" Michael asks, nodding toward Daniel's empty beer and catching the bartender's vigilant eye.

Clara Smith finishes, the notes still hanging in the air like liquid honey. Daniel turns and nods at Froggy Green, the bartender, who smiles with genuine affection. "You all wantin' the same thing, Mr. Daniel?"

"Yeah. Thanks, Froggy. What are you having, Mick?" Daniel asks, turning to his brother and catching his eye for a moment.

"I'll have the same as Danny, thanks." Michael says, nodding to Froggy and adjusting himself on the bar stool.

They are the only two white men in the night club, and although Daniel is comfortable and at ease, Michael is less so. "I don't get the attraction, Danny," Michael says, indicating the room with a nod of his head.

"You don't have to," Daniel says, shrugging slightly while lighting up a cigarette. He inhales deeply and then slowly pushes the smoke from his lungs, watching the pale grey stream make its way up toward the dim lights above the bar.

The band starts up again and the music soars encouragingly through the room, vibrating through their bodies, soothing and exciting at the same time. "But I gotta admit, the music is pretty good," Michael says, his eyes trained on the band.

Daniel nods. "That it is."

The drinks arrive. From the corner of his eye, Michael watches Daniel down the bottle, the liquid measured in the effort of his Adam's apple, moving almost rhythmically to the music. He can hardly recognize his young brother, who has returned from the First World War immersed in a deep pool of silence. At times, the Daniel Michael he knew seems to have disappeared, leaving a stranger in his wake. Daniel frequents the black nightclubs, soothed by the sounds of the new music that has made its way up the Mississippi from the Deep South, flourishing in cities like New Orleans, Cincinnati, New York, and Chicago.

Reconstruction, Jim Crow laws, and the First World War have encouraged the migration of black people from the soil of the rural south to the pavement of the urban north, their second diaspora. They have brought with them the pain of their history, the strength of their spirit, and the music of their souls. The drum beats of Africa, the melancholy of the spiritual, the syncopation of the marching band, the history of the folk song, the pining of the blues, all becoming a homogeneous mix in the melodious, discordant vernacular of American jazz, original and raw.

Jazz calls out in creative chaos; it is the sound of a burgeoning country, of a people scrounging to find an identity within different ethnic societies. In its musical strains, Daniel hears the struggle of the individual spirit, the struggle of a people, the struggle of an evolving nation. The painfully discordant notes add to the fullness and depth of the music; they speak of a people struggling to find harmony and meaning in the confusion of becoming. An adolescent country becoming aware of her feelings, her growing needs, her surprising desires;

it is an exciting, confusing time full of pain, introspection, extravagance, love, desire, elation, and despair, a time of lost boundaries, of disillusionment, of loss, of hope. All this is reflected in jazz. In the music, Daniel finds some escape from the memories of the Western Front, from the months of rain and chill and mud, of trench warfare, and the menace of the Forest of Argonne. Daniel, frightened and bewildered, exhausted and disillusioned, is one of over a million American men who, alongside their tired and broken Allies, pushed the German army from France entirely.

In the new music of the age, Daniel finds a way to forget about the weeks of attacking and retreating, the taste of fear in his mouth, and the feel of heavy stone in his gut as he and the other desperate young men he commanded put their lives at risk day after day. Exposed to artillery mortar, machine gun, rifle fire, and gas, Daniel's regiment, the seventh infantry, lost twenty-eight hundred of its three thousand men in twenty-eight days. He cannot expunge the horror, the stench, the revulsion that he felt surrounded by the decomposing bodies of boys who would never live to be men. Their faces were contorted or surprised, or sadly peaceful in the chaos of the Dante-like inferno around them. Worse yet were those with no faces at all, lying in goading parody of human bodies, grotesque and hypnotizing at the same time. They were all etched into his mind with indelible ink. *And for what?* The question haunts him through his waking hours. Only music can offer a distraction.

"Danny?" Michael's hand is on his arm, his voice layered with concern and apprehension. Daniel focuses on the voice, pulled toward the present, toward the secure darkness of the night club, toward the music, toward life.

"Yeah, Michael, I'm good," Daniel says with a weak smile, an effort on his part to dissipate the fear in his brother's face. "I'm making it through." Daniel forces a tone of joviality into his voice, into his consciousness. "So, are you looking for me for a specific reason, or are you just looking for me?"

Michael, relieved, smiles his crooked smile and leans against the bar. He turns his attention to the business at hand, suddenly much more comfortable. "Dean wants a meeting with ya'."

"I'm hardly back from one war and O'Bannion wants to enlist me in another?" Daniel asks, his eyes meeting his brother's for a moment.

"Well, word is that Torrio's got a new wing man, a guy called Al Capone, and they're building strength on the South Side. I think Dean wants to use your superior intellect, if you know what I mean."

"I already told you to tell him that I'd do the books. I doubt anyone's touched them since I've been gone. There's no big rush."

"I don't think it's about the books, Danny," Michael says, looking from Daniel to the stage, his measured words cutting through the music.

"Then what?" Daniel asks, turning toward his brother, genuine interest in his voice.

"Have ya' heard about that amendment? Some Bible thumpers and the women's sobriety movement are trying to push it through in Washington."

"Prohibition?"

"Yeah." Michael nods. "I'm telling ya', with the war and everything, those lily whites have been able to force their opinions through, and now we're looking at a dry country. Can you imagine?" Michael asks incredulously, shaking his head and taking a long pull on his beer.

Daniel finishes his beer and nods to Froggy for another. "So, what does this have to do with me? Dean wants me to go to Washington and argue the case against prohibition?" Daniel laughs.

"Not quite," Michael says, his smile fading quickly. "I think he's setting up connections in Canada so if and when there's no liquor available here, Dean can bring it down from the north."

"That sounds interesting but tell me, since when did Dean get so far thinking?"

"I think Torrio is bringing out the best in him."

Daniel laughs. "I didn't think that was possible."

"Actually, one of the snitches told Dean months ago that Torrio was setting up his own connections in Canada in case the amendment passes. Which he thinks it will."

"Well, he'd know. Torrio answers to Mike Merlo, and everyone knows Merlo has a pack of government men on his payroll."

"Yeah, that's what Dean figures. Merlo's probably given the nod, and Capone has been busy as a blue-arsed fly setting everything up for Torrio. So, Dean's been busy trying to get the jump on him. He figures he's got a good connection in Canada, and he has something all hooked up. He just needs a representative to go up there and seal the deal."

Michael stops to take a drink and then continues, his enthusiasm evident. "And Dean's under the gun, so to speak, to beat Capone in setting this up. There'll be millions to be made, Danny, and not much risk. Merlo don't like violence."

"Yeah, Mike Merlo doesn't like violence, but he plays both sides of the fiddle, and that's always a dangerous game, especially with hot heads like Torrio. And who's this other guy? Capone?"

"Al Capone. He's a Brooklyn boy from the Five Points gang. Came to Chicago and started out as Torrio's bodyguard, but now he's wielding his own power in the South Side. He's a new breed."

"It doesn't sound good to me, Michael. Merlo's Unione Siciliana is a power to be reckoned with, and we're just a bunch of Micks from the North Side. O'Banion is no match for the likes of Mike Merlo and Torrio."

"Merlo won't let anything get outta hand, Danny. His political reputation won't allow it. He's the only reason there ain't more blood on the streets."

Both men drink, the music momentarily forgotten.

"Where in Canada is this connection?" Daniel asks, fingering the bottle in front of him and watching the condensation slide down the side. "It's a big country."

Michael swallows a mouthful of beer, then turns his head and burps. Turning back, he answers, "Montreal."

"Montreal?"

"Yeah, they speak French there. And since you've been to France..."

Daniel barks out a laugh. "I don't speak French."

"No, but you've been to Europe, you're educated, and you're intimately acquainted with the French." Michael lifts his beer in salute, as if everything is settled.

"The only thing I've been intimately acquainted with in France is the mud," Daniel says with no hint of humour in his voice.

"Weren't you in Paris?"

"Yeah, when I was on leave. I spent my time in bars and brothels like any red-blooded male." Daniel smiles.

"Didn't you have to speak to those French women? Tell them what to do? Or did they already know?"

Daniel's eyes dart toward his brother as he takes a drink. He lets the question hang in the air like the smoke from his smoldering cigarette.

"Come on, Daniel, you're knowing what I mean," Michael says, slipping into the brogue, a sign of intimacy he knows his brother cannot ignore. "You got sophistication and smarts. You're an officer who passed that army test with flying colours. The rest of us are just bums. We don't know our arses from our elbows. And what else will you be doing with yourself, Danny boy, now that you're in your civvies?"

Daniel smiles despite himself. His brother's patter never changes. Plus, the distraction of working with O'Banion might take his mind off the war. "Okay. Set it up. I'll meet with Dean and hear him out."

Michael smiles, thumping Daniel's shoulder hard. "Good!"

"Now shut up, Mick. Let's listen to some jazz. Did you know Jelly Roll Morton is coming here next week?"

"He is?" Michael answers, nonplussed.

Daniel smiles at his brother's lack of interest, and pushes on. "Yeah, why don't you come with me and hear him? Jelly Roll Morton and the Red Hot Peppers. They'll be at the Green Mill Jazz Club on…"

"Yeah, I know where it is—North Broadway. It's Capone's club in our territory, Daniel." Michael raises his eyebrow and looks across his beer at Daniel, his voice hard.

"It's music, Mick. It knows no territory, and it's the only thing I can really enjoy since I got back." Daniel looks down at the drink in his hand, the smile at the corner of his mouth belying the seriousness of his tone. "It helps me hold on; it gives me hope for the human race."

"If you say so, Danny."

"All you have to do is listen to it, Mick. It's music that transcends the human condition at the same time as it recognizes it for what it is."

"Oh boy-oh! You're getting a little too deep for me!" Michael laughs with embarrassment.

"Well," Daniel shrugs, "sometimes, there's nowhere else to go but inside. And guess what you find when you look there, Mick?" Daniel continues without waiting for an answer. "That music. Blues and jazz. The power of the human spirit to overcome and celebrate in the face of all the struggles that life has to offer."

Michael is aware of the music's effect on his brother. Daniel's distance, his moody silence, the turmoil that has been swirling around him since his return from France has disappeared. Daniel's smile has returned, reaching his eyes and bringing a little of the old Danny to the present moment.

For the first time since he returned from the war, Michael feels comfortable enough to probe Daniel's thoughts. "It was bad over there," he says softly. It's not quite a question.

He hasn't pushed Daniel for details about the war; until now he has been unable or unwilling to acknowledge Daniel's lingering pain, present in every moment.

"It was bad," Daniel answers, his words as flat as his eyes. He pulls on his beer, swallowing his anger and disillusionment along with the alcohol.

Falling into an awkward silence, Michael avoids looking at his brother; he doesn't have the language or the understanding to help Daniel, and his impotence frustrates him. Daniel is one of the many hollow men returning to a life without meaning, desperate to find it. Some turn to alcohol, some religion, some family, some deviance, all of them looking for a lifeline, a mooring. After a moment, Michael shrugs and continues, "Well, if the music helps."

"It does," Daniel says quickly.

Michael nods, wishing there was some way, anyway, he could help ease his brother's pain. "Do you want another drink?"

Daniel laughs, spurting liquid from his pursed mouth, aware of Michael's desperate need to give him something. He wipes his chin and swallows, "Yeah, I'll have another drink." He grabs Michael's shoulder. "And don't worry, big brother. I'll be fine. We come from hardy stock."

"Hey, Daniel, enjoying the band?" A slim, good-looking black man stops beside the two brothers and places his hand on Daniel's shoulder.

"Yeah, Tommy. Thanks. You getting up later?"

"Well I brought my horn so I'm hopin' to blow." Tommy laughs.

"I'll stay to hear that," Daniel says, smiling into the other man's dark eyes.

"Who was that?" Michael asks as they watch Tommy making his way past the bar and its patrons.

"That, Mick, is Tommy Ladnier, one of the world's best jazz trumpeters," Daniel says, his eyes following Tommy until he disappears behind the stage. "Born in Louisiana but raised in New Orleans—the city where it all came from," Daniel says, nodding to himself.

"You seem to know him pretty good, Danny boy."

"Yes, that is my privilege," Daniel says and then looks at Michael. "You'll have to stay and listen to him. Then maybe you'll understand what I'm talking about."

The music starts again, and the brothers listen in silent companionship. A blues tune soars around them, its scale intentionally forced over the major chords, distinctively dissonant. The conflict of tonalities pulls at Daniel's soul, painful and soothing in equal parts; it is somehow able to touch him, to free him from his misery. "All right, you come with me to hear Jelly Roll Morton, and I'll meet with Dean. I'm not promising anything, but the distraction can't hurt."

"Agreed!" Michael laughs, nodding at his brother.

THE GANG'S HEADQUARTERS has moved to accommodate its growing needs. Now, they operate out of William Schofield's flower shop on North State Street, across from Holy Name Cathedral. Dean has a growing interest in horticulture; he finds the growing, clipping, and arranging to be a calming pastime. He sets his girlfriend Viola up as the shopkeeper and turns the rooms above Schofield's into the headquarters for the North Side Gang. It is here that Daniel finds himself. The usual suspects are in the front room of the headquarters when Michael and Daniel enter, smoking and talking in hushed tones. Vincent Ducci is the first on his feet, stubbing out his smoke and looking Daniel up and down, a wide smile across his dark face.

"Danny Boy! How are you doing? It's good to have you back. I heard you gave those Jerries hell over there."

Daniel accepts Vincent's handshake and looks around at the others. "Nice to be back, Vinny. See you boys haven't changed much. Hymie still taking all your money at cards?"

Hymie Weiss laughs and extends his hand. "No. The boys like to gamble their money away at the Clarke Street poolroom. Tennes is running a racing form outta there. He's got control over the whole telegraph service, so he brings in the daily returns on racetracks throughout the country."

Daniel whistles one long note. "Nice work if you can get it." He looks around at the men. "I guess the neighbourhood boys have all been busy while some of us have been off fighting the Kaiser."

"You got that right, Danny," Bugs Moran continues. "Between Tennes with the gambling and Big Jim Colosimo with the prostitution, Torrio and Dean are gonna be fighting for the only thing left: booze." They all laugh. The virtue of vice.

"It looks like I'm the answer to your prayers then."

"Well, we're hoping so," Dean O'Banion says as he emerges from the back room, a smile on his face, his hand extended in greeting. "How's it going, Daniel?"

"Good. Thanks, Dean." He accepts the handshake.

"So the conquering warrior has returned." Dean is still smiling.

"So to speak." Daniel's reply is clipped, his eyes unable to meet Dean's.

"Let's go to the back room and talk, Daniel. It's not much, but I use it as my office."

The office is bright; two large windows set in dormers look out onto the street, and the light spilling across the floor catches the corner of a large metal safe, its door partially open. There is a mahogany table and chair, dark and polished and facing the door. The table is empty except for an ornate anniversary clock and two books lying haphazardly on the corner. A settee is placed against the south wall, and two straight back chairs face the table. "Take a seat, Daniel." Dean indicates a chair and moves behind the mahogany desk. "Do you want a drink? I think it will be appropriate for our talk."

"Okay. What have you got?"

Reaching into the bottom drawer, Dean produces a bottle of single malt scotch and two glasses. "Only the best."

While Dean pours the scotch, Daniel picks up the books. A snort of laughter escapes him. "The Holy Bible and *The Art of War?* Unusual bedfellows, wouldn't you say, Dean?"

"They're not as contradictory as you would think." He hands Daniel a glass. "The Bible is full of struggle and conflict, people wanting and fighting for territory, and *The Art of War* is a meditation on dealing with your enemy in times of struggle. I suppose the big difference is that the Bible teaches that God is on the side of victory while Sun Tzu teaches that restraint and good planning ensure victory. Guess which one I follow?"

Daniel smiles, turning the book over in his hand. "What else does *The Art of War* say?"

Dean downs his scotch in one swallow, winces, and pauses before he answers. "To win without fighting is best."

There is a silence. Dean allows the silence to settle before he continues. "So, I hear you're struggling with being back."

Startled at the abrupt shift in direction, Daniel coughs up the scotch. A moment passes before he's able to speak. "Who's saying that?"

"Your big brother."

"Well, what would he know?"

"Nothing compared to you. Like the rest of us here, we didn't go to 'the war to end all wars.' We're pretty occupied here with this war." With a sweep of his arm, Dean indicates the street outside.

"Is that why you didn't go?"

"Partly. That's the biggest part. But another part of me had trouble coming to terms with fighting on the side of the English..."

Dean laughs. "Meaning, the enemy of my enemy is my friend?"

"Yeah, something like that." Dean pours himself another scotch and looks inquiringly at Daniel, who shakes his head. "Then another part of me has a hard time believing in the necessary lie." He takes a drink. "I have no patriotism."

"I'm impressed, Dean. *The Art of War* and now philosophical insights. You're gaining wisdom in your old age." Daniel smiles ironically. At twenty-three and twenty-five, both men are old beyond their years.

"I have to use anything and everything I can. I'm up against worthy opponents in a time with no rules." Dean snorts out a sound close to laughter and stretches out his arms. "This is the opportunity of the new world. We are men without a country because we *are* the country. I can be my own sovereign, and I'm engaged in a serious war. Capone is the new kid on the block, and he's not a boyhood rival—he's from New York and he's running Torrie's organization like an army. They're even calling the guys on the street 'soldiers.' And they intend to take over Chicago by force."

"I thought Mike Merlo doesn't like violence?"

"Yeah, but Merlo can't be everywhere. This Capone is a new breed; he plays with no holds barred."

"So, what does this have to do with me?" Daniel can barely contain his contempt at the use of the word "soldier." "Michael said you want me to make the connection for you in Canada. I can't do that without all the background information."

"That's true." Dean pauses, leaning forward, unsure how to continue. "Look, Daniel, nobody's trying to belittle your efforts and those of millions of other men who put their lives on the line. I have nothing but admiration for you. I couldn't do what you did, fight for an ideal, to keep the world safe for democracy, as old Woodrow Willy would have us believe. That's not immediate enough for me, and, to be honest, it doesn't mean anything to me. I watched my parents suffer in a so-called democratic country, working themselves into early graves surrounded by squalor and with nothing more than empty dreams. It was the same for your parents, Danny. That won't be my life. Or Michael's, or any of the guys out there." He points to the adjoining room where the men are waiting. "We'll fight for that."

They fall silent, surrounded by the ticking of the anniversary clock, the muffled noises of the street, and the murmured voices of the men in the other room. Dean has been unknowingly describing Daniel's unspoken fear: that the death and dying on the fields of France, on the fronts of Europe and in the villages of Russia, the accumulated cost measured in human life both military and civilian, measured in full scale destruction of land and property, may have been for nothing. Futile. Daniel is overcome by a sense of helplessness, of impotence, a loss of control; in the silence, his feelings of disillusionment sharpen into deceit and manifest into anger.

"You did what you had to do, Danny. The Allies won." Dean says, breaking the silence and bringing Daniel back to the moment. "The ends justify the means."

"And now you're a Machiavellian?" Daniel scoffs.

"All I know is that sometimes, good men do bad things in the belief that it's for the greater good."

"And the problem with that, Dean is that belief can so easily be manipulated."

"Yes, that's what I know, Danny. I think it's called leadership."

"Propaganda is more like it."

"Call it what you will. It's a tool."

"A tool? That's a joke." Daniel laughs but with no humour. "Tell that to the men that died in Flanders. Tell that to their families! We have all been used!" Daniel's voice rising with anger. "Used like fodder!"

Dean says nothing as the two men sit in silence, more pronounced after Daniels outburst. Then, picking up the bottle, he offers one to Daniel who nods his acceptance."

"All is fair in love and war, Danny boy."

"That's what you think, Dean."

"That's what I know."

Daniel shakes his head, his mind wheeling and darting around Dean's words, his anger palpable, flushing through his body and colouring his face. "So, what do you want with me?

"I want your loyalty. I want your intelligence. I want your bravery."

"Hell, you're not asking for much, are you?" Daniel spits out the words, his smile not quite reaching his eyes.

Dean nods. "No more than Uncle Sam asked of you."

He is right, of course. Wasn't the war brought about by the same competitive urges that individuals experience: acquisition, pugnacity and pride, the desire to control, to dominate? Yes, Daniel thinks. Uncle Sam, the state, is a living organism rife with all the baser human instincts of its inhabitants, but none of the restraints.

"He asked too much."

"Ours not to reason why, eh Danny."

"Yes. Tennyson was right, ours but to do and die."

"Some men find that noble."

"Some men are fools!"

"Yes, I agree!" Dean laughs, throwing back another shot. "And that's what I count on."

For Daniel, there was nothing noble to be found in the mud of France, where men shit themselves in fear, cried like children, or prayed to a God who had long ago forsaken them. That the Allies won the war means little to him. More was lost than won, but he knows that the stories will never be told, not the true stories; instead, things will be coloured and shaded, cleaned up and made acceptable.

"I need a representative. I need you to be my liaison with the connections in Montreal. It's behind the scenes. You'd have your own autonomy. You would be making decisions for me, creating a future and I need someone I know and trust."

Dean's proposal brings with it a feeling of immediacy. It is something he can see himself doing, something intriguing, even entrepreneurial and something, Daniel thinks, could help push the despair, the scenes of France, so vividly alive in his mind, to the periphery. He could, for a time, exchange one war for another, if not as a soldier then as an ambassador, an advisor.; there is only the individual, the here and now. Dean's offer is the armour he needs to be able to centre himself in a world that has tilted on its axis and is pulling him toward oblivion.

"Look, Daniel. You can think about it for a few days. You'll never be on the front lines in my organization. You can continue with the books and as an advisor, but I would like you as my representative. I need a personal contact in Montreal. If this amendment gets through, it'll be a licence to print money, and I'll want to get the jump on Torrio and Capone.

"No, Dean. I won't need a few days," Daniel answers, his gaze steady. "I've got nothing to lose."

"And everything to gain, my boy!"

When do you need me to leave?"

Dean smiles broadly, relief evident in his face. "Is next week okay?"

"Yeah, that shouldn't be a problem." Daniel nods. "I can start on those books, and you can fill me in on the details between then and now." Daniel gets to his feet and extends his hand across the table.

Dean accepts the handshake and replies warmly, "Welcome home, Daniel."

5.

"I THINK HE KNOWS."

"About us, you mean?" Leland lifts Ruby's hand to his lips. She feels the pressure and wetness against her fingers; her body reacts, a tightening in her abdomen, a flush to her face.

"Oh, Leland, what are we doing?" she asks with vague concern, running her hand through his hair, along his broad forehead. The question is always there, haunting her every waking moment, at times leading to such panic that she becomes curt and distracted with everyone around her. She has become an open sore, too vulnerable to be able to concentrate on anything but the need she feels. It grows with the intensity of lust, painfully alive and soothed only by the presence of Leland. He is a cooling balm on the heat of her confusion. With him, she is no longer aware of the pain that leaves her breathless and hurting. Being with Leland calms her mind, anchoring her safely in the whirlwind of emotion her days have become. With him, the world stops and she becomes, not the mother, not the wife, not the daughter, but Ruby Grace, existing fully in the moment.

She has stolen the time to be with him, taken it from her children, her family, feeling guilty and desperate at the same time. And her guilt makes her reckless, the sex between them driven and intense. She pushes past boundaries, wet and breathless for more, meeting Leland on a level that neither of them has ever experienced. He revels in her appetite and she in his creativity and openness, exploring each other with a thirst that cannot be sated. There is a wicked, almost violent undertone to their love making; but it is love making, a sharing, a communion, a recognition of soul. Afterward, lying wrapped in the lull of satiated release, there is no turning away from each other, or from the bond that holds them.

Leland stops his playful kissing and nipping of Ruby's neck, and sits back to study her face. The back booth of the night club is hidden from sight and lit only with a small, red, pot-bellied candle holder that flickers steadily, illuminating Ruby's distress in the sharpened angles of her face. Shirley Horn's song, "It Had to Be You," is playing in the background, her voice slow and sultry, the piano and saxophone sliding smooth against the brushes. *"It had to be you ... could make me be true ... make me be blue ... wonderful you."* Leland, picking out the lines, smiles to himself. The words are so apropos, the song so beautifully sad.

"Oh, my Ruby Grace. You need an answer, don't you?" He looks steadily into her eyes; into depths he can't reach.

Ruby nods, afraid to speak, holding Leland's eyes with her own, trying to force what is in her heart into him.

Leland takes her hand again, sighing deeply, the romance of a moment ago replaced by the levity he knows Ruby needs. "I told you already. Leave John and marry me and let the cards fall as they may."

"Just like that?" she whispers.

"What else can we do?" Leland places both hands on the table shakes his head. "We can't go on like this. You can't go on like this."

"But John? The children?" she asks, pleadingly.

"John and the children." Again, Leland folds his arms across his chest and nods. He is an interloper in her world, holding open a door to something else, but he feels her reluctance, understands her confusion. She is balancing precariously on the ball of decorum, conformity leaving her unable to move one way or another. His suggestion, his answer comes from selfish frustration.

Ruby leans back against the seat; her body is clammy, her mind racing. She is where she hoped never to be. But from the first moment, it was inescapable, this running off the rails, this catastrophic train wreck. She hasn't wanted to look. She has been pushing the reality out of her mind, out of reach, unwilling to contaminate what has grown between them, what is growing within her and what she can no longer deny. She wants to be with him, needs to be with him, will die without him. Closing her eyes, she begins silently to cry, her body moving gently with the rhythm of her sobs.

LISA LEANS TOWARD HER GRANDMOTHER and shakes her gently. "Nan?"

Ruby's eyes open wide. She's surprised by the brightness of the rail car and the concern on the young woman's face. "Where is Leland?" She looks around, unfamiliar with the scene she has so abruptly found herself in. Was she dreaming? *Yes.* As she gathers her thoughts and settles into the present moment, the images of the night club and the ache in her chest begin to slip away, leaving only a flavour, a whispered impression of something she can barely recognize. Now there is this young woman leaning toward her. *Who is this again? Surely, I know her.* Looking down, she sees a book in her lap and a hand, aged and arthritic. *This is me in old age. And the young woman…. She's too young to be my daughter. She must be my granddaughter. Yes…. Lisa.*

"Nan?"

"Was I snoring, lovey?" Ruby slips the glasses from the end of her nose and places them on the book in her lap, the movement centering her in the present.

"I think you were just dreaming." Lisa smiles, relieved by the recognition she sees in Ruby's eyes.

"More like reliving a nightmare. Ha!" Ruby laughs with relief.

"Was it a bad one?"

Thinking, Ruby turns to the window, her mind struggling to recall the dream as it drains from the crevices of her thoughts like sand. "No." She shakes her head sadly. "More like bittersweet." How unfair, she thinks, these dreams of youth trapped in her mind to be relived in the harsh isolation of age.

"What is it, Nan?" Lisa asks, watching the past flickering behind her grandmother's blue eyes, holding her captive.

"Lisa!" Ruby laughs, surprised again by her granddaughter's presence. Reaching for the younger woman's hand, Ruby continues. "Funny isn't it? When I was young, I could never remember a dream if my life depended on it, and now these dreams feel more like reality than my waking life does. Well, they are my life, aren't they? They're my memories unravelling themselves like a reel of film, burning through the projector with no one to control it." Looking at Lisa and sensing her concern, Ruby continues with a chuckle, "Old people! We're not much fun. Are we, lovey?"

"Well, *you* always are." Lisa replies, patting Ruby's hand in a gesture of reassurance.

"Good. I'm glad you feel that way. Now just remind me— where are we right now and what are we doing?" Ruby smiles, keeping the moment light, focusing on the present.

"We're on the train heading for Chicago to see your daughter, my aunt Phoebe. Do you remember?"

"Chicago. I was born there, you know?"

"Yes, I know."

"Phoebe was born in Montreal. Francis, my first son; Phoebe, my second daughter." She nods, remembering her children as babies.

"You mean your only daughter."

"No. Phoebe was my second daughter," Ruby says, her eyes fixed intently on Lisa's. "I had another baby girl, still born. We named her Julia Rose. Francis was born soon after."

"Nan?" Lisa is hardly able to get the word out, shocked by

the information. "I never knew about this. Mom, Dad, Aunt Phoebe ... none of them has ever mentioned this to me. You have never mentioned it. Why? Why wouldn't I know about this?"

"It's all right Lisa, Lovey. Don't sound so hurt. It was a long time ago."

"But do they even know about this? I mean your other children? My dad? Why wouldn't he tell me?" Like her thoughts, Lisa's words tumble over one another, scrambling for some familiar ground.

"He wasn't born yet. None of the kids were born yet. It was my first baby." Ruby turns to the window, watching the countryside moving by. Then, almost to herself, she adds, "And life has a way of moving on so quickly." She turns back to Lisa and smiles. "Your aunt Phoebe sounded excited that we were coming."

Lisa is hesitant, still feeling overwhelmed by the new information. "Yes. After the initial surprise, at least. I mean, you know aunt Phoebe—she's pretty buttoned up. She doesn't go anywhere unless she's planned it at least two weeks in advance." Lisa is speaking almost absently.

"No!" Ruby shakes her head, smiling. "Spontaneity was never Phoebe's strong suit. Even as a little girl she liked everything planned out. She certainly didn't get that from me, did she? Ha!"

"No, Nan. In that I'd say you two are polar opposites. Actually, you're pretty different in every way."

"I suppose that's what happens with children. They try to become the complete opposite, to distance themselves from their parents."

"I guess to a certain extent that's true. Even Dad needs a strong sense of order in his life, unlike me."

"Or me. That's probably what made them the way they are. The way I am." Ruby falls silent, her thoughts gathering around her like a storm. When she continues, her voice is hollow with regret. "Oh, Phoebe, trying to distance herself, becoming someone so different from me, as different as day and night. Polar opposites. I think it's my fault."

"Your fault? That she's a planner?" Lisa laughs.

"No, that she needs to feel secure. That she needs to feel in control. As mothers we try to do the best we can...." Ruby falls silent, caught up in a sequence of moments that stretches to the edges of her memory.

"And I'm sure you did, Nan."

"Did what, honey?"

"The best you could for your children."

Ruby's voice drops. "Yes, that's what I've always said, but sometimes I wonder."

"Oh, Nan. You were an excellent mother who loved her kids and put them first. I wonder how you did it sometimes. When you were my age, you had three kids and a career. And you had lost a child. I can't even imagine."

"I don't know if that's true, you know, that I put them first. Did I, or is it just easier to think and say I did? I'm not really sure if we thought of children in those terms back then." Ruby nods to herself as both women gaze out the window, following their separate thoughts, their separate stories. When Ruby continues, it takes Lisa a moment to recall the conversation, and she is pleasantly surprised at her grandmother's continuity. "Well, it's good that you can't imagine losing a child. I hope you have only beauty in your life, Lisa, but even with life's trials and hardships, it's always beautiful. That's what life is, a harsh and private beauty ready to overwhelm us at any moment. That's what keeps us going, isn't it? This life and the beauty we can make of it."

"The beauty in life? Yes, I guess that does keep us going."

"Or finding the beauty, creating the beauty. It's always there, you know."

"Well, I suppose some people are better at finding it than others."

Ruby takes stock of her granddaughter, the movement of the train rhythmically soothing. "So, lovey," she continues, "are you one of the people struggling to find the beauty?"

Lisa stays quiet, unsure how to articulate her feelings or even if she should. Her grandmother is old; her mind is slowly being stolen by dementia. Her father only humours her, keeping everything light, and her aunt Phoebe has always seemed distant with her. Lisa's own mother never talks about anything meaningful to Nan, feeling somehow that the old shouldn't be involved in the concerns of the young.

As though she has read Lisa's mind, Ruby laughs. "Don't worry about telling me anything, lovey. You can burden your old Nan anytime you like. That's what grandmothers are for. That's the reason there are grandparents, so the younger generation can unburden themselves and we can hopefully put the problem into perspective. I can't guarantee that I will remember what your problem is the next day, or the next minute," Ruby laughs, "but I know that I can give excellent advice. At my age, Lisa, the filter of decorum and civility has pretty much dissolved. My advice is tempered with the truth of age; it's as close to the truth as possible." Ruby readjusts herself in the chair, easing her weight from one hip to the other. "Come on, girl, out with it now."

Lisa smiles at Ruby's determined look.

"I'm listening, lovey."

"I don't know, Nan. This might be out of your realm. I don't know if you would understand. Your life was so different; the time you lived in was so ... I don't know ... far removed from today. Women in your time, they had everything set out for them; their decisions were already made. You were a mother and a wife...."

"You forgot to say a wife three times." Ruby nods.

"Yes, exactly. A wife three times, and here I am at thirty-one. I'm not married, and I don't know if I want to be married. Well, part of me does and part of me doesn't. And..."

"So, this is what's bothering you? That you're not married yet?"

"No, it's not that. Well, that's part of it. But..." Lisa turns in her seat and looks into her grandmother's calm, compelling eyes. Maybe she should be telling her mother this and not Nan? "Oh, forget I even said anything, I'm just going around in circles here and sounding pretty silly."

"No, you don't sound silly, lovey. You sound confused about something. We have all felt like that at one time or another. Even women like me, who, as you say, lived in a time when everything was set out for us." Ruby chortles. "When I was young that was what confused me the most. My life was already set out, as if I had no choice in the matter—ha! If I had had a choice or even thought I had a choice, I probably wouldn't have been married three times."

Lisa, deep in thought, watches the sunlight falling across her arm. She feels the motion of the train, and the hard knot of worry in the base of her stomach, and something else that she can't place. Pulling herself together, she looks at Ruby. "Are you hungry, Nan?"

"You'd think that since I've been married three times, I would be the type of woman who doesn't like to be alone, but it's quite the contrary," Ruby continues as if there has been no lull in the conversation. "I enjoy my own company; I always have. The marriages were as surprising to me as a January thaw...."

They are quiet, both women lost in their own thoughts. Lisa is thinking ahead, consumed with anxiety and concern; Ruby is thinking back, always thinking back.

A January thaw is a surprise, that's for sure. And marriage and children—another surprise. I can't say that I should have never married John Grace—otherwise I would never have become Ruby Grace—but I felt the unhappiness, felt I was missing the beauty. I was Ruby Grace. I had a growing awareness of myself, but it was an awareness of loss. Just at the time that I began to know a little bit about who I was, I was lost in the day-to-day demands of being a wife and mother. Struggling against something, but not knowing what. It wasn't John and it was John. It wasn't the children and it was the children. It was a slow seeping away of potential, a potential unknown but deeply felt. How different Ruby Grace would have been if not for Leland James. Everyone needs someone as I needed you, Leland. You were like a divining rod pulling at the centre of who I was, bringing to the surface what was already there. I would have been lost without you. Do my children have this? Do my grandchildren?

Ruby brings herself back to the present moment. "Lisa, let's go to the bar car. My legs could use the stretch, and we could both do with a little drink."

"That's the best suggestion I've heard all day. I wonder if they'll be able to make you a vodka gimlet."

"Ha! It doesn't matter. They don't taste the same as they did when I was young. Nothing does. I suppose my taste buds are worn out along with everything else. The only thing I can taste anymore is salt, but it's not good for my high blood pressure." Ruby throws her hands in the air.

"I know. It's just not fair." Lisa smiles at the tirade.

"And I'm not complaining, mind you. Just stating the facts. Time was I could enjoy a vodka gimlet and eat a few pretzels. Now I can't taste the damn drink, and eating the pretzels I'm taking my life in my hands. Ha! Maybe we should just sit in the bar car and let me go out with a bang!"

"Well, that's always an option." Lisa stands, waiting for Ruby to struggle up. "What's wrong, Nan? Are you okay?"

A look of pain passes across Ruby's face like a shadow, sharpening her features and settling in the lines around her mouth. Lisa sits back down, taking her grandmother's hand. "Nan?" Concern raises the corners of her voice.

"It's nothing, nothing. My left leg was asleep. Now it's prickling with pins and needles." Ruby extracts her hand from Lisa's and rubs her upper thigh.

"Do you need me to do something?"

"No, not unless you have a magic elixir to turn back time. This may take a while." Ruby looks at Lisa, eyebrows raised. "Sorry."

"No problem. We'll just take our time. It's not like we're following a tight schedule or anything. We've got all the time in the world."

"I thought that once." Leaning forward, Ruby uses her cane to help herself up, then reaches for Lisa's hand. "I suppose we all think that don't we—that time is on our side? 'But just when did time, that diaphanous material, fray into rush?' I forget where I read that, but I've always remembered it." Ruby stands and gently shakes her foot, watching the offending appendage as if willing the blood to move. "You always think time is on your side, and then one day you find yourself on the other side and time is suddenly against you, pulling on the rope like a tug of war. Suddenly you're scrambling to hold on for dear life, all your good intentions and someday plans forgotten in the immediacy of your battle."

Ruby, aware that a look of helplessness has settled on Lisa's face, continues, "I'm sorry, honey. I didn't mean to get so melodramatic. It happens when one becomes maudlin, and I'm getting that way with age. Everything is beginning to take on a new meaning. And I don't think living in that so called 'retirement home,'" Ruby's voice raises sharply, "helps in any way. Everyone is old there! Ha! Sometimes I look around and I wonder: what are all these old people doing here? Is it a Saturday afternoon and I'm in the foyer at intermission? Did we perform at an old age home and this is the reception? Then I remember: no, I'm here. This is me. I'm one of these damned old people!"

Ruby's voice has gotten louder during her tirade. Although there are only a handful of people in the car, they have turned to look at Ruby and Lisa. Lisa smiles and nods, dropping her voice as she answers, hoping her grandmother will take the hint. "Oh, Nan. I never knew you felt like that. It must be confusing."

"Confusing as hell!" Ruby answers loudly. "But what's worse is when my mind finally lands in this body…" she stops, places her hand on the backrest of a chair, and looks at Lisa, "…and I think, just a minute, this can't be right." Ruby laughs, looking around. "Well hello and good day to you all." She nods at the passengers who are watching her, their faces pinched with interest. "Getting old is just such a bother. Don't let this happen to you." She nods to each one as if from the stage, then turns back to Lisa. "Okay, I think we can make our move now. You lead and I'll follow." Ruby points with her cane in the direction of the bar car.

Lisa laughs with unguarded emotion, enjoying this moment. She moves along the aisle, nodding and smiling at the other passengers, her embarrassment of a moment ago forgotten in the humour her grandmother seems to bring to every situation. Then, deferring to her grandmother in mock salute, she raises her voice to include the entire car in the fun. "To the bar car we go, Ruby Grace!"

6.

MONTREAL IS COLD, a cold unlike anything Daniel has ever experienced. In the brief time it takes him to walk from the cab into the newly completed Ritz-Carlton Hotel, it snaps his nose hairs and numbs his face. Earlier that day, when the sun, shining from a cloudless sky, had warmed the air to a more tolerable temperature, he walked the streets of Montreal. Although wide and snow-covered, many of them in various stages of development, they somehow reminded him of the streets he walked in France; one area in particular was reminiscent of Place du Tertre in Paris. The architecture here was more eclectic, yet retained enough of the classical to lend weight to the city's atmosphere. He stopped in the Place d'Armes square as though he was being held in place, lost in a frozen landscape of memory.

The New York Life Insurance Building, standing at eight storeys high, was Montreal's first skyscraper—erected thanks to Elias Otis and his elevator, which had opened up futuristic possibilities for the world. The very first of these skyscrapers was in Daniel's hometown. The Home Insurance Building, completed in 1885, was a familiar beacon for Daniel who, loving architecture, often marvelled at mankind's ability to design and construct. For him, architecture, like art, represented the beauty of the human soul. Facing the Place d'Armes square was the Notre-Dame Basilica, its Gothic Revival design amongst the most dramatic in the world. Walking inside, Daniel found himself assailed by unexpected emotion. The god of his childhood, so omnipotent and undeniable, had been lost in the cold mud of France, the battleground where his idealism, his morality, and his faith were sacrificed in the immediacy of survival. But entering the church, Daniel suddenly encountered that lost god again. He was shocked at his own visceral reaction to the church. The basilica, almost ephemeral in its beauty, was too much to take in. Its vaulted ceiling rose above him, absorbing and alienating, calling to a primal need to believe in something bigger than himself, while at the same time reinforcing a rage he can't articulate. He staggered from the building into the harsh light of a winter sun, inebriated with emotion.

Now, at six o'clock, the evening closes in like a raven's wing, dark and claustrophobic, the omnipresent cold re-establishing itself with a vengeance. The people he passes, often deep in conversation with each other, are definitely speaking French. Although he can't understand the words, the cadence, the accentuated lifts are recognizable. Except for the painful cold in his extremities, he can almost imagine he is in France, Bordeaux, or Paris, walking with the guys from the regiment and looking for some fun: fast French skirt or good French wine, or both.

His contact is Pierre Montcalm. *Of course, what else would his name be?* Daniel thinks as he hurries through the front doors of the hotel, thankful to be out of the evening air. The hotel lobby is elaborate and opulent, and Daniel, removing his fedora, looks around as he unbuttons his coat and straightens his tie. He is duly impressed. His face feels numb, but in the heat of the lobby, his feet and hands begin to tingle with returning blood.

There is a small band playing in the deep recesses of the lounge to his right, an atmosphere he recognizes. He thinks about a drink. Debating whether or not to enter the lounge, he is unaware of a man, short and neat but powerfully built and impeccably dressed, who has seemingly appeared from nowhere beside him. "Are you Daniel Kenny?"

"Yes," Daniel replies, curt with surprise.

The man smiles, his eyes dark, and quickly extends his hand. "Sorry. I didn't mean to startle you. I am Pierre Montcalm. Welcome to Montreal, Monsieur." Pierre is clearly bilingual: his English is flawless, and his pronunciation of "Monsieur" is impeccable.

"Thank you, Mr. Montcalm. And no, you didn't startle me. Your approach was just unexpected. Where did you emerge from so suddenly?" As the words leave his lips, Daniel can see the double French doors of the restaurant. Following his gaze, Pierre nods. "I had a perfect view of the lobby entrance, and it was not difficult to spot you, my friend." Pierre laughs, clapping Daniel on the back. The movement is so natural and affectionate that it leaves Daniel feeling charmed.

"Am I that obvious, Monsieur?" Daniel smiles nervously. "Perhaps we shouldn't be conducting our business out in the open like this?"

"No, no. Not to worry. You do not look as though you are here for anything other than to meet an old friend and enjoy a meal. And perhaps to warm up, no?"

"Yeah, I have to admit I'm pretty cold."

"You do, however, look Irish." Pierre continues as if Daniel hadn't spoken. "And with a name like Daniel Kenny, I expected nothing less!" He laughs again, thumping Daniel on the back. "Come now. If you have warmed up sufficiently, you can check your coat and hat and allow me to buy your meal. Then we'll talk."

"Thank you, Mr. Montcalm." Daniel replies, his eyes darting around the large lobby and then back towards the lounge.

Following his gaze, Pierre smiles. "You are enjoying the music?"

"Well, not this music particularly, but I do enjoy being in lounges, night clubs. I don't know if you are familiar with jazz, but that is the kind of music I like. In fact, I think I've fallen in love with it."

"Oh, *oui,* I know jazz. Montreal is a surprising city, and there are many clubs with this music."

"I'm pleasantly surprised to hear that. I mean, I didn't know that jazz had made it to Canada, I thought it was an American anomaly."

"No, it is here. The St. Antoine district has three clubs where you can hear jazz every night of the week. If you like we can make arrangements to visit them; I am well acquainted with the proprietors."

"Yes, I would very much like that. Thank you, Mr. Montcalm."

"Please, it is Pierre. Now perhaps we will sit and eat and get down to the business, as they say. And not to worry." Pierre continues, trying to assuage Daniel's obvious trepidation. "Our business is not illegal, at least not yet, and not on this side of the border."

"Not yet?"

"Yes. These laws, they change back and forth, back and forth. It depends I think on who is running for office, no? I have been in this business for years, one way or the other."

"One way or the other?" Daniel asks over his shoulder as he hands his coat over the counter to the coat check girl. She smiles shyly at him.

"Yes, importing liquor from other provinces, from other states. Filling the need during this country's dry spells. Now we export to you. The routes are the same, my friend; it is the direction that has changed!" Laughing again, Pierre leads Daniel into the restaurant. It is busy and dark—an atmosphere charged with informal, unrestrained conversation—and Daniel relaxes into the anonymity of the place.

"Quebec has never been dry," Pierre continues, seating himself at a small table and lifting his glass. "The French are a civilized race. We have always understood that liquor is the lubricant of society. Through liquor, we avoid friction." He drinks and smiles. "But the laws of the land are changing, no? The Volstead Act now prohibits the consumption, the sale, or the importation of liquor in any state in your country. These ridiculous measures!" Pierre shakes his head and looks directly at Daniel. "They will only enable the entrepreneur to become rich!" He laughs with excitement. "And, that my friend, is capitalism at its best."

"Entrepreneur? So that's what you call it up here." Daniel says, looking over at Pierre and nodding slowly.

There is something compelling about this man; he has a European charm flavoured with a new-world realism and a sense of proportion in his ironic humour. Daniel cannot help but like him. Over their meal, he enlightens Daniel on the subject of Canadian and American prohibition laws, his knowledge of the subject encyclopaedic. "The routes for rum running have been established for years. It is almost as if the government planned it. Wouldn't you agree, Daniel?"

Daniel lifts his glass of Rémy Martin. "It's preordained."

"*Exactement!*"

"So, where do we go from here, Pierre? Will we be signing a contract and establishing a payment plan? You obviously have the experience; in fact, I'm quite humbled by your knowledge."

"Well, it is my business, and up until now it has been a living. But what is to come may well make us both rich. The demand for beer and whiskey will be unprecedented. The law may change toward virtue, but man's vice does not."

"Will you be able to supply the demand? It will be more challenging than in the past. Where will you be securing the liquor?"

"I have a partner, Simon Bigman. Don't laugh, that's his real name."

"Wow. I would call that destiny."

"Yes, you may be correct. He is a Russian Jew from Western Canada. His family was prominent in Russia but fled during the anti-Semitic program. They settled, or maybe I should say they were placed, in Manitoba. They have done a little of everything, from trading horses to running hotels. They have connections to Hirsch and Rothschild." Pierre nods as if clearing up an important point. Daniel looks back blankly, realizing he is missing something.

Pierre shrugs. "They are Zionists. Their business dealings have no borders and are little concerned with government rhetoric. The Bigman's are the ones who bought the Canadian Pure Drug Company. During the War Measures Act, they sold liquor through the loophole of *medical purposes*." Pierre raises his eyebrows for emphasis. "Up until this year, they were the sole importers of whiskey from your country."

"So, you're saying that they're well connected?"

"Yes. To say the least. Now with prohibition in America, the Bigmans have simply turned from importing to exporting. It is that simple! They also import from Britain. They have strong ties to the government there." Pierre smiles genially at Daniel, who is enjoying his drink and the conversation. "Simon has been in Montreal only a short while but he has the connections and he has the capital." Pierre sips his cognac falls silent for a moment, appraising Daniel. "You will like him," he continues.

"When will I meet him? Is he joining us?" Daniel sits up, eager with anticipation.

"No, no. Not tonight. Tonight, is for us to establish contact, which we have done. Dean O'Banion said I would like you, and he is correct. I do. We will work out the payment schedule and the best routes—Detroit is never a problem. Once on the American side, your men will have to work out the best routes to Chicago. It will not be hard. Times are difficult, and men are more than willing to get steady, dependable work. We are the wholesalers; you are the retailers. It is a good business."

"How long will all this take before we get the first shipment in Detroit?"

"Well, that will depend on a couple things. How quickly you can establish your men and have them ready? Remember, this is not new to us. Also, we will have to agree on a payment schedule. But don't worry. We have a few days to work it all out."

"Good. When shall we meet again, then?"

"I am having a dinner party tomorrow evening. I would like very much for you to attend. I'm sure there is no one you know in Montreal. You will be able to meet Simon and some of our other retailers. After dinner we can discuss further business in the privacy of my drawing room." Pierre nods at Daniel, and then continues. "We also have a very charming niece staying with us. She is my wife's sister's daughter from the east, come to experience the big city. She is very pretty and charming." He looks at Daniel out of the corner of his eye. "You never know, maybe she will see something in you. Besides, your presence will make an equal number of men and women, and my wife will be pleased with this."

"Well, thank you for the invitation, Pierre. I look forward to meeting your niece. What did you say her name was?"

Pierre laughs. "I did not say! Her name is Jeanie, Jeanie Lehman." Pierre rises from his seat and adds, "I will pay the bill and call for cabs."

Minutes later, Pierre joins Daniel who has been waiting outside the front doors of the Ritz, stamping his feet, his hands pushed deep into the pockets of his coat. The two cabs pull up at the same time. "Bien." Pierre extends his hand, "I believe things will work out well between us, Daniel Kenny. There will be a cab outside the hotel for you at seven o'clock tomorrow night. I will see you then."

Watching Pierre moving toward the open cab door, Daniel calls out, "Should I bring anything tomorrow night?" He raises his shoulders to emphasize the question.

"No, nothing." Pierre laughs and then adds, "Perhaps a warmer coat, no?"

Daniel nods in agreement. "Yes, maybe a warmer coat."

DANIEL ARRIVES AT PIERRE'S DOOR shortly after seven. He is wearing a new wool coat and carrying cut flowers that have been well wrapped against the Canadian cold. He adjusts his fedora, thinking of the fur hat the salesman at the store had suggested. He has noticed quite a few people wearing fur hats, a smart choice in the face of such bitter cold, but his fedora will have to suffice for the few days he will be here. The coat was a must, and it was certainly worth the money, if only to keep him warm for the few minutes he stands on the stone portico waiting for the magnificent mahogany door to open.

Soon, a middle-aged woman—obviously the maid—greets him, taking his coat and hat and indicating a set of white pocket doors. A hum of conversation punctuated by laughter emanates from the room, and Daniel hesitates before sliding the door open. He feels awkward and self-conscious, worried that this social encounter may be too much to handle. He's noticed that he's not felt warm lately; since France, he's become sensitive to the cold. His feelings also seem uncontrollable at times, leaping here and there, straying of their own volition, as if disconnected from him. In certain situations, feelings of distress rush in, stimuli overwhelming, heart pounding in anticipation; he becomes over sensitive to his surroundings, feeling trapped and frightened and vulnerable. He finds a reprieve from this in the dark, broody atmosphere of the night clubs he frequents. They afford him a place apart, a reprieve from his own thoughts, but away from their familiar atmosphere, he is left to deal with these emotions on his own. Breathing deeply, he wills his heart to slow, his nerves to calm. There is nothing on the other side of the door to be concerned about, and he can't let his anxiety dictate his life. He hears his father's voice: "Have no fear, Danny-boy." With a conscious effort of will, Daniel slides open the door.

The room is well lit and warm, with an open fire at the far end. The murmur of conversation of a moment ago halts when the door opens, and all eyes for a brief moment are on him. *What will they think if I just take a step back and slide this door closed?* The thought crosses his mind as his eyes meet those of the young woman standing directly in front of him. She reads the indecision in his face and smiles with understanding. They will both remember this moment, this quiet exchange, this unspoken understanding. Words, as well as physical affection, will always be important between them, but it is this laconic communication, this sharing without words, that will bind them, one to the other, in silent orbit.

He is introduced around the room. A blur of impressions swirls around him, but clears and sharpens with the introduction of Jeanie Lehman. They are seated together during dinner, but after the intimacy of the shared moment in the drawing room, there is an awkwardness between them. She is small and fair, and Daniel is painfully aware of her presence at his side. He has never felt at a loss for words before, especially with women. His brother and his friends always teasing him about his blarney with the women, but this Jeanie Lehman has arrested his abilities. His interest in Simon Bigman and the business at hand has waned. He has experienced the power of a female presence before, but never to this extent. He is aware of her movements out of the corner of his eye, and he is amused by his own reactions. He wants to take her hand and hold it in his own, push it against his mouth, smell her, taste her.

"I understand you were in the war, Mr. Kenny?" Lenny Davis, who is sitting at the end of the table to Pierre's right, asks. With the shock of the direct question, Daniel realizes that he has been silent for much of the meal. The others turn, anxious for his answer. Mike Frank—Sardinian born but of Italian descent and the head of the Frank Gang, the Calabrian faction of the Black Hand—and his wife Louisa are directly across from Daniel. On the other side of Louisa sits Simon Bigman. His comportment belies his beginnings; his family's history of selling, trading, and bribing, as he sits confident and easy in the opulent room. Simon Bigman will become one of the new country's leading businessmen, a wealthy, influential and powerful man. In later years, he will become a philanthropist;

pulling around himself the cloak of civility and respectability, just as the country will learn to reinvent itself through the retelling of old stories.

Daniel is unsure of the political feelings in the room, of the attitudes toward "the war that would end all wars." He is unsure of his own feelings about his part in the war, what it means to him, what it will come to mean. Was it nothing but a heartbreaking and pointless conflict? It was imperialism taken to its extreme—millions dead, millions more crippled physically and emotionally. An entire generation shattered, and for what? The Canadian effort was enormous considering her scant population. He knows of Vimy, of Passchendaele, the human cost. American casualties and deaths seem trifling compared to that of other countries. He feels cornered by this simple fact, confused as to his feelings. He took part in the war; he was a soldier who took and gave commands, that was all. "Yes. I was, Sir." he answers Lenny Davis's question, his voice ringing flat in his own ears.

"Did you see much action?"

Daniel looks down the table at Lenny, a Paris born Jew who is working to establish himself in the young country as a man with connections. Daniel looks down, stroking the smooth polished steel of his dinner knife. He is contemplating the question, the question that has been asked of him so many times and with such idle curiosity, or perhaps morbid voyeurism, he's never sure, either way, the question always throws him off balance, bringing into focus scenes he has pushed into the depths of his mind, leaving him feeling angry and frustrated.

"Mr. Davis, I think our guest would rather not speak of such things during dinner." Sophie Montcalm, Pierre's small but confident wife, comes to Daniel's rescue. Continuing quickly, she adds, "There are too many opinions at this table to make this a suitable topic of conversation."

"My wife is correct, no? We French know when to leave well enough alone."

"Wasn't that your attitude toward the war itself, Pierre?" Davis asks, raising his wine glass and looking at it intently.

"The riots in Montreal over conscription would attest to that, would they not?" Pierre answers, his smile repudiating the strength of his convictions.

"Enough, gentlemen! This is not the place for such a discussion," Sophie continues, looking severely at her husband at the other end of the table, her voice firm with redirection. "Have you heard of the poet Emile Nelligan, Mr. Kenny?"

The conversation unfolds like a work of art; in moments spattering exchanges erupt between the guests, the hum of voices becoming a palpable lubricant. Daniel drums his fingers on the table. Jeanie leans forward and places her hand lightly over Daniel's, stilling its movement and quieting his mind. "Don't take any heed of Mr. Davis. He is a cantankerous man who likes nothing more than to stir the pot."

Daniel turns and says the one thing he has been thinking the entire evening. "Could I call on you sometime, Miss Lehman?"

Jean Lehman is from New Brunswick, and at eighteen, is anxious to experience the world. Montreal is an exciting city with many opportunities, and it affords her a social life that her home town does not. Daniel Kenny is another surprise the city has to offer. His blue eyes rimmed with black lashes are exquisite, and his brooding attitude intrigues her. "Please, call me Jeanie, Mr. Kenny. After all, we have been formally introduced."

"All right, Jeanie." Uttering her name brings a smile to his face. "And please call me Daniel."

"Do you ever get Danny? You look like a Danny."

"I do get that, but it feels somehow childish to me now. I prefer Daniel."

She returns his smile. "Very well, Daniel." She lowers her head, averting her eyes. She is embarrassed at her reaction, at her immature prattling. *You look like a Danny! What a ridiculously silly thing to say. Who looks like a Danny?* Her chest feels tight, her throat constricted. This must be what it feels like to have your heart in your mouth, she thinks. She would like to speak to Daniel again, not just to erase the stupidity of her last comment but to hold his attention, to look into his eyes, to watch his slow smile make its way across his handsome Irish face. Rushing over topics, she rejects one after the other as inappropriate or silly until finally she settles on one. "How long will you be staying in Montreal, Daniel?"

"Well, that will depend." He breaks into another slow smile as he takes in her high colour, cheeks flushed with the heat of the room or his attention; he's unsure of which but hoping for the latter.

On what? Jeanie thinks but dares not say, "*On me?*" Instead, she asks, "On the business with my uncle?"

"Yes."

Looking at him, she smiles at the unspoken words, at the meaning passing between them, the emotions. Is it the war that has done this? Is it the lack of young men, the horror of the returning dead, that sharpens the need to reach out and take what is given without reserve? she wonders. Daniel Kenny, young and handsome, is her future. She knows this. The knowledge is buried deep within herself—past the pounding of her heart, past the rush of emotion, in the pit of her stomach. She knows this with an undeniable precognition that reveals itself in impatience.

"Can you meet me tomorrow, Daniel?"

Daniel's mind rushes ahead to the business concerns they will address this evening, when the men adjourn to the study. In the following days, he will have no plans except to wait for the concluding details before he returns to Chicago. "Yes. Where?"

They are speaking quietly, with a nonchalance neither one feels. Daniel's answer is louder than he expected, drawing enquiring smiles from around the table. Nodding, he continues, his voice softer but still full of its previous intensity. "I don't believe I have any plans for tomorrow. Could you suggest something, perhaps?"

"I would be more than happy to accompany you at your convenience and show you the sights of the city." Jeanie lowers her head to disguise the excitement she feels.

Yes, I would like that. I want to spend as many hours as possible with you, Jeanie Lehman, Daniel thinks. He replies, "Yes, thank you. I would appreciate that, Miss Lehman. Would the afternoon suit you?"

"Yes, around three?"

"I will look forward to it." Daniel nods and picks up his glass.

As if on cue, Pierre stands and looks around the table. "Gentlemen, I believe we shall retire to the study. I have brandy and cognac. We can talk business and allow the women their own time."

AS HE ENTERS THE WELL-LIT STUDY, Pierre sweeps his arm in a grand gesture. "Sit, gentlemen, sit." Deep burgundy leather chairs are pulled around a fireplace that glows amber. A large oak desk on the north wall faces the room, and to the left is an expansive bar lined with bottles of varying size and shape. "What is your pleasure, Daniel?"

"What would you suggest?" Daniel seats himself, shaking his head when Simon offers him a cigar.

"That will depend on what you like—something sweet, something smoky, or something to bite the back of your throat?" Pierre laughs over his shoulder as he reaches for the bottles. "Would you like a whiskey? I have one of Hiram Walker's better brands here."

"Yes, Daniel," Simon says between puffs. "Walker is one of your own countrymen, chased out by the growing temperance movement.

"Dismantled his distillery in Detroit one day, crossed the lake, and set it up in Windsor the next!" Mike Frank adds, picking up the story.

"I think that would take a little more than a day," Daniel says.

"We can get nothing by you, Mr. Kenny." Pierre winks as he hands Daniel his drink.

"There is something quite ironic about all this, don't you think?" Daniel takes his glass, nodding his thanks.

"You mean, our drinking while we discuss the topic of prohibition?" Simon asks.

"Yes."

Pierre laughs. "The idea of prohibition is an English thing, Daniel. We French have never had to worry about where our next drink will come from, or indeed if it will be there at all."

"Is that because you're French, Pierre, or because drinking is part of your Catholic religion?" Lenny Davis asks, taking his drink from Pierre.

"*Exactement!* It is a sacrament—the breaking of the bread, the drinking of the wine.

"No law will stop the consumption of alcohol," Davis continues. "We've seen that over and over again. Any country that declares itself dry is setting itself up for exploitation."

"Exploitation is a bit harsh don't you think, Lenny?" Simon says with a dry laugh. "We are simply entrepreneurs who see a need and are obliged to fill it."

"That is thinking in the noblest of terms, Mr. Bigman." Mike Frank agrees.

"Perhaps that is why they call it the noble experiment, no?" Pierre laughs.

"Well," Davis continues, "if it is an experiment, it's failing. We have been successful in supplying dry states and provinces for years."

"How do you get it across the border?" Daniel asks, looking at the men in the room, men used to getting what they want.

Simon Bigman laughs loudly and taps his cigar into the ashtray. "With a few bribes here and there. Anyway, how well can they enforce this law when there are hundreds of miles of open border between our countries?"

"And the lakes—they're wide open, Daniel." Mike Frank nods.

"The desire to legalize temperance has been with us forever." Simon squints his eyes through the smoke.

"Yes," Lenny Davis adds, "and where would the true businessman be without the Puritan? As we know, value is increased through scarcity."

"It is the way of the world." Pierre nods in agreement. "The Volstead Act creates a need, and one way or another we will be filling it for some time to come, gentlemen."

The men around the room nod and remain quiet, their thoughts varied and diverse. Simon Bigman breaks the silence. "These are chaotic times we live in. Messy times we have lived through, where the value of human life has been nullified." His sentiments move through the room like the pungent odour of his cigar. "What has been lost? What has been gained?"

"I think much has been gained." Pierre states as he looks around the room. "We sit here tonight, a Parisian Jew, a Russian Jew, a Sardinian-born Italian, an Irish American besotted now with my lovely niece, who is herself a product of a Scottish and German marriage. We represent the European nations at war against each other months ago, and here we are tonight in congenial acceptance."

"Perhaps it is the flavour of the new world: forging our own national identity with combinations of others," says Mike Frank.

"And it is so much better, no?" Pierre adds.

"It makes you wonder about the point of war, if there is one," Frank muses.

"The point of war is to eliminate fascism, to stop it from taking root," Lenny Davis answers, his intensity a cold presence in the room. "Evil can only happen when good men stand by and do nothing!"

"Perhaps you are right." Daniel nods, his eyes on Davis, his mind a thousand miles away.

"Let us return to the business at hand, shall we, gentlemen?" Simon entreats, nodding slowly, sensing the distance in Daniel's eyes.

"Yes! We drink and we discuss the business that has brought us together, no?" Pierre says, taking Daniel's empty glass and moving to the bar to refill it.

The business is interesting and amiable, and Pierre keeps the atmosphere jovial and social. Daniel appreciates this; he finds Lenny Davis somewhat intense and tiring, and he can't stop his mind from wandering back to Jeanie and the intimacy of her presence. It is as if he knows her, has already experienced a lifetime with her. Meeting her tonight has allowed him to reflect upon the hollowness he has been feeling; he understands now that the feeling of emptiness is simply her absence in his life. Or is it? Could it be that easy? Is her presence in his life preordained? It seems absurd that such a quick encounter, such a minimal brush against another individual, can cause such a cascade of emotion, such an awakening of possibility. New thoughts and feelings dart like minnows in the depths of his soul.

When the men emerge from the study, hours have slipped by and the women have left or retired for the evening. They part in the small hours of the morning—Pierre Montcalm, Lenny Davis, Michael Frank, Simon Bigman, and Daniel—their smiles and handshakes forging the future, shaping the past.

Daniel can hardly remember returning to his hotel, his mind is so full of the evening. He remembers the men in the room, turning the world toward their own ends with an ease that seemed like child's play. Men with the ability to change and shape, influential, powerful men. And the soft brown eyes of Jeanie Lehman.

That night, he cannot sleep.

7.

"MY PARENTS MARRIED within two weeks of meeting each other. Amazing isn't it? But I suppose what is more amazing is that they were together for all their years and still very much in love." Ruby gazes out the car window, unaware of the countryside, pale greens and golds, struggling through the winter chill. The bar car is busy, low conversations spiked with occasional laughter percolating above the muffled sounds of the track. Snaking through the countryside on its steel rails, the train is comforting in its repetitive motion, soothing, almost hypnotic.

Lisa waits, watching Ruby, who is now lost to the world of memory. She thinks of her grandmother as a link to the past, to her own understanding of herself. Speaking softly, pulling Ruby back to the present, she says, "I never knew that, Nan."

"Knew what, lovey?" Ruby turns quickly, surprised by the comment.

"That your parents married within two weeks of meeting each other."

"Why, yes, they did." Ruby's unspoken question—*how did you know that?*—hanging in the air between them.

"It was a different time I suppose." Lisa continues gazing out the window and nodding.

"Yes, it was a different time." Ruby is silent again, pulled back to the still pictures and movie reels of her mind. When she continues, it is with an abruptness that surprises Lisa.

"It was after the war, when life must have felt very tenuous, when you had to reach out and grab it without the luxury of waiting for it to come to you." Ruby grabs the air in front of her, bringing it to her breast. "They met in Montreal after the war. Met and married within two weeks."

"I guess it must have been exciting. That time." Lisa nods and then adds after a moment, "And simple. Maybe the war did that for people, you know, made life feel immediate."

"Yes, there must have been that for them, finding happiness after war." Falling silent, Ruby watches the countryside slipping by, her face partially reflected. "My mother always seemed so content," she continues almost to herself, "while I, well, I have always felt I was living life with some sort of urgency, waiting for the next thing to happen."

"Really, Nan? I feel like that too sometimes, but mostly I feel like I'm being pulled along through life, bumping along like a pebble in a stream, wondering where I'm going to end up next."

"No, Lisa you can't feel like that, honey." Ruby, turning, pats her granddaughter's hand and laughs. "You've got your education and your job with the paper. You have given yourself your life's direction."

"Actually, Nan, I'm not working for the paper anymore. I took a buy-out, and now I'm freelancing for a while."

"Is that why you're feeling at such loose ends?"

"No, it's more than that." Lisa falls silent, pulled into her mind, distracted by indecision and the continuous attempt to push her thoughts to the far ends of her mind. She's plagued by her floundering relationship and her growing disappointment with her career, but even more urgent is the need not to allow her mind to alight on the one decision she needs to make. It grows heavier in her mind with every passing mile, growing heavier in her womb with every passing day.

Aware of Ruby patiently waiting for an explanation, Lisa continues almost absentmindedly, "I don't think journalism is really for me. I didn't really choose it; I just fell into it more or less and I don't really think it's what I want as a career."

Ruby nods her understanding, sensing a deeper sadness but reluctant to prod further. She has never been driven by not knowing. She could let sleeping dogs lie, so to speak. In this way, she was the opposite of Leland James, who, like a kid with a stick, couldn't help poking at a nest of hornets. He always had to have an answer.

"But what would make your parents leave Chicago so suddenly in 1924?" she remembers him asking. "How was he so easily able to set up a business, buy a home, even a summer home?"

"I don't know. It was just something my parents never spoke about."

"But Ruby, aren't you curious? Aren't you just dying to know the story behind a big move like that?" With Ruby's silence, Leland pushes on. "You know, I asked him once, asked Daniel why he moved from Chicago to Montreal. We were at the Reservoir Club. You know the one, off Front Street? And I don't know whether it was the music or the whole atmosphere, but he started to tell me something but then thought better of it."

"What did he tell you?" Ruby asks, her interest piqued.

Leland pauses, remembering the evening; the dark, cellar like atmosphere of the bar; the haze of smoke and noise; the man sitting beside him and the intimacy of the moment....

"You know, son, a decision is not always about one thing. It is never just about one decision; it is a series of decisions, one leading to the next. And then suddenly you have already made half the decisions before you know it, before you're even aware of it." Daniel takes a sip and then studies the ice in the glass, tipping it this way and that, watching the effects. "You grow up in a neighbourhood and it becomes what you know, who you are. It was a different place and time, growing up in Chicago back then. There were no rules, no road maps. There

was just the neighbourhood; family relationships, friendships, business, and life all revolved around it. Sometimes the lines blurred, and you would be led down a path complicated by loyalties. It's a lot to know, and sometimes it's more than you want to know." Daniel nods to himself. He has become a pool of stillness in the noise and blur around him. Then, almost in a whisper, he continues "I made decisions, some of them good, some not so good. But I made them. I'm responsible for them...." Then he looks up from his glass and over at Leland, almost in surprise. "I think I need another drink, I'm starting to sound like a broken record. How about you, Leland? Let's have one more for the road, as they say."

"Your father, Ruby. He is just so interesting." Leland shakes his head.

"I never know what to think about him," Ruby answers, taking Leland's hand in hers.

"I think he was a man trying to make it in a country just starting to land on its feet. It must have been mindboggling, living in Chicago just after the turn of the century, going to war as such a young man, and then trying to be a husband, a father, a businessman. He is a good man, your father." He turns to look at her and smiles impishly. "You get your looks from him, you know—your black Irish looks and your black Irish temper." He laughs and, taking her chin in his hand, he tilts her face upward, looking into her eyes before kissing her. Ruby laughs at his playfulness, his intensity.

SHE SMILES, A LAUGH ESCAPING HER. "Ha!"

"What's so funny, Nan?"

"What?" Ruby turns to Lisa, her smile lagging around the corners of her mouth.

"What were you laughing at?"

"Oh, I was laughing at Leland."

"Leland?"

"No, no. Don't worry." Ruby responds to the alarm in Lisa's

voice. "I was just remembering Leland, I should say. Laughing at his memory."

"You loved him the most, didn't you, Nan?"

"Yes. I loved him the most." Ruby's gaze turns inward, drawn to the richness of the memories emanating around her like an aura. "Leland died, and I thought I couldn't go on, but I did."

"You remarried."

"Yes, I married Jack in 1978. I was no spring chicken. Jack was a good, steady man, and I had known him for years. I knew him when we were both young and living in Montreal. Leland had been gone for two years when I bumped into Jack at the Toronto Symphony one evening—imagine my surprise. He had an apartment in Toronto and had just bought a home in Peterborough. When I told him I was living in Peterborough, he couldn't believe it, couldn't imagine me living in provincial Ontario. I told him it wasn't so bad, and we laughed. It broke down barriers, for both of us, that laughter. He had moved his business to Peterborough after his divorce, and he was out on a date that evening. The next thing I knew, we were dating!" Turning to smile at Lisa, she adds, "He said he'd loved me for years. He told me he was shattered when I married John Grace, and that it was our destiny to be together. I guess he was right to a certain extent. I mean, who would have thought that we would both end up living in the same town after all those years, I ask you? Anyway, we ended up together, happy and very comfortable; money was never a problem. I even got to enjoy my life with Jack. He wasn't Leland James—nobody could replace Leland and what we had together, what we've always had and still have," Ruby finishes with a sigh.

"And Jack didn't mind you performing, your involvement in the theatre and everything?"

"How could he? It was who I was. By the time I met Jack that night, I had been reincarnated as a local stage star. He knew me as a singer, and he must have taken my evolution into musicals and stage work as a matter of course. I remember when he came to see me in *Hello Dolly*—my voice was still as strong as ever then." She smiles broadly and nods her head. "I loved the theatre, and performing came naturally."

"Well, I guess singing on stage and acting in the theatre have a lot in common," Lisa muses.

"You're right, honey. For singing and acting to be believable, genuine, they have to come from your soul; you have to make it your truth before you can offer it to someone else. And my god, it was fun! Ha! Musicals, comedies, dramas. I did it all. I even got myself an agent in Toronto and had small parts in three movies."

"Dad said you were the biggest thing to come out of Peterborough."

"Oh, I became a big fish in a little pond. And I was married to one of the most respected businessmen around. Jack took his company public in the eighties and never looked back. Yes, Jack was a good man, good company, but he was never Leland."

"Why? What was it about Leland, Nan? Your first husband, Grandpa Grace seemed like a nice man. I don't really remember him or Leland. I remember Jack and he was always nice. He loved you and you loved him, didn't you?" Lisa watches Ruby's face. She is amazed by the life her grandmother has led, a life of breaking boundaries, of determination, of guts.

"Yes, I loved Jack. He was a good man, but I didn't love him the way I loved Leland." Ruby sighs, and Lisa waits. Finally, after a few long minutes, Ruby continues, "I was afraid to divorce John and marry Leland. I didn't want to feel the way I did in my marriage, but I was afraid of getting a divorce. Looking back on it now, I think fear was what motivated me the most. I don't know why—I just always felt fear, like an anxious knot in the pit of my stomach. I married John because I was afraid of success, afraid of failure, afraid to continue in opera. Then, in my marriage, I was afraid to love, afraid to be hurt, afraid of not being loved in return. I suppose I was afraid that who I was, was unlovable." She falls silent, and Lisa reaches for her hand. Ruby's confession, her articulation of her fears, gives Lisa a glimpse of the woman her grandmother once was—fearful, hesitant, so unlike the woman she knows.

"Leland James. What was it about Leland?" Turning to Lisa, her eyes glowing with a flush of nostalgia, Ruby continues, "John Grace and Jack Richardson were good, steady men, like the tortoise. And Leland was like the hare. Leland lived moment to moment, and his love for me pulsed through his veins with every beat of his heart. Life and love were intense with Leland, and I knew I couldn't live without that, without him." Ruby, turning, speaks out at the window. "It sounds melodramatic, doesn't it? And it's not true. I could have lived without Leland, but then my life would never have had depth. It wouldn't have been my life." Looking out the window, into the landscape of her past, Ruby continues, her voice monotone, her eyes unfocused.

"He was funny and fearless. Maybe it was that, the fearlessness that was such a part of him. With Leland, I could feel the extension of myself in ways I had never known before. I could see a self that I had always been afraid to become, a self that expanded spiritually, sexually, intellectually, socially." She nods to herself. "Yes, all those ways."

These were the thoughts that, in quiet moments, circled her mind, private and beautiful. They were thoughts of Leland, an ordinary man, who directed her to all that was within herself, who taught her how to understand her own truth. The knowledge was easy to avoid, to bury within. She needed him to coax them from her, to witness them, to unearth them. Things that were always there.

Perhaps he acted like a magnifying glass? A kaleidoscope? Life with him was more colourful, more intriguing. Somehow it was always more present, more focused. He was her diviner; together, they were regular people with an extraordinary gift, able to find water in the depths of the earth by holding a simple branch. They weren't extraordinary in themselves. They were flawed and average, fighting weight problems or bad breath. Yet together they unearthed potential, they unearthed life. They knew what was hidden and where it was, and only they could draw it forth.

Nodding to herself, Ruby continues, unaware of her surroundings, drawn into her memory. Her story is deep, faceted, and easily recognized. Her voice, cracked and thin at first, picks up the richness of the singer, the storyteller, the performer, drawing Lisa along with the ease of the train itself. "Every year, when my brother and I were young, my mother took us back home with her to New Brunswick. We looked forward to that, getting away from the city, being with family. Daddy had no family. 'We were all he had and all he needed'—that was how he'd put it. So, summers at the farm were special: grandparents, aunts, and uncles and cousins to play with, running in the fields, building forts, and riding the old swayback mare. Ha! Such fun for a child.

"One summer my grandfather—Grampa, we called him—was getting a new well. It was all he talked about, the well—where it would possibly be, how deep, how cold. Yes, it was all he talked about, the well and the drought that had set in. The whole idea of a well was strange to us. The farm already had a well in the front yard, and our chores included bringing in water to the house. But Edward and I had always lived in the city; we never thought about water, about where it came from, how it got to us—it was just something that came out of a faucet when you turned it on. But Grampa's excitement had infected us, and we began to wonder about the new well. Grampa said that someone would be coming out to the farm to show him where to dig, and we waited with great anticipation for the man to come.

"It was a sunny, cloudless day, and Edward and I were playing under the trees at the side of the house when a man in a rickety old truck came to the farm to determine the exact location of the new well. We were more than interested, since

Grampa had never explained anything to us about how to find a well—we had only a vague idea that it was going to be somewhere in the back paddock, near the livestock and fields. The man was not very old, although it was hard to tell. His face was weather beaten, his teeth brown and worn when he smiled, and—every once in a while, to our great amazement—he would lean forward and release a great stream of yellow liquid from his mouth.

"He met Grampa on the porch, pushing his hat back from his forehead, talking and pointing in the general vicinity of the back paddocks, nodding and spitting and nodding some more. Then, after what seemed like forever, he walked back to his truck and starting rummaging in it. Out from the tools and pieces of this and that, he extracted an old forked branch of a tree. Edward and I looked at each other, wondering what on earth he was going to do with it. Would he use it to mark the spot? And how would he find the spot, the place unseen and waiting under all this land, where the water runs, cold and clear, the water that will help Grampa through the drought?

"The man walked out to the paddock with Grampa, the branch dangling from his hand like a mysterious wand. We two kids trailed behind, our anticipation growing with every step. When we got past the chicken coop, just before the big barn, he stopped. He took the branch in both hands like the bars of a bicycle, and, holding it loosely in his fingers, he began walking in measured steps around the whole area. We were captivated, too enthralled to speak or even to laugh. It was a bizarre sight: this strange little man, walking around the yard with an old branch of a tree in his hands, his eyes partially closed, his head tilted toward the sky, and his face as set as a hound dog on a scent.

"He walked back and forth, back and forth like that for ages, sometimes slowing, always intent, almost hypnotic. Just when Edward and I had begun to lose interest, the branch began to quiver. It became a living thing in his hands, trembling and pulling like a leashed animal desperate to break free, its head craning forward and down. The man's arms, moving in spasms, were ridged and tight with the struggle. We couldn't take our eyes away from him as he fought for control of the branch that only moments ago had been nothing but a stick, and now seemed possessed by something we couldn't see, pulling and tugging, alive as if by magic. Just when I thought the earth was surely going to open up and swallow him whole, this man with the magic stick dropped one hand, pushed back his hat to wipe at the sweat that had gathered on his brow, and waved my Grampa over. 'Dig here,' he said.'"

Ruby falls silent, her eyes bright with the memory of that day, with the child she was, with mysteries unfolding before her. She smiles at Edward, Grampa, and the farm as they recede from her mind.

"Nan?

"I was afraid to succeed, afraid to love, afraid to know myself." Ruby turns, her eyes sharp as she looks at Lisa. "Leland was my divining rod. With him, I became who I already was." Nodding, she looks down at her hands, thin and liver-spotted, the skin transparent, the veins gnarled like old roots. She continues after a moment, her voice resonating gently in the car, her mind like the countryside around her, moving into the past. "I always think of Corinthians when I think of Leland: 'but when that which is perfect is come, then that which is in part shall be done away.'"

"That's beautiful, Nan," Lisa answers above a whisper, breaking the silence. "I don't think most people experience a love like that."

"Yes, that's true. Had I not met Leland, I would never have guessed that love could be like that." Sipping her drink and then gazing out the window, Ruby continues, her voice warm with emotion. "I miss it, you know, the intimacy, the nakedness, the comfort. I suppose in a way Leland seduced me with that, the freedom I found in my own sexuality."

"Wow, Nan, that's pretty progressive!" Lisa, almost breath-less, struggles to find the words to express her dismay. "I never knew that, well, that sex was..."

"What, honey, do you think your generation invented sex? Ha! How do you think you got here?"

"No, it's just that..."

"It's been around for a long time, a long time, in all its glory and guilt." Pausing, Ruby turns toward the window, her thoughts hurtling by like the countryside reflecting in her eyes. "I suppose that in embracing that part of myself, I could embrace who I was. Sex was so reserved with John Grace; he was a good man trying to live by some sort of so-cial ethos. I don't think Leland ever felt that pressure, or if he did, he dismissed it. He was a maverick. He lived by his own rules, and it was seductive to be around someone who could be like that. And he was right, ha! The only good thing about living a long time is seeing how the whole world can change; everything can turn upside down in a matter of years. Female sexuality was never discussed in my day, not in what was considered respectable society. You had to wade into the whole thing with trepidation, knowing something was there but never sure what. Then it all changed, and now women can jump in with both feet! They're even expected to! Well, let's just say that Leland threw me into the deep end, and I learned to swim quite well." Smiling, Ruby winks, patting Lisa's hand as though she is a child too young to understand the complications of the adult world. "With Leland, I ex-perienced all that, all of life, all of myself. When I started seeing Jack, it wasn't as if I was letting go of any of it; it just became another chapter, one that would have meant nothing without the chapters leading up to it."

"Nan?" Lisa asks when she can find her voice. "Have you ever told my dad about any of this?" She waves her arm to indicate the breadth of what her grandmother has just shared. "Or aunt Phoebe and uncle Frank? Do they have any idea about...?" Lisa lifts her hand, unable to formulate the right question.

"You mean about my sexual liberation?" Ruby answers nonplused.

"Yes."

"I don't know." She takes a deep breath and settles deeper into her chair, her body tired with the effort it takes to communicate these days. "I don't think I ever really talked to the kids about things like that. I regret that. Maybe if I had been more open, more receptive.... I don't know. You always pull at the truth, you know, pull it and shape it into something different, something acceptable, respectable. I shaped it into what I wanted it to be, what I needed at the time. Who would want to know about a grown woman's sexual awakening, her growing understanding, or her struggles?"

Dropping into silence, both women are consumed by thoughts that are difficult to articulate. Ruby feels the need to share something of herself, the only thing she can offer, with her granddaughter. "When I was married to John Grace and falling in love with Leland, it was a confusing, chaotic, exciting time for me," Ruby continues, her voice weakening with fatigue, or maybe regret. "It was a time of discovery, a time of loss. The divorce took up all my waking thoughts, I was consumed by the need to be free. Nobody knew that I was having an affair; it seemed I was right in the middle of it before I had even realized I had made that decision. I couldn't turn away from what I found with Leland—I tried. I really did. But I couldn't, and the only decision left to me was to divorce." Sighing, Ruby continues with an effort, her words coming to Lisa as if from a dream. "My life with Leland felt like it was something apart, nothing to do with my children, or my parents. Who could understand? It was such an event to confront my parents with the disappointment of my failed marriage. I can still hear my mother's voice the day I told her about the divorce."

"WHAT DO YOU MEAN you're divorcing John?" Jeanie's voice is tight with shock, her eyes darting from her daughter to her husband.

"Ruby. You've just had your third child. You can't divorce your husband. It's just not done." Daniel's words seem to put an end to any further discussion, but Ruby stands defiant. Looking at his daughter and shaking his head, he continues, "John has never beaten you. He's a good solid man. You are not divorcing John Grace, and that's final." Daniel's blue eyes flash as he shakes his head, snapping open his evening paper. They are on the front porch of the summer house in Maine, the children settled for the night, the late summer sky brooding with fading light.

"I am, Daddy. I'm a grown woman, and I've made my decision."

"Oh, just like that?" Daniel asks, looking over his paper, unwilling to engage in this discussion any longer.

"No, not just like that. You know John and I have been unhappy for years, really, from the day we were married."

"And whose fault is that?"

"Yes, all right—it's my fault. I just can't be what he wants. I've tried, Dad. I've tried, and all I ever feel is unhappy." Ruby turns away, looking out into the evening light, the heat of the day hanging along its edges, the sound of crickets and bullfrogs enveloping them in musical silence. She has made up her mind as surely as night is falling, and she knows her father will comply, will eventually succumb to her wishes. He has always found it difficult to deny her anything, the child he longed for, the daughter he wanted.

Daniel, now ensconced behind his paper is unable to concentrate. He always imagined himself the father of daughters, surrounded by women. Before Ruby was born, Jeanie had endured two miscarriages, and disappointment had taken up residence in her face. Fear and caution marked the duration of her third pregnancy. After eight months of trepidation, Ruby emerged, screaming with health, a small, beautifully defiant fury, her colouring like Daniel's own: pale white skin, fine black hair that grew in gypsy curls, and dark blue eyes that he was reluctant to look away from. It was Ruby's presence that allowed him to function so clearly on one of the worst days of his life. His brother's death had been wanton and cruel, but the reality of his daughter—held snuggly against his chest, her head tucked under his chin, the weight of her three-year-old body—had anchored him in the present. There was nothing he would not do for her.

"Lots of couples are unhappy, Ruby," Jeanie says, her voice returning to her. "Married life is like that sometimes. You just make the best of it. You raise your children, you work alongside your husband, and you get by, day by day. You get by. You have a duty to your family. That's all there is to it."

How can Ruby explain to her mother that she doesn't want to just get by? That she doesn't want to live her life out of duty, a life that screams, "Is this all there is?" That she can't go on living her life feeling like an outsider?

It is Leland and his prodding, his incessant questioning, his need to get to the core of Ruby Grace that forces her to finally look long and hard at her life, at the life she has accepted, like her childhood catechism, without question, without wondering if there could be something more, something bigger.

After the crushing disappointment with LaLiberté—her career stalling, never really taking flight—she had allowed fear and disappointment to lead her into the safety of marriage.

The brilliant and renowned Alfred LaLiberté, who had worked with the finest musicians in Europe, who had taught at the best studios, had offered himself as Ruby's vocal coach after hearing her sing. He was an impassioned task master, strict and rigorous in his teaching, his love of music evident in his every thought. He taught for and expected perfection, and he believed he had found it in Ruby. She was a dedicated student with a talent whose depths were yet to be reached.

It was only a matter of time until she achieved recognition; he knew this, but Ruby wavered. He understood that it was fear that had chased her into the arms of John Grace, and he grieved for her future as a singer, as an artist.

"You are still young," he said. "We will continue to practise, and you will have another chance soon." LaLiberté urged her not to give up; he told her that this period was simply a slight setback and that with continued hard work she would one day grace the world stage with her undeniable voice. He had tried to persuade her to take John Grace as a lover, to explore that part of her life, but to remain single. "Famous women have done it for centuries, my pet. Take your lover but remain free, unencumbered. An artist is married only to her art!"

But it had been two years of constant vocals training, engagements, and receptions, with no recognition. It was demoralizing. She was tired of being the solo artist; the pressure, the isolation manifested in nausea and weakness. LaLiberté's coaching, his relentless optimism, was too much to handle alone. Marriage seemed like an escape to a safer haven, a quiet lull in the ocean of ambition, and Ruby was too young, too inexperienced to break with social convention. She moved into marriage like a mooring ship, bumping with the choppiness of the sea, into the safety of the slip. But havens too quickly become prisons, and her new husband was not as she had imagined he would be. He was not a supportive bystander, encouraging her operatic dreams, helping shore her up to continue the drive toward success and prima donna status. No, John Grace wanted a wife, a mother for his children, a partner and supporter for himself. John, as much as he appreciated her growing celebrity and artistic bent, was a traditional man. Their discussions about her continued singing and vocal training soon turned to heated arguments, belittling and damaging.

"Oh, for God's sake, Ruby, grow up! You have children to think about. Don't expect me to come home from work every night to you gone and the kids either at your parents or with a sitter!"

"It's not every night, John. It's only three times a week. I can move the lessons to the mornings and then be home for you."

"And what about the expense of this whole thing? And the time commitment? The concerts and the engagements, Ruby? I don't want this. I'm trying to get ahead, to go somewhere with Decca. It's me who pays the bills, the mortgage, and you're out pursuing what? A career that has already passed you by?"

She was stunned at John's words. They were her own fears, ringing in her ears with a truth that seemed to take the strength from her knees.

Once Ruby married, LaLiberté never had anything but encouragement for her; he never acknowledged out loud that he had been right about the effect her marriage would have on her career. The day before leaving for Toronto, she stopped by his studio. It was late morning, and Ruby had dropped the children at her mother's house for a few hours, under the pretence of packing, and rushed to Kings Hall on Montreal's main street, anxious to see him one last time.

He was in his office, perusing scores, sheet music littering his desk like giant confetti. He was playing music in his head, concentrating, following the notes and rhythms with the precision of a conductor.

"Am I disturbing you, Laylay?" Her pet name for him jumped to her lips.

Looking up, his eyes took but a fraction of a moment to focus before his face blossomed with recognition. "No, not at all, my pet. You could never disturb me."

"I leave tomorrow. John and the kids and me." Her words hung in the air between them, a broken footbridge. She rushed on "We'll be renting a nice older home in Yorkville. I can take transit to the Conservatory. I intend to continue my training." She was embarrassed by her prattling, painfully aware of every nuance of the moment, the smell of the small office (polish, mildew, and cologne); the dust particles, turning in the shaft of light falling across the desk; and LaLiberté's gaze, calm but concerned. "It's what you want, isn't it, Laylay? That I should continue my training?"

Laughing, he stood and moved around the desk, taking her hands in his. "Not for me, my pet, but for yourself. You must pursue the things you want in life, not what someone else wants, and certainly not an old, foolish man like me."

"But you've been so persistent. So ... so demanding. I thought you would be pleased."

"I am pleased. If this is what you want. But it is difficult to serve two masters. You must decide what you want and follow that path without distraction. It's a difficult thing for anyone to do." Still holding both her hands in his, he looked into her eyes with frank regard. "You are young, my pet, and if you saw clearly, you could see your way to the finest stages in Europe."

There was a feeling of heaviness in the room; or perhaps the heaviness was in her heart. She could think of nothing to say, and he gently dropped her hands, returning to his seat behind the desk. "I will tell you, my pet, the saddest thing in life is to settle. To give up everything in pursuit of a dream, even if you don't achieve it, is still a richer life than to simply accept. You are an artist, Ruby. You will find that to accept a path that is not your own will be difficult."

She had wanted to cry, fall into his arms like a child, and bury her face in his chest. She had wanted him to make everything better. But he was not speaking to her like the child she had been. Standing before him, she feels very much alone. The feeling tightened her chest, constricting her throat.

"You will find your way, Ruby. We all must, and we all do. We will write, my pet. We will stay in touch. I cannot lose my star pupil!"

With an effort, Ruby nods. There was so much she would have liked to say, but her voice was lost, like her lost saints, she thinks. Finally, she spoke, breaking the awkwardness that had filled the space between them, the words moving past the tightness around her heart. "We will stay in touch."

Then she moved down the blurring hallway toward Rue St. Catherine, the lump in her throat painful, her eyes smarting. She passed two young vocal students on their way to the studio, their charts held against their eager bodies, their voices harsh with enthusiasm.

"NAN? NAN, did you say something?"

"Did I say something?" Ruby asks, her mind clouded and sluggish with sleep, her chest tight with anxiety.

"I thought you did." Lisa watches Ruby struggle, feels the desperate need to connect, to reach back in time, to pull out the woman she never knew.

"Nan?"

"I thought it was the end of my life that day, but it was only the beginning. The beginning of another life, another chapter. And I was the author. Ha! Funny how it takes a while to figure that one out!"

Turning to Lisa, her eyes lucid with understanding, she continues, "And that's what you have to know, Lisa. We are the authors of our own stories. We direct them, we live them, and, ultimately, we recall them, for ourselves and for others. So the decisions we make are always the ones we are supposed to make."

Lisa's face creases in confusion. She feels as if her own thoughts of the past twenty minutes have been jolted to a halt with the clarity of Ruby's statement and with the significance of the moment. She wonders if there is an underlying meaning or order to the chaos of life, if the harsh and private beauty of someone else's life can bring insight and direction to her own. Or is her desperate need for guidance making Ruby's words feel more profound than they are? Either way, her grandmother's advice resonates so profoundly that Lisa's eyes sting with emotion; she is suddenly unable to control the thoughts she has been holding so tightly in check. She is shocked and relieved to give them voice. "Nan..."

The strain in Lisa's voice alarms Ruby slightly. She is still getting her bearings, unsure of the moment. She turns to take in her granddaughter, aware that Lisa is crying but confused as to the reason.

"Lisa...." Ruby says soothingly, awkwardly reaching to take Lisa in her arms. "Oh, honey, what is it? Have I upset you with all my prattling? You just can't listen to an old fool like me. Ha! It just comes out of me sometimes. I have no idea what it is I'm even going to say!"

Lisa's mind, whirling with thought but stifled by emotion, simply lets herself lean into the warmth of her Nan. How often as a child had she sought the comfort of her grandmother's arms: a scraped knee, a dead gold fish, a break up with a boyfriend, an argument with her mother. And now here she is again, once more seeking Ruby's comfort.

"Oh, Nan." Lisa laughs weakly through her tears, her voice a thin reflection of her pain. "You're not an old fool."

"Well, I am, to be blubbering on and having you in tears." Stroking Lisa's hair, she tucks it behind her ear and sighs. "But maybe you better tell your old Nan what the problem is. What's got you so upset that you're falling apart like a cheap toy at an old woman's musings?"

Sitting up, Lisa fumbles for a tissue. Blowing her nose, she takes a moment to calm the sea inside, whose waves are crashing against her chest in painful heaves.

"Well, child? Out with it. What's got you all tied up in knots like this?"

"Nan, I found out last week ... well, I think I knew before.... I just ... Nan, I'm pregnant." Lisa stares at the tissue balled up in her hand as if the words were written there.

Ruby nods. "I see." She is silent for a moment. "And you don't know if you want to have the baby?"

"It's just such bad timing. My job, or lack thereof," Lisa

rolls her eyes, "and my relationship with Steve. Just my whole direction in life—it's so, so ... I don't know! It feels as if I've lost control."

"Well, control is only an illusion, ha! We can control our lives no more than we can control our biological urges. We think we have control of our own decisions, but God knows what influences those decisions: our childhood, our insecurities, our needs, our desires? Sometimes life is just one big falling house of cards. Ha!"

"Thanks, Nan! That doesn't make me feel any better!" Lisa wipes her tears. "Besides, I thought you just said that we were the authors of our own life. How can I write my own destiny when I don't have control over it to begin with?"

"I did say that, didn't I?"

"Yes, you did!" Lisa blows her nose for emphasis.

"Well, I suppose what I mean is that although we think we make decisions and choose what our life should be, where it should go, so much of that is just mere chance. What's that word... serendipity? Who we meet, where we go, the opportunities presented to us? I guess you could call that destiny. What we do have the control over is how we make it our own story. How we turn it into something positive. In that way, the decisions we make will always be the right ones."

Lisa sighs. "I think you're talking about rationalization there, Nan."

"Well, yes, and the stronger your powers of rationalization, the better your life. Ha! You know, in life, if you can rationalize, then there is no room for regret."

"I don't know. That sounds like cheating to me. You can't live your life without regrets."

"Where did that rule come from?" Ruby turns so quickly to face her that Lisa laughs, wiping at her tears, the tissue still in her other hand.

"It's not a rule. It just seems that in this world, nobody can escape death, taxes, and regrets. Come on, Nan. You must have regrets. We can't gloss over life with a magic wand that makes everything perfect, legitimizing every decision or action we've ever made. What's that famous saying, 'an unexamined life is a life not worth living?'"

"Oh, I don't know, honey. I think that's a rabbit hole, re-examining your life, pulling it apart with regret. Sure go ahead and look at your life, examine it in retrospect, but not with regret. What would be the point? It's already done. Leland always said that regrets are for the past. To live with regret is to never move forward. And if there's one thing I know about life, it's got to move forward. You have to go on—there's nothing else for it!"

"That's true, Nan, but who lives a life without regret? Regret for what could have been, or maybe what should have been?"

"Coulda, woulda, shoulda. Ha! What you deal with is where you are and what you have, not what could have been."

"But if you don't have regrets, you will end up making the same mistakes over and over again. There's got to be accountability. Accountability for the decisions we make."

"The decisions we make," Ruby repeats, nodding to herself.

"But I think you're right that the decisions we make are influenced by our own needs, our own insecurities, our own ideas of right and wrong." Lisa breaks the silence, her words as urgent as her thoughts. "I'm pregnant, and maybe subconsciously I wanted this, wanted to force some direction into my life."

"I understand that feeling all too well. Ha!" Ruby says. "So then, you want the baby." A statement rather than a question.

"Maybe ... no ... I don't know. All I know is that now that it's a reality, it feels like it's hanging over my head like a dark cloud. I don't know if I want this. I don't know if I can even handle it. What kind of a mother would I be?" Lisa says, almost pleadingly. She turns away.

"Well, you couldn't be any worse than me." Ruby looks at Lisa, her eyes flat as slate.

"Oh, Nan, that's hardly true!"

"Is it? Is it hardly true? Now that we're falling down the rabbit hole?"

Lisa takes Ruby's hand, pulled by the tone in her grandmother's voice. "I didn't mean to upset you, Nan."

"No, honey, don't apologize for that. That seems to be the problem when you get to be my age: nobody wants to upset you. Well, I've lived this long, a little upsetting isn't going to make me or break me! And Leland was right—regrets are for living in the past. But these days, that's where I seem to find myself anyway! Ha!"

Ruby shakes her head, absently caressing Lisa's hand as it lays in her own, her mind wandering through the years. An image of Phoebe as a child comes to the forefront, then her daughter as a baby, and now her granddaughter carrying a baby. "Life is too hurried; we rush past it too quickly, never knowing what is important until it's already gone by. And where are we rushing to so quickly?"

"Aunt Phoebe and Chicago?" Lisa teases, trying to lighten the mood that has descended on Ruby, threatening to pull her into yet another silence that Lisa cannot penetrate.

"Phoebe. Phoebe was a good child. A good baby. Hardly cried, you know. I would hear her in the mornings, in her crib, months old and laughing and cooing to herself until I came in to get her. Never demanding."

"She was a little cutie too, Nan. I love that picture of the three of them: Dad as a baby in Aunt Phoebe's lap while Uncle Frank looks on."

"Phoebe told me once that I was too busy pursuing my own life to be concerned with hers...." Ruby nods to herself as she stares out the window, her eyes focused but unseeing. In a monotone voice, deep in reflection, she continues, "But I don't think it was that. I think deep down, at the baser level, I was afraid of my daughter."

"You were afraid of your daughter?" Lisa's voice, loaded with incredulity, is just above a whisper. Now the question has been laid out between them, exposed and blatant.

There is a silence that seems to expand the distance between them, between expectancy and reluctance, between understanding and admitting, between elucidation and fear. For Ruby, it is a fear of exposing the darkness of her innermost thoughts, inexcusably hurtful and damaging thoughts that she has been unable to escape. Phoebe carrying the pain of a childhood emotionally marginalized, striving to be accepted, to be understood, to be nurtured and indulged, to be loved.

"Nan?" Lisa is insistent, afraid that Ruby has slipped from the moment, afraid to lose the thread of understanding. She is looking for a glimpse into her aunt's strained relationship with her mother, with her brothers. "You were afraid of your daughter, Phoebe?"

"Would you ladies like another drink?"

Ruby and Lisa look up at the same moment, the attitude in their features, the tilt of their heads, matching them through generations. They are both shocked to realize that they are still in the bar car, their drinks and surroundings forgotten in the heat of the moment.

Ruby smiles up at the attendant, her stage presence ever at the ready. She nods. "Why yes, dear. I'll have another of whatever I was drinking, and my granddaughter will have a milk."

"Nan! I don't want milk!" Lowering her voice and looking around the car, Lisa continues. "Do you have Pepsi?"

"Yes, in the can."

"Great. I'll have a Pepsi. In the can. Thank you."

Turning back to Ruby, Lisa can see that the insight is lost, the veil falling back in place, her grandmother's cheerful expression replacing the darker one of moments before.

8.

THE NORTH STATE STREET flower shop bell rings as Daniel opens the door, hurrying in from the cold November morning, his three-year-old daughter Ruby in his arms. Closing the door with his foot, he swings Ruby up and through the air in one fluid, athletic movement. Childish laughter floods the room, and Dean O'Banion, entering the shop from the back room, laughs at the expression of sheer joy on Ruby's face. Swinging Ruby again in a long arc, Daniel slows his movement and deposits her firmly on her feet before him. Ruby's face is flushed, both from the cold morning and the excitement of the ride, her dark hair escaping the confines of her woollen hat. She beams with adoration up at her father, happy to be out with him and away from the house on Maple Street, where the blinds are drawn and the rooms are quiet and sad.

She knows her brother is gone; she's just not sure where. His clothes are still there and his crib is still in his room, where mommy sits rocking, waiting for him maybe, his favourite teddy bear on her lap. Ruby knows it's his favourite because even though he can't speak yet—except for the *"da, da, da,"* that makes her laugh—every time she holds Teddy up to him, he always reaches for it. Sometimes he reaches so far forward that he topples right over, rolling like a sausage onto his stomach, his hand still reaching for Teddy, his smile showing two small white teeth breaking the gum. He never cries, her little brother; he is always smiling, and his smile gets even bigger when he sees Teddy. That's how she knows....

"And how is our beautiful wee princess today?" Dean O'Banion asks, crouching down and taking Ruby's chin in his hand, his face large and looming before her. "Oh, you sure are a beauty, aren't you, Ruby girl?" He lapses into his phony Irish accent. Kissing her forehead, Dean stands, smiling at Daniel. He is dressed in the white smock he wears when he arranges flowers, his shears still in his left hand. "I imagine she'll keep you busy with the boys in a few years."

"Yes, I'm sure she will," Daniel answers, smiling down at his daughter.

"How's Jeanie doing?"

Daniel shrugs the smile from his face. "Better, I think. The flowers were magnificent, Dean. Thank you."

"No need to thank me, Daniel. My heart goes out to you and Jeanie." Reaching out, Dean places his hand on Daniel's shoulder, but the intimacy is too much for both men. Daniel, twisting out of reach, takes in the massive amount of flowers for the first time; roses—white, yellow. and red—sit in buckets of water crowding out the floor. More flowers than he has ever seen overwhelm the counters and spill from basins. He spots geraniums, orchids, and baby's breath, along with even more that he couldn't possibly name. The smell is an overwhelming mixture of pleasant and sickening.

"What's going on? Getting ready for a big wedding or something?"

"No, no." Dean coughs out a laugh. "Just the opposite. Mike Merlo finally gave it up to cancer. His funeral is tomorrow."

"Yeah, and I'm still nervous about that, Dean." Hymie Weiss, walks into the room at that moment, talking as if the conversation had never been interrupted. "You should make peace with Torrio and Capone; you should offer some restitution for Sieben's."

"Oh, Hymie!" Dean turns, laughing. "Why would I make

restitution for the proudest moment of my life? Torrio don't scare me, and he won't tell me what to do. To hell with them Sicilians! That's what I say. If Torrio won't clear those Genna brothers off my territory, he's asking for trouble."

"Yeah, well you're bringing it to him! Not that he don't deserve it, Dean. But throwing Torrio to the Feds? Well, he's gonna be coming back for blood."

Hymie's eyes cut from Dean to Daniel. He nods curtly, his features set, his tone dismissive. "Your brother's upstairs, Daniel. I think he's excepting you."

"Thanks, Hymie. I'll head up," Daniel replies, relieved to be leaving. The room that only a moment ago seemed so joyful with colour and good wishes is now heavy with foreboding, the feeling as tangible as the sickly-sweet odour of roses hanging in the air.

Swinging Ruby up into his arms, Daniel moves past Hymie and Dean and into the back room. He passes the cold storage and rushes to the stairwell, taking the stairs two at a time to the office above. The weak, milky-white November sunlight spilling into the upstairs office is bright and almost too harsh for Daniel as he emerges from the darkness of the stairwell. Michael is sitting at the table by the window with Bugs Moran. Laying before them, a handful of metallic objects.

"What the hell is going on here?" Daniel asks, his voice tight with bewilderment and fear.

"Oh, Danny, my boy." Michael laughs, quickly putting a gun down on the table and stepping forward, blocking the scene from his young niece. "I didn't know you'd be bringing the princess. Let's move into the office and Bugs can clear off the table." He steers Daniel, with Ruby still in his arms, toward the office door.

"So how is Uncle Michael's wee princess today?" Michael continues in a soothing tone. "Have you come to visit me with your Da?"

Ruby nods, unsure if she should speak, sensitive to the

sound of her father's voice, so different from what she is used to. She has heard this new voice more often recently, in the darkened rooms at home. Instead she looks around, realizing with excitement that she has been here before. Last time, she slid on the chairs and jumped on the cracked leather couch, which she can never do at home.

"What's going on, Michael?" Daniel asks, placing Ruby down; his voice is less harsh, but his eyes never leave his brother's.

"Nothing good, let me tell you." He pauses. "How's Jeanie?"

"Better ... the same.... I don't know." Daniel shrugs, the thought of his wife, her despair that lingers like the smell of over-ripe fruit in a house already pungent with loss. "It's hard to know what to do."

The silence stretches between them, connecting them, separating them. Unspoken thoughts circle them. Their mother's death had been quick and quiet; she had slipped from the world without a ripple, followed closely by Daniel's son, James Joseph Kenny. Baby James. Daniel's mind touches the memory like a tongue pressing a toothache—pain, the reminder of reality. Jamie's small body, listless with fever, lying in Jeanie's arms, his eyes helplessly beautiful. Where is the rhyme or the reason, Daniel wonders? He shakes his head, dislodges the memory, and returns to the present. He knows there is no other way. Forcing his thoughts forward, his voice when he speaks is ragged and foreign, a stranger's voice.

"So, what is the nothing good that's going on, Michael? Hymie is downstairs with Dean, and the friction between them is pretty evident. Then I come up here, and you and crazy Moran are handling hardware?"

Ruby is exploring the room. Running her fingers over the smooth leather couch, pulling out books from the shelves, she thinks it would be fun to play house here with someone. Then she remembers Patty, her rag-doll, hidden in Daddy's coat pocket.

"Daddy, can I have my doll?" she asks excitedly.

Extracting the doll from his pocket with difficulty, Daniel hands her to his daughter. "Here you go, honey."

Both men watch as Ruby takes her doll to the dormer window. Chatting to herself, she arranges her doll into the corner and begins to tell an elaborate story; she is lost to the world of her imagination. Daniel is surprised by the strength of emotion he feels surging through him every time he looks at his daughter— his history and his future together in one small, fragile being. She is tenacious, this child of his. Jeanie finds her headstrong, but Daniel knows she will need that kind of strength to face a world as unpredictable and, at times, unfair, as this.

"Take your coat off, Daniel, and sit. I'll pour us a short one and fill you in. You've had your hands full the last little while, and a lot has happened."

Throwing his coat over the arm of a chair, Daniel sits. "Isn't it a bit early for a short one?"

"Are you arguing with the doctor, lad?" Michael hands Daniel the drink.

"No." Daniel shakes his head, smiling at the old joke. "I guess I could use it after all. I think I'd like to get lost in the bottom of that bottle."

Michael nods in understanding and sits across from his brother. Extracting his cigarettes from his pocket, he offers one to Daniel, who shakes his head. "How's the job going? Any more promotions?" Michael asks, lighting up and inhaling deeply.

Before he answers, Daniel lets the scotch fill his senses, enjoying the burn as he swallows, almost thankful for the harsh bite. He is feeling more present than he has in months. "No," he answers. "Not for a while, I think. McKinsey is expanding the company quickly but cautiously. Financing and accounting as a business is a new idea for local manufacturers, but they're starting to realize that it's a necessity."

"You'll still be able to do the books here, though?"

"Yeah, I can't see that ever being a problem. The company is getting more and more clients, and business is booming, but

I'll always be able to help Dean, although I haven't looked at his books in a while."

"So, there is only one way but up for you." Michael laughs. "I always knew you were born under a lucky star."

"Well, I don't know so much about that." Daniel's eyes cloud and his gaze falls on Ruby, who is busily chatting to her doll. She has struggled out of her hat and coat, and they lie beside her, the sun falling across them, the smoke in the room drifting up like lost dreams.

"So, let me fill you in on things here, Danny-boy," Michael hurries on, uncomfortable with his brother's pain sweeping into the room like a cold draft.

"Yeah, what's going on?" Daniel nods, anxious to busy his mind with other concerns.

"Mike Merlo died."

"Yeah, Dean said. That's too bad. But what's the problem?"

"Well, Merlo was the only one standing between Dean and Torrio. You know Merlo—he was the president of their Unione Siciliano or something." Michael shrugs at his mispronunciation. "Anyways, his word was law for those guys, and Merlo don't like violence." Michael shrugs. "Now that Merlo bit it, Hymie thinks there'll be serious trouble. Capone is ruthless and Torrio listens to him. Hymie thinks big trouble is coming."

"Torrio is the head of the organization over there, isn't he? Remember we used to call him *torero*, the bullfighter. I always thought he was competent. Why is he listening to Capone?"

"Capone has got a one-track mind. If you ask me, he would love to take over the whole operation. So, I figure Torrio plays along with him and keeps him close.

"So, what's Hymie so worried about? I thought things were going well with Torrio."

"Yeah, they were for a while, but the Genna brothers started moving in on our territory and Torrio wouldn't do a goddamned thing about it. The Gennas are selling their liquor at three dollars a barrel, and we sell ours at between six and nine. Their liquor is total shit, but they're selling it on our turf. When Dean found out he hit the floor running; he told Torrio to keep his goons out of the North Side or else." Michael takes another drag, stubbing the butt into the brass ashtray to his left. Shaking his head, he continues, "Those Genna brothers are a mean bunch. There's five of them, and I think Capone is their captain. They're Torrio's army, but they're a power unto themselves. I don't know if Torrio is actually behind the move into our territory, or if he really can't control the Gennas. Anyways, we had a sit down about it and it didn't go well."

Michael leans back, sipping his scotch, his mind drawn back to that evening. He remembers the look in Dean's eyes, stone cold and piercing, as he stared down Torrio with the bravado of the fearless, or the foolish. More and more, when he allows himself to go there, Michael feels the cold sweat of worry. Dean is a good match for Torrio, but it's Capone who pulls the air from the room.

"Daddy. Daddy!" Ruby calls from her world by the window. A smile lights up her face, engaging and open. "Daddy, come see the house I made for Patty! Daddy!"

"All right, my Jewel, I'm coming," Daniel answers, looking at Michael and smiling. "She's only three and already I do her bidding."

Michael shrugs, laughing. "That's women for ya'. They start young."

"Well, this is quite the structure, honey." Daniel crouches beside her and inspects the stacks of books piled up around his daughter. "Maybe we should just straighten out a few—that way the walls of your house won't topple in on you. All right?" Daniel straightens the walls of Ruby's ambitious doll's house. "There. That's better."

"Can you play with me, Daddy?" Ruby strokes Patty's hair and looks up into Daniel's face; she hasn't felt this happy in a long time.

"Later, honey. Let Daddy spend some more time with uncle

Michael, and then I'll take you and Patty for a nice lunch. How does that sound? Do you think Patty would like that?"

"Oh yes," Ruby answers seriously. "Patty has to eat her lunch to grow up strong."

Daniel laughs and returns to Michael, whose amusement at the exchange shows in his smile. "You're a good father, Danny."

"You taught me well, Mick."

There is humour in the exchange, but Daniel means every word. His eyes meet Michael's. The two brothers smile, and in a single moment, their history passes between them: Michael's youth sacrificed to bigger concerns, his struggle to take their father's place, setting himself up as the barrier for Daniel and their mother against the harshness of life.

Too old before his time, Daniel thinks, looking at his brother. A man before he was a boy and now, thin and greying while still in his prime. Forcing these thoughts from his mind, Daniel asks, "So, where were we? The Gennas taking over Dean's territory."

"Yeah, that's right. Dean has been dissatisfied with Torrio and Capone ever since he helped them take over Cicero." Michael continues, picking up the thread of the conversation.

"I thought that was a done deal? Papa Torrio took that territory almost three years ago. Daniel's facetious use of John Torrio's mob name is not lost on Michael. "Dean was happy to help him out then. So what happened?"

Michael nods. "Torrio is smart. He fixed the elections in Cicero so's he could move his headquarters out of the city limits and away from the pressure of the reformers and Mayor Dever. Dean even sent a dozen of us over to Cicero to lean on the constituency on election day."

"Yeah, I remember all that. So why the trouble over Cicero now?"

"Well, Cicero has become a big cash cow, Danny boy. The South Side is seducing more politicians and cementing its hold on everything moving in and out of the goddamn city. Those goons are becoming more condescending in their attitude. Makes me so mad, I could spit blood! Torrio has more than he can handle: The South Side, the prostitution ring, Cicero, the Canadian liquor consortium." Taking another long swallow, Michael shakes his head, the politics of all of this getting to him. "Then about a year ago, Torrio gave Dean a strip of Cicero territory, just like he was throwing a bone to a dog."

"Yeah, I know that. So what?"

"Well, the earnings in that territory are pretty slim, about twenty grand a month—such a minor concession that it verges on insult. Dean said he had a plan and that he'd beat the Ities at their own game, and he did! Dean has quadrupled the income by leaning on fifty or so of the saloon keepers on the South and West Side, and now we got them doing business in our territory."

Daniel stares at his brother, his mind racing. His throat constricts around his last swallow of scotch, and he has difficulty answering. "This is sounding pretty reckless on Dean's part. I mean, this is heading for serious trouble."

"Yeah, you telling me. Torrio was none too happy at the sit-down, let me tell ya'." Michael swirls the golden liquid in the bottom of his glass, remembering the scene in the drafty back room of the abandoned mill

"DEAN, MY FRIEND," Torrio's voice is low and controlled. A smile plays at the corners of his jackal mouth. "I need some kick-back from your Cicero territory. You cannot undermine me on my own turf—what will the neighbours think? We will agree on a weekly price, and then we will talk about the Gennas." Torrio nods slightly in the direction of Sam and Angelo Genna, who, standing to his left, are far enough away that the conversation remains private but close enough that their menacing glare is undeniable.

Dean, his attitude unwavering, the smile on his face incongruous with the murderous look in his eye, lets the moment stretch on to minutes; the sweat running down Michael's back is the only movement in the room.

"Okay. All right. You drive a hard bargain, O'Banion. No one can ever say you're not a tenacious business man!" Torrio laughs, trying unsuccessfully to dispel the tension in the air. Nodding to Capone, who is seated to his right, he continues, "Perhaps we will offer interests in the brothel. Fifteen percent. You agree to weekly payments for Cicero and take fifteen percent of the brothels in the area. It's a good offer, my friend."

"I'll have no dealings in brothels." Dean breaks his silence, the anger in his voice barely contained. "There are no brothels on the North Side and there never will be. I'll not deal in human flesh." Dean's voice drops to a whisper with the last statement. Leaning forward, he continues, his eyes locked on Torrio's, his jaw muscles jumping. "Remove the Genna dogs from my territory."

Torrio leans back and laughs again, loud, boisterous. "Dean, my friend, I cannot force the Gennas to do anything. It is a free country, is it not?"

Before the words are out of Torrio's mouth, Dean is up from the table. "Let's go, boys." Dean nods to Michael, Hymie, and Ducci. Then he turns and looks back at Torrio, Capone, and the Gennas. "You won't take care of the Gennas, Torrio. I will!"

DANIEL SHAKES HIS HEAD, blood pounding in his temples. "So Torrio won't keep the Gennas under control?"

"Won't or can't. Anyways, we hit two Genna shipments and it was a good haul." Michael smiles, the innocent smile of a child happy with the outcome of his game. "Over thirty grand in Canadian whiskey! But that's not the best of it." He gets up and takes Daniel's empty glass. "You'll need another one for this."

"But we're running our own Canadian whiskey. Why hit the Gennas?"

"It ain't about money anymore, Danny boy. It's about honour. We can't let just anyone walk in and start operating out of our territory. Torrio gave Dean the Cicero territory, and now he's leaning on him for kickback. He won't call off the Genna dogs, and then he insults Dean by suggesting he take an interest in the brothels. You know how Dean is against that—hell, everyone knows!"

Daniel watches his brother, his forehead creased with worry. He's going too far with this, he thinks. *This is still just a game to him. And he's too thin. And lonely.* Daniel can hardly understand what holds his brother so tightly to this life. The O'Banion gang has become his whole world, consuming him to the point of obsession. Michael has no wife, not children, no home life. He is still living in the old neighbourhood, one of the few left from the old days. The gang has become wealthy and influential, all of them except Michael, moving with growing families out to more prestigious areas, into homes they could never have imagined a few short years ago.

The American dream is coming to fruition in barrels of Canadian whiskey and syndicated crime. Although the syndication is yet to become fully realized, Daniel knows it's headed in that direction. The neighbourhood gangs have become more and more organized. They have transformed from groups of delinquent children to deadly serious organizations with levels, with routes, with influence that reaches from one area of the country to the other, one continent to another. They export whiskey from The Distillery Company of London, in Britain to the Liquormans in Canada, who then act as middlemen, importing and exporting to and from America. Their main contact is Arnold Rothstein, who will eventually become the godfather of organized crime. Within a decade of the Roaring Twenties, the syndication will be peddling heroin, cocaine, and other illegal substances through the same means—the same wholesale, transportation, and retail system developed to bootleg booze during prohibition. Daniel can't predict the specific outcome of their activities, but he can feel the power and deadly intent growing as these gangs organize and legitimize themselves through corruption.

Daniel takes a deep breath as a sudden realization passes through him. He thinks of himself as a moral man; he thinks of his brother as a good man, although perhaps too caught up in the machinations of the city's gangs. In France, Daniel saw moral men doing immoral things; the compass somehow never finding true north, and war called for desperate measures. *Is this war?* He looks at Ruby sitting in the sunlight at the window and thinks of Jeanie. Handing him his glass, Michael interrupts the reverie.

Michael is smiling at the story he is about to tell, warming to it like a cold man before a fire. "Things pretty much settled down after that. There were a few more sit-downs, and Dean promised to keep the status quo, but we hit the Gennas two more times and nothing happened. Torrio didn't even come after us for restitution for the score, Dean went to Torrio with a proposition, telling him he wanted to retire."

"Dean's retiring? Good idea. Maybe you should consider it yourself, Mick. Buy a big house down by the lake and find yourself a wife!" Daniel, suddenly happy at the turn of events, can't keep the excitement from his voice.

Michael's look is flat, his voice clipped. "Dean's not retiring. He told Torrio that he was so's Torrio would buy him out of Sieben's."

"Sieben's?" Daniel thinks for a moment. "Oh yeah, that's right. Dean owns fifty percent of that place. Gambling and alcohol, always the best money makers." Daniel's irony is lost on Michael.

"Yeah, that's the one. Best money-maker on the North Side. Well, Dean got tipped off that they were gonna raid the place. I mean, Torrio ain't the only one with politicians in his pocket. So, Dean convinces him that he's ready to retire and work at the flower shop with Viola—he's always here anyways—and that he wants Torrio to buy out his shares.

Daniel shakes his head, his thoughts racing. "I find that hard to believe. That Torrio would think Dean is ready to retire. God knows he's got the money to retire, but Dean's addicted to this." Daniel lifts his arm, but he's suddenly not sure what he's indicating. The room, the criminal world, the influence, the power?

"Well, maybe he did, maybe he didn't. But I guess he figured Dean wanted to sell his shares for whatever reason. And you know Torrio—he's always up for an opportunity to increase his holdings in anything and everything."

Daniel nods. He doesn't know Torrio and doesn't want to; he's happy to stay on the periphery of things. He's frightened for his brother. The momentum of Michael's lifestyle seems to grow exponentially with every passing day; it's like a vortex of power, sucking morality from a man with dizzying speed, a game of chance with an inevitable outcome and the highest possible stakes. Daniel feels the weight of worry, cold and gnawing in the pit of his stomach.

Still unconvinced by Michael's story, he asks, "So, what happened?"

"Torrio had his lawyers there. He paid. Dean signed."

"Do you know how much?"

"Half a mil."

Daniel's whistle is low and long. "Sweet Jesus!"

"Dean signed over his shares, and now Torrio owns the Sieben, lock, stock, and barrel. They met there the following week to finish the details. They were sitting at the table in the back of Sieben's with the lawyers, the deed done, so to speak"—Michael slaps his knee, anticipating the punch line—"when they got raided. Chief Collins and his captain, Zimmerman, and the boys in blue came hauling in and arrested twenty-eight guys, including Dean, Hymie, and Torrio. They also confiscated thirteen trucks loaded with liquor."

"Dean got arrested?"

"Yeah, but because he ain't got no interest in the brewery,

they can't hold him. He knew that would happen, and he also knew what they'd do to Torrio."

"What?"

"They handed him over to the Feds cause it was Torrio's second arrest for violating prohibition. Torrio was caught with some egg on his face, boy! It was the best sting I ever heard of!"

"Torrio must be beside himself. This is serious, goddam business, Michael."

"I'll say. But that guy plays his cards pretty close to his chest. Hymie is worried sick. He thinks Dean is thumbing his nose at Torrio and there'll be trouble."

"What does Dean think?"

"Dean thinks it's the best prank he's ever pulled. Told Hymie not to be so frightened of those 'gutter rats,' as he calls them." Michael laughs.

Daniel is quiet, watching Ruby, who has looked over at the sound of her uncle's mirth. She smiles at Daniel, and he returns the smile automatically, his mind struggling with the ramifications of what his brother is telling him. "I don't know, Mick. It's not that funny. It sounds pretty serious. I think Hymie is right. Dean should call a truce, make peace. Torrio isn't going to take this lying down."

"Yeah, you're probably right." Michael says, sobering up. "And now Mike Merlo ain't here to balance things out. Merlo prefers talk to violence, and all those Italian boys bend their knees to him."

"What do you think? What are you going to do?"

Michael looks at Daniel, smiling in reluctant acceptance. "What can you do? Dean is the way he is. For months now he's been saying 'to hell with the Sicilians.' He ain't gonna start playing ball with them now."

"You're going to have to be careful, Mick. Maybe the gang should break up for a while."

"No, nothing is gonna happen right away. They still gotta bury Merlo. Torrio's boys have already been in here ordering roses like they're going outta style. Torrio's order is almost ten grand! And James Genna and Carmen Vacco ordered a seven-hundred-and-fifty-dollar wreath to be picked up today. Things will be quiet for a while. They gotta bury their king."

"If you say so," Daniel answers, unconvinced. "But I think I'll take the books home with me and work from there for the next few weeks."

"Good idea." Michael stands, taking Daniel's empty glass. "Why don't we go grab some lunch? I've got to feed Ruby something or she'll go all day without eating."

"No, Danny, but thanks for asking. I got some work to do with Bugs, and it's a bit early for lunch for me."

"Okay. I'll nip out with Ruby and grab some lunch and be back in an hour or so. You want me to bring you back anything? I hate to sound like Ma, but you need some meat on your bones."

"Yeah, you do sound like Ma!" Michael laughs at the serious expression on his brother's face, a look he'd recognize anywhere. "Sure. I know I won't get anywhere with you unless you have it your way. If you're going to Grady's, bring me back whatever the lunch special is." He looks at Daniel. The space between them is charged with emotion, brotherly concern, familial assent, and something else. "Do you feel better now?"

Daniel shakes his head, laughing. "Honest to god, Michael, you are worse than a child. I'll bring you back something. And you better eat it!"

HOLDING A PAPER BAG—the lunch special from Grady's—in one hand and Ruby in the other, her sleepy weight comfortably against him, Daniel makes his way back to Schofield's.

Memory is a funny thing, easily disrupted and confused by traumatic events. The horrors of France never come back to Daniel as one chronological story; instead, without warning, they seep into his conscious mind like oily liquid, spreading in a deep pool of disorder. Bright, disjointed moments come back to him highlighted in surreal imagery, frightening in their unreality, as his mind rushes to understand, refuses to accept. He knew something was wrong before the door to Schofield's had closed behind him. The stillness? The feeling of total emptiness? The smell? All of these things and something else, something indescribable, unrecognizable but present.

The shop bell rings above his head, jovially announcing his entrance. He is aware of Ruby's weight in his arms, her body warm against his chest, her sleepy breath on his neck, and her small whimper, a response to the tensing of his muscles

"Dean?" Daniel calls out, circumspect, hearing nothing but the thin fall of his voice. It is hard to breathe after the cold air of the street. He feels overpowered by the heat of the flower shop and by the cloying odour of so many roses and something else he recognizes, sitting at the edge of understanding, the slight metallic smell of blood. He knows what he will find. And then, he is standing over Dean, whose body lies at the side of the counter, his eyes open in a look of surprise. Blood covers his face, his chest, his stomach, the floor around him, the corners of his mouth.

"Shh.... It's okay, honey." Daniel reassures Ruby, who has stirred in his arms.

A cold sweat has broken out all over his body; his coat feels heavy and restricting. He knows he is reacting to the horror; his body is reacting to the perceived threat. His vision narrows and he fights to control his breathing, willing his heart to slow and focusing his attention on his sleeping daughter. Tucking her head under his chin, he moves in a hypnotic state past Dean's body and to the back room. The back door is open half way, the pale noon light falling across the floor and along the wall. Jimmy Dolan, the boy Dean employs to clean up and make deliveries, sits on the bottom step. He doesn't notice Daniel approach him.

"Jimmy. Jimmy." Daniel places a hand tentatively on the boy's shoulder. Moving out of the flower shop has steadied

Daniel's resolve, but he struggles to raise his voice above a whisper. "Jimmy, son. It's me, Daniel Kenny."

The boy looks up, his eyes focusing with effort. "Mr. Kenny?"

"Yes, Jimmy. What happened? Where's my brother?"

"I don't know, sir. I was just coming back and leaning my bike against the wall like I always do. I was going in to tell Mr. O'Banion that I'm back when I sees one of those Jewett's touring cars pulling up in front of the shop. I didn't think nothing of it at first, but I just stays behind the door here." Jimmy stares off.

"Jimmy. Jimmy!" Daniel shakes the boy's shoulder gently until he sees recognition settle into his eyes. "Then what happened?" Daniel asks soothingly, leading Jimmy like a blind man back to the moment. "What happened after you saw the car?"

"Three men come in. All three of them walking together right up to Mr. O'Banion," Jimmy continues without looking at Daniel, his eyes focused into the distance. "The one in the middle is kinda tall, with a fedora and a long coat. Mr. O'Banion moves out to shake hands and asks 'em if they're from Mike Merlo's. They're smiling, and the guy in the middle says, 'Yeah, that's right. We's here for Mike's flowers,' and he takes Mr. O'Banion's hand and pulls him in close and the other guys kinda surround him and they just start shooting him and before he even falls they're coming toward the door and I move back and they push open the door and go up the stairs...." Jimmy's words trail off, and he drops his head into his hands, taking deep ragged breaths.

"It's okay, son. Can you get up? I think you should head home. I'll deal with this." Daniel helps Jimmy up. The boy seems stunned, but there is little he can do for him. "Will you be alright to get home by yourself?"

Jimmy nods, then holds out his hand toward Ruby and strokes her cheek. "She's frightened."

Ruby's face is white, her eyes large and luminous under her hat. She looks at Jimmy without seeing him.

"She'll be fine." Daniel covers Ruby's face with his hand, tucking her tighter under his arm and against his chest. "Are you sure you can make it home?"

"Yeah. I'm all right now."

"Walk your bike home and remember to take deep, even breaths. All right? And Jimmy? No need to mention this to anyone yet. I'll deal with this. All right, son?"

Jimmy nods, hesitating before he leaves. "I heard shots up there too." He indicates the office with a nod of his head; his eyes, locked with Daniel's, flicker before he turns. When he moves through the back door, the weak light is momentarily obliterated, and then he is gone.

Daniel climbs the stairs, a prayer like a mantra filling his thoughts. *Please God, please God.* His blood pounds in time with the chant. Pausing in front of the door, he tries to gather his thoughts, which are fracturing like glass before him. Ruby must be his only concern. He should leave now, follow Jimmy out the back door and into the afternoon light, but he is worried for his brother's life. He already knows what he will find, but still he is compelled to push open the door.

Michael is on the floor. There is a chair next to him, which looks to have toppled over as he grappled the air while falling back. Unlike Dean, he has not been shot at close range. This shooting was hasty; it stopped Michael in his tracks as he headed through the office, keeping him from intervening in the violence downstairs. He is not dead; his chest rises and falls with an effort that Daniel recognizes.

"Michael?" Keeping Ruby's head turned away, he kneels over his brother and watches Michael's eyes flutter open. "Michael?"

"Danny?" His voice is choked with the sound of liquid.

"Yeah, Mick. It's me. What the hell happened? Who did this?"

"I didn't know them, but they're Torrio's boys. They said they were here for payback...." Michael's coughing halts his story, racking his body with violent tremors.

"Don't talk, Mick. I'll call for help. We'll get you to the hospital."

"No, Danny." Daniel can feel the stickiness of his brother's blood as Michael grabs his hand, his grip tightening with immediacy.

"No.... Don't ... call. Listen ... to me."

"Michael...." Daniel shakes his head, his eyes searching Michael's.

"No...." Struggling for speech and breath, Michael pleads for understanding. Tears slip from his eyes, bright with urgency. "Listen to me ... please." His words are sluggish, his breathing shallow, his heart slowing. Daniel nods his compliance, unable to answer.

"You have to leave Chicago...."

There is a long silence. Daniel knows his brother wants to say more, but the effort is monumental. It takes everything he has. "Take them ... and leave."

Michael's words hang in the air. His breathing is a harsh rasp as his lungs fill with blood. It's a sound Daniel has heard too often. Micheal's eyes close and then open again. He struggles to stay focused, stay conscious. The last of his energy is being given to this moment. There is nothing now for Daniel; the world has been narrowed to this experience, this place, the few inches between brothers. He strokes back Michael's hair and looks into his familiar eyes, into his brother's face strained with pain. "The ... safe.... Take the money...." Michael's eyes close, his face chalk white, the bones beneath pushing forward. With an effort, he opens his eyes. "If they'd a come in a few minutes earlier, the safe woulda been wide open." He begins to cough, holding his hand over his stomach. Daniel holds Ruby's head against his chest with one hand and supports his brother with the other. When he has calmed, Michael continues, "Better you take the money and get out, Danny. The boys will think it was swiped by Torrio." He nods. His eyes close briefly, but he forces them open again. "Do it now ... Danny." His voice is a command, familiar and forceful, demanding a younger brother's compliance.

"I'm doing it, Michael. I'm doing it," Daniel replies, taking Michael's hand in his.

"Good, Danny. Good." Michael relaxes, his ragged breath slipping from his body. His eyes are open, but Daniel can already see the emptiness behind them.

He stays with his brother, he's not sure for how long. It's not until Ruby moves that Daniel realizes he has been frozen in place. Ruby squirms in his arms but she is quiet, watchful. Reaching out, she touches the hand of her uncle, still held in Daniel's own. She begins to hum a song, a nursery rhyme that Daniel recognizes but cannot name. His thoughts have deserted him, scattering like starlings roused from a tree and circling beyond the horizon. Now, they return with a clarity that heightens his awareness. Gently, he lets go of Michael's hand and takes Ruby's. Holding it against his chest, he rocks her back and forth, looking around the room for the first time. He wonders how long it's been since he stepped through the front door. It seems like hours, days even, but could only have been minutes. How long would it be before someone else comes into the flower shop and finds the bodies? Standing, he is cramped and sore. His arm aches with fatigue as he holds his daughter, pulling her tighter into his chest..

"Ruby," he whispers, moving her from one arm to the other. He goes into the back room and around the desk to the safe. He knows the combination, and he runs the tumbler with one hand, Ruby snug in the other.

The safe is full; the smell of money wafts up to him in the small stuffy room. His mind racing, he begins to scan the office for something to carry the money in. There is nothing on the desk, but then, behind the credenza, he finds an old leather satchel. His from his school days he thinks, vaguely amused.

It is awkward, holding Ruby and filling the bag, but he does it, stacking the money in as neatly and quickly as he can. He begins to sing the song Ruby was humming, "*Ring around the rosie, a pocket full of posies,*" distracting them both from the present. The sun has changed its angle; the afternoon has moved on. Before leaving the office, he thinks to take the last ledger. It's more to carry, but he has been seen carrying ledgers back and forth from the flower shop for years. It seems natural, and he grasps for anything that can bring a sense of normalcy to this day, anything that can quell the sea of unease churning in his stomach. He is anxious to leave, to be out in the street and on his way home. The office is eerily quiet, heightening the sounds from outside: the traffic rumbling by, children's voices carried through the tunnelled streets and floating up from blocks away, dogs barking echoing from distant corners of the unheeding city. All of this, and the room itself, make the moment surreal. He wishes he could walk out with his eyes closed and not have to see his brother's body. He doesn't want that final image of his brother to stain his memory forever. Moving into the room, he stays as far away from the area as he can, talking and singing to Ruby in soothing tones, focusing on his daughter and her safety. The stairwell is in semi darkness as he heads down; the back door is not quite closed, and the sunlight illuminates a strip of floor like a pathway to freedom. This is the quickest way out.

Now the fear of discovery tightens his chest; blood thumps through his ears, making it difficult to concentrate. If he can make it out with the money, he and Jeanie can leave Chicago and start a new life. They could return to Canada, to Montreal. He can set up his own business, a new home. A life away from this, he thinks, taking one last look along the hallway and into the flower shop, the odour of roses and death hanging heavy in the air. Ruby retches at the smell, then vomits her lunch over her hand and onto Daniel's chest and arm. Her visceral reaction urges him outside and into the sunlight of the November afternoon. As quickly as he can, he escapes the flower shop and all it contains.

The bodies in Schofield's are not discovered until early evening, when Viola, Dean's wife, drops by to help with the orders for the next day. Within minutes, the flower shop is swarmed with Chicago's finest, making notes, taking pictures. Jimmy Owen will be interviewed, and the three men's description will be circulated. It will be years before the main gunman is named. Frankie Yale, a New York mobster, and two others, John Scalise and Albert Anselmi. The *modus operandi*, three men shooting victims with a handgun at close range, will come to be known as the Chicago handshake. O'Banion's death will begin the bloodiest and most violent era in Chicago's history, culminating in the St. Valentine's Day massacre on February 14, 1929.

If we are present at some historic event, can we hope to comprehend it? Can we even remember it with accuracy? Perhaps retelling it as a story is the only way we can make sense of it, make it acceptable, make it real, or as real as we imagined. Jimmy will tell his story to the police, to his parents, to his neighbours, to his children and eventually his grandchildren. The tale will be told and retold, embellished, improvised, and glamourized. He will always remember the part he played in the history of the Chicago gangs, the death of Dean O'Banion, the end of the Irish stronghold on the North Side, and the beginnings of syndicated crime in America.

9.

"HOW'S THE PEPSI?" Ruby asks over the rim of her glass, eyebrows raised

"It's fine."

"Should we order some pretzels, or do you think that would be pushing my luck?"

"Nan!" Lisa smiles.

"So, finally, a smile."

"Sorry. I'm preoccupied and not very good company. Now that I've told someone about my situation, it seems more real than ever. I can't ignore it anymore. I have to make a decision."

"Well, you don't have to make it right this minute, do you? Let's weigh the pros and cons. Shall we?"

"It would be easier if you could just tell me the right thing to do." Lisa's voice is edged with exasperation.

"Oh, I can't tell you that, honey. Only you can know the right thing to do. I can try to give you some advice, but really, advice is something you ask for when you already know the answer, but wish you didn't!"

"Maybe that's why I haven't asked."

"Maybe." Ruby nods, preoccupied. "Maybe…" she repeats, her voice trailing off, her mind pulled by an irrevocable force into the past.

"MAYBE THE RIGHT THING to do is to do nothing." Daniel Kenny's eyes are flat as he turns from his daughter.

"I can't just do nothing, Dad." She shakes her head in defiance. This is not what she wants to hear.

"You have responsibilities, Ruby. You are a mother and a wife!" Daniel says almost dismissively.

"I'm more than a mother and a wife." Ruby's voice breaks with frustration.

"SO?" LISA NUDGES HER GRANDMOTHER gently, bringing her back to the present.

"So, what?" Ruby answers, unsure who is speaking.

"Do you have any advice, Nan?"

"Do I have any advice." Ruby repeats. Her eyes dart around the bar car as she attempts to recall the present moment.

"Yes," Lisa says slowly, aware of Ruby's struggle, the force of her effort to regain equilibrium. Like a drowning victim grasping a buoy, Ruby grapples for something concrete.

"You were going to give me some advice."

"Some advice on what, honey?"

"Nan," Lisa continues patiently, aware of her own need. "I was telling you about my present situation. About me being pregnant and..."

"And you aren't sure what to do, are you?"

"Yes, exactly. And I was wondering if you had any advice, if you could, I don't know, maybe give me your opinion, your thoughts?" Lisa places her head in her hands and draws them along the sides of her face. She turns to Ruby, a tired smile on her face.

"Oh, yes." Ruby takes Lisa's hand and pats it with a sigh. "You need some advice."

"Yes, I need some good advice." Lisa says with relief.

Ruby laughs. "Oh, I know, old people are supposed to have good advice. But really, what is good advice?" She looks out the window. "It's just someone else's opinion of your situation. Those opinions are always coloured by our own perceptions of ourselves...." Turning back to Lisa and smiling, Ruby continues, her voice and her mind strengthening with the focus the present moment is demanding. "I suppose at my age I do have some experience with situations. Damn, my whole adult life has been a situation. And I guess what you're asking me to do is evaluate my situations, my life, and glean some insight that may help you with your. Is that right?"

"I guess. At this point, anything would be helpful."

"You know, honey, I don't know how helpful I can be. All I can tell you is that you can never live without regret. I think a life without regret is a life not lived, because life is about making choices. If you choose one thing, it means you don't choose the other and it can leave you wondering, "what if?" It can leave you with regrets. But if you live a life of 'what ifs', you will drive yourself crazy. You have to make your own decision, and when you make it, follow it and don't regret it. Don't divide your energy, don't divide your thoughts. Make your decision and don't look back. Whatever decision you make, it will be the right one for you. It always is. Besides, I find that retrospect gets far too shaded by rationale most of the time and it becomes impossible to tell the difference between what really happened and what you remember."

Lisa shakes her head. "That's a bit jaded, don't you think? Especially for you, Nan."

"Well, I think that at my age, I'm past lying. I don't mean hurtful, conscious lies—I mean the lies we tell ourselves in order to keep up the façade. Who we think we are is often so removed from who we are that the twain shall never meet." Ruby shakes her head before continuing. "Can we make them meet? Should they meet? Ha!" She looks directly into Lisa's eyes. "And who do we become if they do meet? Stripping away all our rationalizing, all the stories we tell ourselves, our last line of defence. When we find ourselves standing in the harsh light of truth, whom do we see? What are we left with? Maybe all we are left with is some good advice?"

"Well, for my sake, I hope so." Lisa laughs.

"I wonder if it's worth it? I wonder if we really can end up being honest with ourselves?" Ruby picks up her drink, watches the light playing through the ice.

I never became the soprano I wanted to be. There was a passion in me, but not to the exclusion of everything else. Not like the passion of the genius living only for her art. Was it because I was a woman, biologically and socially hampered? Was it because the art was not all consuming and left room for love? For it is true, I loved Leland with a passion, a passion that still burns.

"Who would I have been without Leland?"

"Who would you have been without Leland? Is that what you just said?" Lisa, confused by the new direction but interested, gently urges her grandmother. "Nan?"

"When I was eighteen, LeLiberté was so excited with my developing soprano voice that he encouraged my training and set out a three-year course of study. His plan was for me to work toward a scholarship in music at McGill and eventually perform on the world stage. They seem like highfalutin aspirations now, don't they? And I can hardly reconcile the young hopeful girl I was with who I am today. Even the photos of those days look like they're of someone else's life. Who was I? Who am I? And who do I become in the telling?"

Lisa, trying to follow the thread of Ruby's thoughts, answers tentatively, "Maybe you find meaning? Maybe, truth?" Then she adds hopefully, "Maybe you become someone who can give good advice?" Lisa laughs, breaking the tension. She is watching Ruby carefully, unsure if her grandmother is even aware of her presence.

"Maybe you're right, honey! Maybe all this looking back can bring some meaning, and meaning always brings its own sense of satisfaction, doesn't it? And maybe I can end up giving you some good advice along the way! What's that thing you said—an unexamined life is a life not worth living? Well my life was worth living, let me tell you!" Ruby lifts her glass to her lips and drinks in deeply, appreciating the bite of the liquor, the sweetness of the tonic, savouring the moment. When she continues speaking, after wiping at the corners of her mouth, there is conviction in her voice, the timber of the storyteller, the actor.

"Should you marry your young man? Should you have this baby? Is that what you want, what you need, or is it just the next logical step in your life? Do you love him, and to what extent, and will that love last? Will it grow? The love grew between Jack and myself, although it was different from the love I experienced with Leland, and the love I felt for John. I'm not sure if what I felt for John was love at all. When I met John Grace I had just turned eighteen and I was still studying vocal with LeLiberté. He thought I had a talent; I was unsure but willing to believe him...."

"RUBY, MY PET." LeLiberté's voice, is deep and rich, his accent lyrical. "That is enough for today. For Wednesday, I want you to think about the importance of the jaw. Remember to drop it and allow the note to form from the diaphragm." He indicates his abdomen with his hand and then lifts it easily to his face and out toward Ruby.

"Yes, I will, Laylay. I promise to run through my scales every morning." Ruby gathers her sheet music as the late daylight from Rue St. Catherine falls in rays across the wooden floors, slanting up and along the piano legs, illuminating dust particles. The street noises that float lazily up to the second floor window signal the coming evening.

"Good, good. This too is important," says LeLiberté, almost absent-mindedly at first, and then with sudden presence. "Ruby, do you have a moment before you rush off to your bridge party or dance or whatever keeps you so busy these days?"

"Yes, of course!" Ruby laughs. "I always have time for you. You and opera are my only true loves!" Her smile is radiant in its conviction.

"You know, I would like you to continue studying with me. I see a future for you, my pet. You may attain that which so many can only dream of: an operatic career!"

"Oh, yes. It is my dream." Ruby's pulse races at the idea, her face flushing with pleasure.

"I would like to bring someone in to hear you. He is an old friend; we studied together in Europe, and I hold his opinion in the highest regard. Hopefully he will hear your potential, as I do."

Ruby clasps her hands like a little girl as LeLiberté continues. "Have you spoken to your parents about McGill?"

Ruby hesitates. LeLiberté is planning for another year of study with him before she is admitted to McGill University, but the cost is becoming a burden to her parents and the money she makes at Moore's Music is minimal at best. The plan is exiting and inspiring, but how feasible? Her parents are well off, but not rich, and university is expensive, almost inconceivably so.

"Well, my pet?" LeLiberté looks over the top of his glasses, his eyebrows raised inquiringly.

Ruby shakes her head. "No, I haven't spoken to them yet."

"Well, you must. We should be, how do they say, setting these wheels in locomotion. You may be able to receive a scholarship of some kind, but you must speak to your parents and begin looking into this."

"I will. I promise." Ruby picks up her sweater and purse, and turns toward LeLiberté with genuine affection. "I must run now," she says, and kisses him quickly on a cheek in desperate need of a shave. "See you Wednesday, Laylay!"

"Yes, Wednesday!" he calls after her, then shakes his head and turns to Peter, the accompanist, who is still seated at the piano. "Youth, it is wasted on the young, is it not?"

"Yeah, it always is." Peter nods. "Do we have time for an espresso before the next lesson, Maestro?"

LeLiberté checks his watch. "Yes, a wonderful idea. Let me get my chapeau!"

RUBY DOESN'T SPEAK to her parents about McGill. She continues to work and to sing—in the church choir, at concerts as a solo soprano, and with LeLiberté—but university seems like too daunting a financial burden. Ruby is the apple of her father's eye, the oldest and only surviving daughter. There is only Ruby and her younger brother Edward, and their lives have been comfortable and privileged in many ways. Until recently, Ruby hadn't thought much about money. Her parents were always well off, with a large home in Outremont, a summer home in Maine and occasional trips to the continent. Her father was a successful accountant. The depression did not seem to affect them, at least not that Ruby can remember. There was never any scarcity in their home, never any want, and, except for May's death, no sadness. Ruby can hardly remember Jamie, who died as an infant, but May's death is present in her mind as the saddest of memories. Any time her thoughts light upon those days—the dying, the wake, the funeral—she can see only her father, his hands, competent and gentle as he cuts a ringlet from May's hair and presses it into their family bible, smiling at Ruby, his only remaining daughter, his little jewel. This part of the memory is too painful: the sad smile on her father's face, the resignation and the love, coming together in a look of defeat. He looks so unlike himself, the man in the memory, that he slowly becomes someone else, her brave unshakable father, changing so imperceptibly that years later, it is hard to credit his eventual fragility to this moment.

This summer, Daniel and Jeanie are in Maine with Edward. Ruby loves spending the summers in Maine, but this year she has her job and her many concerts, and it is getting harder to leave her friends. Montreal in summer is a bustling, exciting place; it holds Ruby spellbound on the threshold of adulthood, in high heels and short skirts, the antithesis of the barefoot daughter she would be in Maine. She misses her family, but she feels preoccupied by her own life, running full speed toward her bright and promising future.

Hurrying from the studio, Ruby runs toward the bus stop, her thoughts racing ahead toward home and the outfit she will change into for her date with John Grace, her excitement growing with a force of its own. He is four years older than she is, and he seems more worldly compared to the boys she has been seeing. When he finally kisses her, the mysteries of her body open; she feels the tugging in the pit of her stomach, the tingling down her spine, the ache between her legs. The immediacy of the moment, the force of physical passion, pushes all thoughts from her head, and she enjoys the feeling, falling unfettered through an abyss to breathless ecstasy.

"YOUR GRANDFATHER was a good man, Lisa. When we met, I was excited about his attentions. He was older, and he had a good job working for Decca records. In fact, that's how we met. I worked in one of the music stores that he supplied. He was an inspirational sales man, your grandfather, and an enthusiastic musician. He loved jazz, understood it the way my own father did. John Grace was probably the reason I turned to jazz after my hopes of a career in opera had drifted away." She takes a sip of her drink, the look in her eye turning inward. "There I was, married with children. Opera is too demanding a life to allow for such personal pursuits."

"Do you ever regret marrying Granddad?"

"Well, you know how I feel about regrets. They are the black holes of our personal universe, sucking in momentum to no end. I did marry John, and at the time I thought it was the right thing to do. I liked the idea of marriage, of husband and wife and happy ever after. But it was over before it ever began. One day I found myself at the kitchen sink, Francis and Phoebe at my feet, John absent on a sales trip, and me, Ruby Grace, stranded in the middle of a life I never wanted, in a city I didn't know. I picked up Phoebe, who cried out at my wet hands, and carried her to the phone. Francis tagged along behind, confused about the abrupt change in the day. I called a taxi and left that afternoon to go back to my parents. They were in Maine, but I knew the schedules for bus, or train, or plane. Ha! My escape route!"

Lisa, about to say something, stops. Her mind is full of the image of Ruby Grace as a young woman, stranded in a life she didn't want.

"I was pregnant, though I may have only been vaguely aware of it. Another baby." Ruby, stares out the window, her memory pulling her into itself. She is, suddenly unaware of the world outside, or of the young woman beside her.

Lisa, afraid to jar her but uncertain about leaving her to her painful reverie, sits quietly beside her grandmother. She has never heard this story before. She has heard her father and aunt talking about their childhood—their words full of nostalgia, the honey that sweetens the past—but this is a time before her father was born, before Phoebe would remember, a time when Ruby was vulnerable with youth and hampered by convention, confused and lonely and fleeing for her life.

RUBY'S FINGERS TREMBLE as she dials the number of the house in Maine, remembering the long summers spent there, the long warm evenings on the porch, the beach, the bonfires her father would make, the wind-up gramophone playing scratchy music while they danced into the night.

"Hello?" Ruby's eyes sting at the sound of her mother's distinctive voice, tentative but sweet.

"Hi, Mom. The kids and I are coming for a visit."

"Oh, that's wonderful, dear. When?"

"I'll be on the late train." Ruby struggles to keep her voice calm.

"Tonight? Isn't this a bit sudden? Is everything all right, dear?" Jeanie's voice turns sharp with concern.

"Yes, Mom. Everything is fine. I just need to see you and Daddy. I just ... I just miss you...." Her voice cracks with emotion. She is worried about putting her parents in a difficult position, but she is overwhelmed by the intimacy of her mother's voice. With effort, Ruby stops herself from spilling out the truth, from laying it down before her mother like the weight it is. She holds back the gravity of the situation, that her daily life has become a tormented existence: being married to one man and pregnant with another man's child.

Daniel is at the train station to meet them. He lifts Phoebe with one arm and hugs Francis and Ruby with the other. Ruby can imagine herself melting into him, lingering under the protective care of his arm, but he moves away, too quickly, looking for the luggage.

"Is this it, then?" He lifts the small case, concern deepening the lines around his mouth.

"Yes. That's it."

"Leaving in a hurry were you, Jewel?"

Ruby buries her face in her hands, sobbing at the use of her baby name; the late-night train station, the children, the few passengers, all is forgotten in the immensity of her emotions.

"Oh, Ruby, sweetheart. Are things that bad?" Daniel places Phoebe on the ground and smiles at Francis before moving to his daughter, taking her in his arms. It will be okay, honey. Don't cry now. You'll frighten the children, and I'm sure they're confused as it is."

Ruby nods and moves away from him, wiping her eyes with the back of her hand.

"Here, honey." Daniel hands her his handkerchief, and Ruby, unable to find her voice, nods again. His handkerchief is soft against her face and smells of her father, of her childhood. The memories sting her eyes again. She swallows against the lump in her chest, her emotions threatening to break the surface, leaving her a crumpled mass of uncontrollable tears. *I can't go there. I can't go there.... I mustn't go there....*

Blowing her nose and dabbing again at her eyes, she smiles, a weak, pale smile. Looking at her father, she nods.

"Good," he answers, nodding. "Francis?" He turns to his

four-year-old grandson. "Take Mommy's hand. I'll take Phoebe and the suitcase and we'll go see Grandma. Shall we?"

Francis nods, his eyes serious and watchful. He takes his mother's hand.

It is not until later that night, when the kids are bathed and in bed, that the adults can talk more openly about the implications of Ruby's hasty arrival.

"So, what does all this mean, honey?" Daniel asks, handing Jeanie and Ruby a glass of bourbon and then pouring one for himself.

Following her parents out onto the small porch, Ruby sits on the Adirondack chair beside her mother. "I don't know, Dad. I just don't want to go back. I think I want to leave John, I suppose." Ruby shrugs, unable to look up from her drink.

"Really, Ruby." She hears her mother's voice beside her, gentle but practical. "What kind of an answer is that, honey? We've been through this before, and I thought it was settled then. Wives don't just leave their husbands. It's just not done."

Ruby sips her drink, then stares into her glass. "Even when they feel like they're dying?"

"Oh, Ruby!" Her mother's laughter echoes in the shadows of the cottage, shimmering like moonlight off the water. "Nobody dies just because they feel like it." She shakes her head. "And separation, divorce, well that's just such a big step."

Turning to Daniel for understanding, Ruby holds his gaze. He has always been the parent who would give in. Even as a child, she knew that if she dug in her heels, her father was no match for her will. He believed in "live and let live" and found it difficult to force his will upon his family. "Daddy, you must understand how I feel. I just can't go on like this."

"I think I do, honey, but it is not just you involved in this. You have to think about John and the children. You have to understand the consequences of your actions. You have to respect the lives entrusted to you: your children and your husband."

"I do respect the children. And I respect John, but he is living his life, pursuing his goals. He's hardly ever home. I feel like my life is over before it has even begun."

"Oh Ruby, that is just not right," Jeanie interjects, looking from Ruby to Daniel and then back again. "Your life is just beginning. You live for your children and your husband. That is what a mother does. And what a wonderful thing it is."

"But it is not enough for me, Mom. I have a right to the life I want. If I'm unhappy, how happy can John and the kids be?"

"You already have all life has to offer, Ruby. There isn't anything more," Jeanie answers, as if explaining something to a child.

"There *is* more," Ruby says quietly, but her mother isn't listening. She rushes on with her own line of reasoning. "Daniel, don't you think Ruby has a full and blessed life? Tell her there isn't anything more.... Daniel?" Jeanie looks from Ruby to Daniel, realizing that he has retreated from the conversation. She looks at Ruby, her face pinched with concern, a world of unspoken communication passing between them.

Leaning forward in her chair, Ruby touches her father's arm, her voice gentle with worry. "Dad?"

Daniel looks up as though he is waking from a dream, his eyes taking in his surroundings. He makes an effort to rouse himself; it is a struggle he is getting used to, one he knows he must undertake. "Ruby, what is it, honey?"

"Are you all right, Dad? You just seemed to wander off there. Where you thinking about your fishing holes?" Ruby laughs unconvincingly.

"Yes, I'm fine. It's nothing, really." Standing abruptly, Daniel bumps the small table holding his drink but quickly steadies it, one hand on the table the other on the glass. "Well, it looks like I need another drink. How are you girls? Anyone for another drink?"

"No, I'm good, Dad. But I would love a tea."

"A tea?" Daniel laughs. "All right, but it will take me a few minutes, you know, boiling the water and all." He turns to Jeanie. "And for you, my dear?"

Jeanie smiles, handing her husband her empty glass. "I'll join you in another drink, honey. But make it a short one."

When he has left the front porch, the screen door banging on its hinges, Ruby turns to Jeanie, her voice a conspiratorial whisper. "What's going on with Dad?"

"I don't know, honey. In the last few years he has been falling into these moody silences. Sometimes they pass quite quickly, but lately they have been lasting longer. Sometimes for days."

"I don't remember him ever being like this, Mom. Has something happened?"

"No, nothing. Well, except for life. He has never been one to talk about the past, and there have been certain things, you know—the war, the babies dying, his brother's death. Your father likes to move on, always looking forward, letting memories slip quietly into the past as if they never really happened." Jeanie rubs her bottom lip with a finger and looks past Ruby to the screen door. Then she continues, finally voicing a thought she has had for a long time but has not been able to articulate: "I think, sometimes, he gets lost in the silence of not saying."

"Mom, what happened in Chicago? I can barely remember that time, but I think, somehow, it was frightening. I don't know why." Ruby falls silent, trying once again to gather impressions, feelings that are always just beyond her grasp, real but unsubstantial, like cobwebs on skin. "Why did you and Dad leave, Mom? Did something happen?" Leaning forward, Ruby takes Jeanie's hand; it is small and thin, like a child's. Ruby has always thought of her father as the stronger one in the family and her mother as the weaker one, but lately she is not so sure.

"Well, life happened ... and death." Jeanie nods to herself, smiles, and then turns toward Ruby. "I'm not sure that there is a simple answer to your question, honey. Your father had a good job. The accounting business was just starting—in its infancy really—and your father was on the ground floor. He also did the books for private businesses. He was always a good provider. But things were difficult. I had had two miscarriages before you were born and then, three years later, Jamie. Then Jamie died. Those years, honey, they seem lost to me. Grief will do that." Shrugging almost imperceptibly, Jeanie pauses. "Your father dealt with his grief in his own way, but some days it was difficult to go on. You get up and put one foot in front of the other, wondering all the time why you're even bothering to continue. It's painful and pointless, but you just keep doing it, and slowly it hurts less and less. And then one day, life begins to have purpose again. I don't know exactly why we left Chicago. I think it was your father's way of getting over Jamie's death, but sometimes I wonder if there was more to it than that."

"Like what?" Ruby asks, just above a whisper.

"Your father's brother, Michael, was killed in a robbery at a flower shop of all things, along with the man he worked for. It was a flower shop with offices above, but they also had interests in a few other businesses around town. Daniel did the books. The day after they were killed, some men came to the house to speak with your father. I knew one of them. They were acquaintances of your Uncle Mike, and I never liked them. They were what you would call 'shady characters.' But your father had a business relationship with them. Anyway, something happened that day that frightened your father, and we left Chicago the day after we buried Michael. It was a good thing too, because Chicago became a dangerous place." Jeanie nods as the memories resurface in her mind's eye. After a moment she continues, her voice bright.

"It was the era, you know. There's no denying that. It was a fun, exciting time. Your dad would take me to the jazz clubs—they called them speakeasies. It was during prohibition and drinking in the club was illegal. But really, that's what made the atmosphere, that and the music. The music was something else! We saw Joe Lewis, Billie Holiday—so many great names!" Caught up in the nostalgia, Jeanie smiles whimsically, her eyes liquid with memory. For a moment, Ruby can see clearly the young woman her mother once was. "We would dress up in high style and go out on the town, and you knew that this was something just beginning, something exciting and important. But there was always a feeling of foreboding—at least for me, young, Canadian girl that I was—that things wouldn't last."

"What would give you that feeling, Mom?"

"Well, there was always the threat of being raided by police, and we all knew that the club owners were mostly criminals. My goodness, if you were selling liquor in any establishment at that time, you were a criminal. I suppose we were all breaking the law. Prohibition was just such a ridiculous thing. It ended up being more bad than good, with all the illegal drinking and transporting of liquor. Chicago was like a dynamite keg just waiting to explode, and we got out just in time." Looking again at the screen door, Jeanie continues, "So, I'm not sure why we left—I don't know if it was from grief, or if it was something your father was involved with that frightened him—but whatever it was, it was fortunate for us.

"We had money. Michael had left your father a good sum, and we used that to buy a home in Outremont and for your dad to start up his accounting business. We moved to Montreal, and we never looked back. It was the best thing we ever did."

They are silent, listening to the summer sounds outside the porch: the soft hum of night bugs, the breeze through the dunes, the ocean against the shore, soothingly rhythmical.

"He has always been so present and articulate," Ruby says, her voice thick with emotion in the darkness. "He was always the one starting the conversations over dinner and insisting that Edward and I join in. Remember the discussions he would start, Mom? He always expected us all to have our opinions on politics or religion. He just loved to be in the middle of a good argument. This is so unlike him." Turning to her mother for an answer, Ruby watches Jeanie shrug, her eyes worried and compelling.

"I know," her mother answers.

"I'm sure it's nothing, Mom. Dad is strong and so are you. Look at all the things you've been through." After a moment, she continues, "Well, I think it's time to turn in."

"Yes I suppose it is getting quite late. It's easy to lose track of time here, isn't it, honey?"

"Maybe Dad is just tired?"

"Yes, maybe."

They are silent for a long time, isolated in the darkness, listening to the movement from the kitchen, Daniel making tea.

"YOUR GRANDDAD AND I separated for the first time that summer, but I knew it was the beginning of the end, in so many ways. I wanted to leave John and be with Leland, and I should have. But I didn't. Not for years. My father and mother were struggling with Daddy's silent moods, which were getting worse and worse. For the first time, I saw my parents as so very vulnerable. I was pregnant with Gary, and it just seemed easier for everyone if I stayed with John."

"But you were in love with Leland James?"

"Yes, I was in love with Leland James. I have always been in love with him. From the very first time I met him, I wanted to be known by him fully, in every way, the good and the bad. And I was. That summer I ached with the love I felt for him. I was in love with Leland," Ruby nods and then continues, almost to herself, "and I was pregnant with his child."

Lisa, taking a drink from her glass, chokes on the Pepsi; the fluid forced up through her nose is sharp and cold. Reaching for the napkin on the table, her mind reeling, Lisa blows her nose, shaking her head to dislodge the feeling. She must have heard her grandmother wrong, or maybe Ruby is talking about something else, someone else. Turning toward Ruby, her eyes tight with the struggle to comprehend, Lisa asks in a voice lowered with confusion. "Nan?"

"Yes, lovey?"

"Nan, did you just say you were pregnant with Leland's child?"

"Yes, I did just say that."

"Did you have that child?"

"Of course I did." Ruby nods as if to emphasize the banality of the question.

"Are you saying that my dad, your son Gary, is Leland's son?" The question hangs, an expectant bubble between them, pierced by Ruby's forceful voice. "Yes, Lisa. Gary is Leland's son."

Lisa understands for the first time what it means to be struck dumb. She stares at Ruby, her mind ricocheting in uncontrolled directions, incredulity and realization staggering across her face. Ruby is calm, looking out the train window as if nothing has changed, her profile in the afternoon light burning into Lisa's mind like a laser; her grandmother's image becomes a shadow on her retina as she looks away, searching in confusion.

"Who knows about this? I mean, does Dad know? Do Aunt Phoebe and Uncle Frank know?" Shaking her head, Lisa answers her own question. "They can't. I'm sure we would all know." Looking again at Ruby, Lisa feels like she is seeing her for the first time, a stranger on the train, revealing secrets from a lost past. Questions struggle for attention, paralyzing in their magnitude, their implications. Her mind runs through the years until she arrives at this moment. Taking in her grandmother with a new perspective, she asks the only question that matters: "Why are you telling me this now, Nan?"

Ruby, whose attention has been absorbed with the struggles of a fly in the sill of the train window, replies without turning. "Maybe it can help you with your decision."

"Help me with my decision?" What decision? Lisa wonders. This new revelation has pushed her own pregnancy into the background. This is something quite different; it is too big to allow room for anything else. "Nan, you have to tell Dad. He has a right to know. He has been going for blood work. He's been having health issues. He's worried. Mom's worried. I'm worried. They have to know that Leland is Dad's biological father. What did Leland die of, Nan? Wasn't it cancer? Dad will have to know; he'll have to be told. We all need to know." Lisa's voice pitches upward as the magnitude of this information rolls over her with a physical power. She shakes her head either with incredulity or to clear her thoughts, she is not sure. The action is automatic, involuntary, as if it is somehow facilitating her understanding.

Ruby nods, still captivated by the fly's efforts, so like her own. "Yes, I must tell Gary."

"No, Nan. Not must—you will! You have to tell him! You have to tell everyone!"

"I think they must already know."

"How would they know if they were never told?"

Ruby turns to look at Lisa, her eyes, pale and large in the sunlight, compel understanding. "You don't have to be told something to know the truth of it."

Lisa is still struggling to understand. "How old was Dad when you married Leland?"

"Gary was around two when John and I divorced, and just starting school when I married Leland. The children were raised with Leland. After the divorce, John Grace travelled more and more for his job and saw the children less and less. I didn't think it fair to burden Gary, to single him out as different, as the reason I couldn't stay with John. There was no point bringing to light something that would hurt everyone."

"Did Leland know?"

"I think he did, but he didn't want to acknowledge it. Saying it and knowing it are two different things. Besides, by the time we married, it was already in the past."

"But, people have a right to their heritage, or at least the right to the know their biological make-up. Dad needs to know about this right away. He has been having stomach pain and now they are doing all kinds of clinical tests. Does that come from Leland? Shouldn't Dad be aware of who his real father is? For his own health? You don't have the right to keep that from him. From me! It's totally wrong."

"It's the sin of omission."

"Omission! It's stealing, that's what it is. Stealing someone's right to know. I understand that it was a different time with different sensibilities, and that it was maybe confusing for you, but still...." Lisa trails off, silenced by the enormity of it all.

"Larceny. Larceny and chaos. It's the way everything begins. Ha!" Ruby barks out a laugh.

Lisa continues as if Ruby hasn't spoken, her voice strained with contained emotion. "And if you knew and Leland knew and at some level my dad knew, then Aunt Phoebe and Uncle Frank knew—what kind of dynamics does that set off in a family? Nan, it's irresponsible!" Lisa's voice is edged with anger.

"Yes, you're right, Lisa. It is irresponsible. Sometimes the things we don't say hurt us more that the things we do say. Another lesson learned and at my age! Ha! And you wanted some good advice from me? Was that what you wanted?"

Taking Ruby's hand, Lisa finds herself overwhelmed with compassion for the woman sitting beside her, still defiant and bold and somehow beautiful in her human frailties. She pushes her judgement aside, but her voice cannot hide her disappointment. "Yes, Nan. I do."

Looking down at Ruby's aged hand lying claw-like in her own, the skin paper thin, Lisa continues, "I guess we do what we do, thinking it is the right thing, doing it with the best of intentions." A silent camaraderie falls between them, finally broken by Ruby's voice, intimate with introspection.

"Sometimes when I was singing, the notes would flow with such passion, such ease, seeming to go beyond the moment; the note, the timing, the meaning, one's self, everything would reach understanding in a simultaneous way, becoming more than the moment. Other times it was a struggle—repeating a passage, a run, until it becomes exact, acceptable, more than passable but never going beyond what it is." Ruby nods to herself. "I can recount my experiences, my story, but is that the truth of my life? Is there not a greater truth that lies behind and beyond our actions? Is it meaning? Is it intention?" Looking at Lisa, Ruby smiles slowly. "And isn't that the road to hell, as they say?"

"Yes, that's what they say, Nan. The road to hell is paved with good intentions." Lisa answers. She looks out the window but sees only the fly that is caught between the panes of glass, still struggling to make its way to the top. "That's how I feel sometimes," Lisa says, turning toward the window and the captured fly. "Thinking one thing and finding out something else, thinking you are going somewhere only to realize that you aren't the one powering anything, that you are just along for the ride, just keeping busy so you don't realize the futility of it all."

"Lisa!" Ruby turns sharply. "That's just a bit too dark, don't you think? It's not where he's going that matters," she lifts her finger to follow the fly's movements, "but that he's doing it at all. Are things that different now because I told you something that you didn't know? Does that make life any less worth living and struggling for? The joy is in the journey, honey. You know that. And the journey is going to be fraught with problems, some insurmountable. And we are going to make mistakes, some monumental. But it's the going ahead and doing of it that lets us know we're alive. There isn't any brass ring in the end. There's only what we learn along the way. And besides, you have to look past the window to really see." Ruby nudges Lisa with her elbow and nods at the vista outside. "Just look at the beauty out there!"

Lisa looks. White clouds move across a clear blue sky, pierced by distant pines. Patchwork fields of pale yellow and earth brown spread across the horizon, filling the window frame with a vibrancy that seems unreal.

"I'll tell Gary. As long as there's a breath still in me, I'll tell him and Francis and Phoebe. We will be with Phoebe today, and I'll tell her. Francis—well, I'll have to write to him. I suppose this isn't something you tell someone over the phone. Francis has been gone so long, living in California now for twenty years. I can't remember the last time I saw him, and that's probably my fault." Ruby takes Lisa's hand and pats it with determination. Holding her granddaughter's hand and drawing strength, she continues, "I'll tell them all. They deserve to know the truth. It won't make things right, but at least they will all know. It will help your father to know the truth. And Phoebe and Francis. Maybe they'll forgive me my ... omissions."

10.

"DANIEL?" JEANIE'S VOICE IS GENTLE with concern. "Daniel, are you not feeling well? You haven't touched your breakfast."

Daniel looks up from his hands and notices the plate before him for the first time. He smiles and shakes his head. "No, I'm fine, love. I have a bit on my mind is all."

"Anything I can help with?"

"No." Daniel shakes his head slowly, trying without success to take the hollowness from his voice. "Nothing. Well, yesterday…" but he cannot find the words to tell her how he found Michael. Sooner or later, one of the guys will show up at his door with the news. Jeanie is fragile enough with the baby's death; she doesn't need to know that Ruby may have seen Michael and Dean's murdered bodies.

"Are you sure?"

"Yes, sweetheart. I'm sure."

"I'll make another pot of tea then. This must be cold." Daniel stops her hand as she reaches for the pot.

"No, don't make tea." Daniel's voice, level with decision, forces Jeanie back into her seat. Turning and looking at his wife, her eyes still puffy with sorrow for the child they lost, he continues, "I think we should move."

"Move?" Jeanie's voice is tight with surprise.

"Yes. I think it would be good for us, as a family, to move. To start fresh."

"But, where would we move to? The North Shore?"

"No, I mean, leave the city altogether." Daniel pushes on before Jeanie can argue. "I was thinking of moving us to Montreal. We could set up near your aunt and uncle. There is more family there for Ruby and for you, and I think that's what we need right now."

"Well...." The idea of moving back to Montreal is surprisingly appealing, a fact that catches Jeanie off guard. Memories of an earlier time rush into her mind, forcing a smile into her voice, the first hint of happiness Daniel has seen in weeks. Encouraged by this, Daniel laughs, one short volley of humour that works like a spell on the moment. "Come here." He grins, pushing his chair from the table and indicating his lap.

"Daniel," Jeanie chides.

"What? You don't like to sit on your husband's lap anymore? Come on, girl, I want to put my arms around you."

Jeanie's face breaks into a smile that reaches her eyes. She hesitates for only a moment. Wrapping his arms around her, Daniel kisses her neck, inhaling the scent of her. "I think we should make the move, Jeanie. And if we are going to do it, I'd like to do it as soon as we can. It will be a fresh start for all of us. We can try for another child if you like."

Jeanie, with the warmth and strength of her husband's arms around her, feels somehow soothed. She never thought she would feel joy again, but now, sitting with Daniel like this, she dares to find the strength to go on. Overwhelmed, she begins to cry, hastily pushing the tears from her face. She nods, unsure whether she is agreeing to return to Montreal or to life itself. She is relieved to have regained her ability to hope.

They are quiet, both lost in their own thoughts yet aware of each other's presence—Jeanie's breath on Daniel's cheek, her hand lost in his. "We'll talk about it later, all right? But I do think it will be the best thing for us."

Jeanie nods and stands, running her hand through Daniel's hair. When she speaks, her voice is hoarse with emotion. "I'll have to check on Ruby. She's still playing with her doll house. She isn't even dressed yet."

"Well, let her play. I'll be in the study—there's some work I have to finish." Daniel rises and kisses Jeanie on the nose, sealing their decision, before heading to his small study off the hallway, his thoughts tumbling ahead of him with dizzying force.

Alone in his study, Daniel feels trepidation rising in his chest again, tight and cold as a fist. His emotions, teetering on the edge of panic, leave him paralyzed for long minutes at a time. What has he done? What has he gotten himself into? At all costs, he must protect his wife and daughter. For the fourth time, he opens the bottom drawer of his desk. The deep oak compartment slides out to reveal the money, its smell, warm and almost metallic, wafting up and flooding his mind with the images of the day before.

"Daniel?"

He closes the drawer and looks up, a forced smile on his face. "Jeanie, what is it, love?"

"Are you all right? Didn't you hear the door?"

"I guess I've been distracted with the books." He moves his hand over the desk, which is littered with paper and open ledgers.

"Well, Vincent Ducci is at the door with another man. They're asking for you." Jeanie studies her husband, concern creasing the corner of her eyes. "Is everything all right, Daniel? You haven't been yourself this morning. And now Vincent is showing up like this, so early on a Saturday morning." She lifts her hand, gesturing towards the front hallway.

"Show them in. I'll find out what's going on. And Jeanie?" Daniel meets her eyes. "Don't worry. Whatever it is, I promise everything will be fine."

Vincent Ducci's large, square frame fills the doorway. His hand is extended in greeting, his eyes hooded. "Danny, how's it going?"

"Good, Vinny. Come in."

"You remember Cherry?" Vincent asks, indicating his companion, who nods slightly, his eyes quickly sliding away from Daniels.

Daniel knows Cherry, otherwise knows as Charles Berry, very slightly. He is one of a number of guys who hang around the flower shop, running errands for Dean, talking big and acting hard, anxious to be seen as something. Daniel has never liked him. Now, as Cherry moves around the room, eyes wandering with covetous hunger, Daniel feels increasingly uncomfortable, on the edge of anger.

"Sit down, boys." Daniel indicates the small couch and chair before the fireplace.

"Thanks," Vincent answers, seating himself in the chair, running the rim of his fedora held between his fingers. "Daniel, I have some bad news." He is still looking at his hands.

"I know."

"You know? Know what?" Vincent asks, his attention sharpened.

"Michael and Dean. Shot." Daniel's voice catches on the last word.

"How did you know?" Vincent's eyes narrow.

"Ruby and I dropped by with some lunch for Mick and," he lifts his hand in a gesture of bewilderment, "I found Dean in the shop and Michael...." Finding it difficult to go on, Daniel looks at Vincent, then out the window. When he continues, his voice is flat, his emotions held tightly in check. "Michael was upstairs where we had left him. He was on the floor, shot in the stomach. He was still alive." Daniel looks at Vincent again. "He died in my arms."

Holding Daniel's gaze, Vincent nods his understanding. He clears his throat, his anger just under the surface. "It looks like Torrio and Capone have sent us a message, loud and clear. I got there just after Viola and before the cops could mess everything up. Whoever did it was serious about it. Dean—three shots point blank, one in each cheek, one in the gut. They must have gone upstairs to the office and found Mick there with the take for the week. They shot him and took everything. Cleaned out the safe."

"This means war, my friends."

"Shut the hell up, Cherry. That's not for you to decide." Vincent's voice is harsh.

"I ain't deciding anything; I'm just stating the facts," Cherry spits back.

"Did you see anyone or anything when you arrived, Danny?" Vincent continues after a moment.

"No, nothing."

"Torrio and Capone are behind this, but I just don't know who they used. Dean's death is a message, loud and clear!" Vincent repeats, his eyes narrowing as he looks into the middle distance.

"Daddy!" Ruby runs into the room, hair still damp from the bath, an empty satchel hanging over her shoulder and bumping against the ground. "Daddy, look! I'm going to school."

"That's nice, honey," Daniel answers abruptly, standing and moving toward his daughter. "But go find Momma. Daddy's busy right now."

"Hey!" Cherry barks from the corner of the room. "Isn't that the school bag from Schofield's?"

"No, it's mine," Daniel answers quickly. "Michael and I both had one. His is at Schofield's. I've had this one for years."

"Oh, yeah? It looks just like the one at the office." Cherry moves closer and squats down beside Ruby. She can feel the man's intensity, dark and disturbing, as she looks into his face, so close to her own. She can smell the sour scent of his breath.

"Where did you get that old school bag, doll?" Cherry asks, his voice too sweet to fool even a child.

"It's Daddy's," Ruby answers, her eyes pulled to the man's yellowing teeth that seem to be escaping from his mouth in every direction.

"And where did Daddy get it?" Cherry asks, taking Ruby's

arms in both his hands, his smile widening in an effort to disarm her.

Dragging her eyes from the stranger and leaning away from him, Ruby turns to look at her father. There is a prickling feeling running up her neck and a tightness in her stomach. She is frightened by the silence that has fallen into the room like a shadow.

"Hey, my little Jewel." Daniel moves to Ruby, takes her hand, and leads her to the hallway. "You look like a big girl going to school. You go find Momma and tell her Daddy is going out to the flower shop."

Ruby nods, confused and frightened, her voice swallowed by the pain in her stomach.

Cupping Ruby's chin in his hand, Daniel turns her face to his, his smile a reassurance. "Go tell Momma that I won't be long."

Without a word or a look back, Ruby runs from her father, pushing past her feelings, anxious to be away from the room and the strange men.

Turning to Vincent, his voice level, Daniel continues, "Let's take this somewhere else."

THE LATE MORNING is overcast and grey as they head for Schofield's. Daniel, in the passenger seat beside Vincent, is relieved to be taking this business away from his home.

"I'll tell you right now," Cherry growls from the back seat, "if I found the guys who done this, I'd give 'em a slow death." Leaning forward, he pulls a gun from his coat pocket and moves it back and forth like a pendulum, laughing. "What do ya' think, Danny? Where would ya' shoot a guy so that he dies real slow? You saw action over there in France. What's the slowest possible death?"

"Why don't you shut your goddamned big mouth, Cherry? And get that thing outta my face or you'll be the one dying the slow death," Daniel answers, pushing the barrel of the gun from his face, his words heavy with bravado he doesn't quite feel.

"All I'm saying is that it's funny, the satchel and all. I mean, I would have never thought that there were two exact same bags as that. Maybe you just brought it home by mistake. Maybe it was full of money, too." Pushing Daniel's shoulder, Cherry laughs, low and dangerous.

"And maybe you should just shut up," Daniel throws back at him.

But Cherry doesn't. By the time they arrive in the back alleyway of Schofield's, Cherry is convinced Daniel has taken the money. Finally, he turns to Vincent. "Come on, Vinny. He was there. He knows the combination. The golden boy walked in and saw his opportunity all laid out for him, nice and easy!"

"Yeah, that sounds right. My brother was lying on the floor, shot in the gut and bleeding to death, and I just cleaned out the safe, stepping over his body while I did it. What do you take me for?"

Vinny glances at Daniel, slows the car down, pulls up along the garbage bins, and reaches for his cigarettes. Daniel is out his door before Vincent has shifted into park. Cherry's wielding of the gun and the taunting insinuations are driving him into a controlled panic. The air, mixed with the scent of garbage and rotting flowers, does little to relieve his anxiety. Daniel moves toward the back door, his face flushed, his heart racing. He hears the sound of a match strike and Vincent, head bowed, takes a drag on his cigarette. Then Cherry is on him. Daniel can feel the cold threat of steel behind his neck. Rage floods his body as he spins, reaching for the gun and taking both of them to the ground.

Cherry's grunt is loud in Daniel's ear. Daniel's senses are heightened, and he notices Cherry's breath against his cheek; the sour smell of smoke and liquor and onions; the course fabric of Cherry's coat sleeve bunched in his hand; the weight of the other man's body, hard as iron as he twists from beneath him; the smell of garbage, stronger now as the two men wrestle for dominance.

"Hey, boys! Break it up!" Daniel hears Vincent's voice, almost cajoling as he moves with predatory speed from his position behind the wheel.

Vincent's attitude, the sickening smell, the physical contact—all this, Daniel takes in, observing from a distance, watching the scene unfold as if he is suspended somewhere above the narrow alleyway. It is all too immediate, too real, like the scenes that fill his mind from time to time, transporting him the thousands of miles back to the mud and insanity of France. He wants to cry, to laugh, to forget why he is rolling around against the hard ground, the desperation of another man pulling him into a place he doesn't want to be.

There is a grunt, a broken half laugh below him, then the sound of a gun, loud and hard against the concrete, and then nothing. Daniel watches Cherry's eyes drain of life, his features almost unrecognizable. His jaw has been partially blown away, and his mouth gapes grotesquely up at Daniel, who feels the other man's body surrendering into death. Then Vincent is moving them apart, calling his name, and finally shaking Daniel back to the present moment.

"Danny, what the hell...?"

Daniel, wiping the blood and bone from his face, points at Cherry's dead form. His voice will not come.

"Come on, help me get him into the car. We gotta get him outa here." Vincent crouches over the body, lifting Cherry up under the arms. "Grab his feet."

Daniel stares, trying to find his voice. "I ... I...." But his mouth is too dry to form words, his mind unable to find them. Again, he wipes at his face, damp and sticky.

"I know, kid." Vincent looks up. His eyes, barely visible beneath his fedora, are locked on Daniel's, forcing contact.

Daniel, averting his eyes from Cherry's face with morbid reluctance, looks at Vincent.

"I know, kid." Vincent repeats. He continues only when he has Daniel's full attention. "Grab his feet and move him to the back of the car. I got a tarp in the boot, and I don't want this waster messing up my car. Danny?" Vincent nudges Daniel to get his attention. "Danny! Hey!" He grabs Daniel's arm with a rough pull, letting Cherry's dead body slump to the ground. "Hey, snap outta it. We gotta move this guy and get the hell outa here." Taking the cigarette that has been firmly clamped in his mouth, Vincent hands it to Daniel. "Take a drag on this; you need it more than I do."

In a daze, Daniel takes the cigarette, inhaling deeply, holding the smoke in his lungs; the effort helps.

"Let's lay this down and roll him into it." Vincent returns with the tarp. "We'll dump him on the South Side and they'll think Torrio's men did it." Vincent nods and then continues, "He took the shot to the head—that's good."

Daniel takes one more pull and then flicks the butt into the alley. In minutes they have Cherry's body in the tarp and in the trunk of the car.

"Okay, let's move." Vincent's voice is edged with excitement as he slides in behind the wheel. Daniel feels dizzy, either from the cigarette or the whole experience, and pauses at the passenger door. Sweat rolls down his face as the world begins to spin around him. Leaning forward, hands on his knees, he vomits, his stomach convulsing upward with a force he is unable to control.

Vinny has started the car, evidently impatient. "Come on, kid. Get in the car." Vinny calls out, leaning over and opening the passenger door.

Wiping the sweat and spit with the back of his hand, Daniel climbs in. His body is slick with perspiration and he is beginning to feel cold and damp.

"You okay?" Vincent backs up, glancing quickly at Daniel's face, which is still white with shock.

"Yeah, I'll live. But…"

"But, what?"

"What are we going to tell Cherry's family?"

"Nothing. What the fuck are you talking about, Danny?" Vincent's face is dark as he glances at Daniel. "This ain't the goddamn army. Besides, Cherry don't have no family. Whatever he had, you're looking at it." Vincent laughs and fishes out a smoke from his pocket.

"I'm sorry, Vincent."

"For what? For this?" Vincent indicates the back of the car with his thumb, his cigarette lit and clamped firmly in his mouth.

"Yeah."

"Cherry was a waster, Danny. He woulda bought it one way or another. Just too bad it was on your watch." He pauses. "And this may work out well with what Hymie is planning."

"Glad I could be of use," Daniel answers with sad sarcasm. His eyes dart toward Vincent, who is staring over the wheel, nodding in the smoke circling around his head, his mind racing forward.

They are driving, but Daniel has a hard time remembering where they are going or why. No, he remembers why. His breath is coming quickly, his heart beating hard in his chest.

"Here." Vincent nudges Daniel's arm, nodding to the cigarette pack he is holding. "Have another smoke."

Daniel, hands still shaking, finally lights the cigarette and takes a deep pull, feeling the smoke burn his throat, his lungs. Holding it in, he finally releases it, watching the smoke stream from his mouth, steadying his heart beat and pulling his emotions out with it. He takes another drag, his hand trembling only slightly as he lifts the cigarette to his lips. "Vinny?"

"Yeah?" Vincent turns. The smoke curling around Daniel's profile catches the light, forming a halo and illuminating the perspiration still on his face. "What, kid?"

Without turning Daniel continues, "I should tell you. I took the money, Vinny."

A beat of silence echoes between them. "Yeah, I know," Vincent answers, his eyes fixed on the road in front of him, negotiating a turn.

"How ... when...?" Daniel leaves his sentence fragmented and unfinished.

"How did I know or when did I know? Is that the question?" Vincent quickly looks at Daniel, his profile moving from shadow to light in the moving car. "I didn't know until I saw the satchel. You know, it's something I seen for years. Seen it so much I never saw it no more. You know what I mean?" He nods to Daniel. "Then I seen it in your house, and, well, the penny dropped, as they say."

"We should go get it, Vinny. Let's go get it." Daniel's voice is edged with hysteria.

"No, Danny." Vincent laughs, his heavy features creasing with the effort. "We're not gonna go get it. Shit is gonna be coming down. Hymie is on the war path, out for revenge. They killed Dean, they killed Mick, *they* took the money. Leave it at that. It won't make no difference. Hymie and Moran have already set the wheels in motion. There will be payback like you ain't never seen, kid. In fact, you ain't gonna see it. Take the money and get the hell outa here. Mick never wanted you mixed up in any of this anyways. And the Cherry thing, nobody's gotta know the truth about that. Let them find the body and draw their own conclusion—that's what people like to do. They'll build a story around one of O'Banion's men found murdered on the South Side. It'll have nothing to do with you, and nobody needs to know the truth. This is the best thing." Vincent looks over at Daniel who is watching the smoke rising from the cigarette in his hand. "You hearing me, kid? Danny?" Vincent places his hand on Daniel's shoulder and shakes him gently as if waking him from a dream. "Danny, forget it now. It was an unfortunate accident. Shit like this happens, whatcha gonna do? Cherry is a no account waster and he shouldn't a' been waving that gun around. He was asking for it. It might work out good for us, but it was an accident, plain and simple and don't nobody need to know about it."

Daniel nods, repeating Vincent's words in his head. *It was an accident. Wasn't it?* He could tell right away, with the first bit of physical contact, that Cherry was no match for him. Daniel had been in hand-to-hand combat, and his reflexes were still sharp, his training lying dormant just under the surface. When Cherry moved in behind him, the gun hard against his neck, it was as if he lost all conscious thought. Forced to play a part he knew well, he did just what he had been trained to do.

Bringing Cherry to the ground was hardly an effort; with his elbow pushed against Cherry's windpipe, Daniel easily wrestled the gun from his hand, and, before he could stop himself, he had blown the other man's head off.

He didn't have to do it. As soon as Daniel's instincts took hold, his body and mind no longer his own, he felt the other man's submission, felt the slackening of muscles against his body. He felt Cherry's hand tapping his arm, almost pleadingly, as if giving in. If Daniel had released his arm from across Cherry's windpipe, he may have heard the man beg for his life.

"Where are we taking him?" Daniel asks, dragging his thoughts back into the present.

"I was thinking 'bout dumping him on the South Side, but I got a better idea. We'll take him to the Green Mill on North Broadway. It's our territory, but the club is owned by Capone.

"That's right, the Green Mill Jazz Club is owned by Capone. I think Michael may have told me that."

"Yeah," Vincent spits out a laugh. "What kinda balls is that? I'll tell ya', Capone is a new breed. Mike Merlo and Torrio and Dean, they're old school. All of us is kids from the neighbourhood just taking what we can from our own territory, but Capone wants it all and he don't care about spilling blood. We dump Cherry behind the Green Mill and it'll look like one of Capone's outfit did him in. Yeah, it's perfect."

"Doesn't Jack McGurn run the Green Mill?" Daniel asks, still sorting out the information.

"Who do you think McGurn works for?"

"I didn't know Capone had any Irish in his outfit."

"Are you shittin' me, Danny?" Vincent looking quickly over at Daniel, a half smile on his face. "Have you ever seen McGurn?"

"No. I haven't been in the Green Mill for a while. Why?"

"McGurn ain't Irish, Danny. His name is Vincenzo Antonio Gebaldi. He changed his name when he was trying to make it as a boxer in Brooklyn. Irish boxers get more fights, so he goes under the name Battling Jack McGurn. He weren't even in no gang until his old man bought it in a mistaken identity by some White Hand gang members."

"What?"

Vincent takes a drag of his cigarette and settles into his story like a bear into a winter's nap. "Yeah, I guess they mistook his old man for Willie Altierri, one of Frankie Yale's men. You know Frankie Yale—he's one of the big bosses in Brooklyn and Capone's mentor. Story goes, Vincenzo soaked his hands in the blood of his dead father and swore revenge on the men who did it. He was good to his word too; he's killed most of the guys responsible and he ain't even twenty-one. Now instead of calling him Battling McGurn, they're calling him Machine-gun McGurn. Capone brought him to Chicago to use as muscle in his outfit."

"Wow, you're just a fountain of information, Vinny." Daniel, with a low half laugh, tries to keep his mind on the conversation and in the present moment.

"Yeah, well it pays to know who you're up against. Anyways, that's how the story goes; that's what they say about him." Rubbing his hands along his pant legs, Vincent continues, "I wonder what they'll say about me after all this is said and done."

They are quiet. Vincent thinks about posterity, and Daniel about Michael and Cherry, and the act just committed. He doesn't want anyone saying anything about his actions, about his part in all this. He needs to move on as if none of this has ever happened and get the hell out of Chicago as quickly as possible. He needs to put all this behind him, in the past, locked away from thought with conscious effort, like the images of France. He needs to escape ... or go mad.

"I'm going to have to bury Michael. Then I'm going to get out of here, Vincent."

"Yeah, that's best, Danny. Nobody's playing by the rules no more. You gotta be committed or you gotta get out. Dean's funeral will be the big one. We can bury Mick quick and quiet, and you and Jeanie and the kid can hightail it." He looks over at Daniel. "Where do you think you'll go? No, don't even tell me. It's best you just disappear without no forwarding address."

The next few hours and days are a blur to Daniel. His mind feels numb, and grief and guilt seesaw back and forth in his gut, making him physically sick. Images return to him, mostly in dreams that seem interminable: two men dying, one in his arms, the other by his hand, their faces and bodies morphing from one to the other, begging and pleading as they die; a tarp, heavy as lead and oozing blood. He watches himself pull at the weight, his arms aching with fatigue, the shadow of dread—as real and imminent as the sound of his pounding heart—always pushing him on, relentless.

A body buried—dust to dust—beside an Irish mother, the last of an unknown country. A body left, splayed on the dirty ground like so much forgotten garbage.

11.

I'M DREAMING. I KNOW I AM because you are here with me. I can't see you, but I can feel your presence beside me, around me. But it is not only you that I feel.... John Grace is here and even Jack. Yes, I can feel their presence, sliding around from one to the other. Dreams are like that; there is never a face, only an impression vague and transient but strong enough for recognition. But mostly it is you that I feel, your presence, Leland—comforting, familiar. I have missed that.

We are somewhere, but I'm not sure where. It is noisy, confusing. Ah, I see now. We are at the side of a busy road and trying to cross it. We must cross it for some reason that evades me, but it is there, the need to push on. Cars are passing by so close, so quickly. I can feel the air they displace moving across me, blowing back my hair, flapping our clothes, a whirlwind. It is dangerous, but we are moving into the centre of the highway—for now I see it is a highway. It's like wading into a deep and swiftly flowing stream, isn't it? It's dark now. There are streetlights and headlights all around while we make our way to the other side. Funny that I'm not frightened. Have I done this before? Do I already know that we will make it across? I have no fear. Perhaps I am favoured by God? Yes, I must be. I feel the confident in this. We are almost there, and I am smiling. I can feel the smile. I can almost see it on my face, as if I am above and looking down. Look back at how far across we have come! Ha! I can see the other side, recognize the other side. Others are there now. I'm not sure who it is, but they are there looking out. Now they're stepping into the traffic. One of the children? Oh, they are so young—maybe five or six—still small enough to lift into my arms, if I could bear the weight. Clearly it's a child, but I'm not sure who. I just know it's one of mine. I feel it now. I'm anxious, fearful for their safety. Oh, Leland, the child! It's Gary who is following us, but who is with him? Who is holding his hand? He is too young to be attempting this. Where is his father? Why is no one with him? I move to the edge of the highway, across from him, arms open wide, waiting, waiting, waiting. I ache for him to make it to me, to hold his small body against my own. I can feel his warmth, his sparrow-like arms around me, his head beneath my own. I'm dreaming I know—my actions and emotions so separate from each other. I feel no recrimination, no overwhelming responsibility, only hope that he will make it to my arms. Suddenly there is movement. My eyes open; I'm awake. I can't move. I push against something hard. My face is cold.

"NAN, ARE YOU AWAKE? We're almost there. We'll be pulling into the station in a few minutes." Lisa leans over, smiling into Ruby's open eyes. "You okay, Nan?" Ruby remains still, slumped against the window pane. "Nan?" Lisa tries again, touching Ruby's left arm lying along the armrest.

I can't move, Ruby thinks. *My arms, my legs, my mouth. I can't move.*

Lisa gently pulls her grandmother to an upright position. "Nan, can you hear me?" Her voice is full of alarm. "Oh my God, Nan. Nan." She looks about and raises herself from her chair, her hand still on Ruby's arm. She calls out, "Someone, I need some help here! Please, I need some help!"

"What is it?" A young man from a seat a few rows back moves to Lisa's side, a concerned look on his face.

"I don't know, but something is wrong with my grandmother.

She isn't moving. She's not talking. I don't know what to do. I think she's had a stroke or something." Lisa's voice is tight with panic.

"I'll go find someone, tell someone. We'll need an ambulance. Try to stay calm, and I'll be right back." The words are barely out before he is gone; in his wake, a rush of air swirls around the occupants of the car, leaving them anxious and alert.

"Can you push her chair back?" asks a woman in a nearby seat. "My name is Sherry—I'm a nurse. Can you push her chair back and straighten out her legs? I think you're right; I think she's had a stroke. Let's make her as comfortable as possible. We're almost at the station; hopefully they will have an ambulance waiting by the time we get there."

"Thank you," Lisa answers, looking quickly from Ruby to Sherry. "She's my grandmother. She's eighty-nine. We were talking together the whole way here. I don't understand...." She shakes her head in disbelief.

"These things happen. Especially to the elderly. Don't worry, we'll get her help as soon as possible."

Holding Ruby's trembling hand, Lisa comforts her grandmother. "It's all right, Nan. It's all right."

Ruby understands the tone but not the words. She tries to respond, but her language, along with her ability to form the words, is gone. All familiarity is gone. There is pain, sharp and localized behind her left eye, and only a vague awareness of her surroundings. Words form in her head with an urgency she does not understand, but her speech comes out in a croaking, choked sounds that frighten her.

In a state of suspended shock, the women wait for the train to pull into the station, for the paramedics and the stretcher to arrive, for the difficult transfer from the chair to the stretcher, from the train to the platform, from the platform to the waiting ambulance. Lisa, fearful the whole time, holds herself together with a calmness that belies the chaos churning beneath the surface. The anxiety and worry cannot be good for the baby, she thinks, holding on to this thought in order to sooth her own emotions.

Sherry, an emergency nurse with twelve years of experience, oversees everything calmly. She is all efficiency and business, helping Lisa stay focused throughout. Still, without realizing it, Lisa is holding on to Sherry like a child as they wheel the stretcher into the ambulance, Ruby firmly strapped down.

"There's only room for one," the paramedic comments as he turns from the stretcher.

"Yes. I'm coming with you," Lisa answers, finally relinquishing Sherry's hand and turning toward her with gratitude. The kindness of strangers, Lisa thinks.

"Don't worry. You're in good hands now." Sherry smiles, her eyes level. She gives Lisa's hand a final squeeze as the medic pulls the ambulance door closed with a metallic thud.

It takes only a few minutes for the ambulance to make its way to Northwestern Memorial, but for Lisa it feels like hours as she sits nervously beside the two paramedics, holding Ruby's hand and watching her grandmother's eyes for signs of recognition or comprehension.

"When did you notice the paralysis?" the paramedic beside her asks, adjusting the oxygen mask over Ruby's mouth, her eyes wild and unfocused above.

"When she woke up. I mean, when I was trying to wake her, about half an hour ago now."

"So, no signs of anything before she fell asleep? She didn't complain of a headache, of dizziness or numbness of any kind?"

"No. We were talking and she was fine. Sharp and coherent. She was telling me about her life."

"No confusion?"

"No, I don't think so."

"How long was she asleep for?"

"I'm not sure, but not long. Maybe twenty minutes. Is that important?"

"We need to establish the time of onset. It will determine

what they can do for her at the hospital. Some drugs have to be administered within hours."

"Will she be okay?"

"We can't tell yet, but try not to worry. We're headed to Northwestern, and it's one of the best neurological centers in the country."

At the emergency room, there are more of the same questions. Ruby is rushed into another area, while Lisa is left in the pale-yellow waiting room, surrounded by vending machines and desperation.

"Excuse me, Ma'am, did you come in with the elderly woman in the ambulance?" A short haired, perky nurse comes up to Lisa, her words clipped, her smile practised.

"Yes, I did. How is she?"

"We won't know that until she has been examined and sent for some tests, but I will need you to fill out a few forms for me." She hands Lisa a clipboard and pen, and points to the nearest chair—imitation blue leather with plastic yellow arms. "You can just bring them to the desk when you're finished." Another smile before turning away.

"When can I see her?" Lisa asks, embarrassed by the vulnerability she hears in her voice.

The nurse calls back over her shoulder. "As soon as the forms are filled out, I'll take you to see her." She turns to face Lisa, compassion on her face, her competence of a moment ago replaced with humanity. "And try not to worry. She is in the best hands, and everything that can be done for her is being done."

Sitting down, the clipboard forgotten beside her, Lisa fumbles for her cellphone. In the pandemonium since the train, she has not thought about contacting anyone, but now with the small weight of the phone sitting in her hand, she feels the need for connection. She'll have to call Aunt Phoebe. They were to meet tonight at the hotel after Phoebe's conference. She'll have to call her mom and dad too, but the first call she finds herself making is to her boyfriend, Stephen. The call goes to voicemail, but just the sound of his recorded voice brings a level of comfort. "Hi, Steve. I'm in Chicago, but I'm calling from the hospital. Nan had a stroke—I think. Well, I'm pretty sure. They're with her now and I'll know for sure after the doctor has looked at her." Her voice breaks with the relief of the connection, with the realization that she is not alone in this. Controlling her emotions, she continues, "Don't worry, I'm okay. I've got to call my dad and my aunt Phoebe, but I just wanted to let you know. Anyway, call me when you get this. Bye."

Now, the rest of the calls, Lisa says to herself. She feels the fatigue of the trip and this experience settling in on her like a physical weight. Phoebe's cell goes to voicemail, as does her dad's. Leaving a similar message on both phones, she is unable to avoid the sound of controlled panic that has edged into her words.

She fills out the forms to the best of her ability, and returns them to the admissions desk. The same nurse leads her through the labyrinth of halls to a small, draped, temporary room. Ruby is lying in the bed, the green hospital gown adding to the ashen pallor of her face. The head of her bed is elevated, and another nurse is adjusting the drip of her I.V.

"How is she?" Lisa asks, her eyes searching Ruby's face.

"Well, she is as comfortable as we can make her."

"Can she hear me?"

"She can hear you. I just don't know if she can understand you. The doctor will be in shortly to explain what is going on."

"She's had a stroke," Lisa says turning to the nurse.

"Yes, she's had a stroke."

"LISA." A HAND ON HER SHOULDER, gentle and familiar. Lisa smiles, opening her eyes and passing her hand through her hair. "Aunt Phoebe. You got my call?" she asks, her voice hushed, stealing a quick look at Ruby, whose eyes are closed and still.

"Yes, I tried calling you back, but I don't think you can get a signal in here." Moving to the bed and taking her mother's hand, Phoebe continues. "How is she?"

"The doctor says she's stable." Leaning forward, Lisa watches the fear and concern pass over her aunt's face. "I'm so glad you're here."

Turning and reaching for Lisa's hand with her free one, Phoebe smiles. "You're doing great, honey. I spoke to Francis and Gary—they're both on their way."

"Good."

"What have the doctors said?"

"A blood clot in the left hemisphere. She might need surgery, but they have given her some drugs to help stop the bleeding and they're going to observe her progress."

Moving the only other chair in the room beside her niece, Phoebe sits, taking Lisa's hand in her own. "Poor Mom."

"She'll pull through this." Lisa nods with conviction. "She's strong and determined."

"Yes, she's strong and determined all right," Phoebe answers, a smile in her voice.

The two women sit in silence, holding hands and watching Ruby, who drifts in a world beyond them. It's a world without distinction, without edges, where light and dark swirl, dipping and reeling, fluidly like water..

"We should go and get something to eat and some rest. I don't think it will do any good if we get sick." Phoebe stands, breaking their vigilance. "We've been here for quite a while, and you're looking pretty wiped, Lisa. We'll come back first thing in the morning with your dad and Uncle Francis, but first let me take you for something to eat."

Phoebe hails a cab just outside the hospital, opens the door for Lisa, and quickly gets in after her, giving the driver the address of the restaurant before she is even properly seated.

"Boy, you seem to know where you're going around here," Lisa says, smiling at Phoebe. She has always admired her aunt; she is so competent, pulled together, and beautiful.

"Well, I have been here for a week, you know, and it doesn't take long to find the best places to eat. I found this great little restaurant called RoSal's the second night I was here. I hope you like Italian."

"Yes, that sounds good." Lisa sighs, leaning into the comfort of Phoebe's company.

THE RESTAURANT IS QUIET; the late supper rush is over, and although many of the tables are full, meals are finished and patrons are lingering over coffee and liquors, satiated and satisfied. Looking more like mother and daughter than aunt and niece—Phoebe's tailored suit and briefcase the antithesis of Lisa's jeans and casual sweater—they follow the hostess to their table.

"I just remembered the luggage. We didn't get it when we arrived. In the commotion of everything, I didn't even think about it," Lisa comments, slipping into her chair and realizing with eager anticipation that she is actually hungry.

"Don't worry; I think we're almost the same size. When we get to the hotel, you can look through my stuff and use whatever you need. I brought so much with me to this conference, you'll think you're shopping at Holt Renfrew's. We can stop off at a drugstore for a toothbrush and anything else you'll need for tonight, then tomorrow we can go to the station. I'm sure the luggage will be there in a holding room or something." Phoebe looks across at her niece. The candlelight plays with the angles of her face, making her look tired and drawn. "You look pretty tired, honey. We'll eat and then head for the hotel. You need a good night's sleep."

"Yes, I need a good night's sleep. It feels like I haven't been to bed in weeks."

"I'll order for us, shall I?" Phoebe asks.

"Yes, that would be great." Lisa, placing her hand on her stomach, leans back into the comfort of the chair, the atmosphere and the presence of her aunt helping to restore her somewhat.

"Did you want to tell me about the trip, Lisa? How was Nan doing leading up to the stroke? Did you notice anything unusual?"

"No, it's so funny; there was nothing to indicate that this was going to happen. Nan was doing really well with the travelling and everything. We disembarked once and that was great. We spent time in the bar car and just chatted and laughed most of the day. She would fall asleep sometimes and be a bit disoriented when she woke, but she's been like that since the stroke she suffered last year."

"I wonder why she insisted on making this trip," Phoebe says, shaking her head, her eyes distant.

"I'm not sure, to tell you the truth, but I think maybe she's feeling trapped." Lisa leans forward. "You know, trapped in the retirement home, trapped in the amount of time she has left. She wanted to see Chicago, to see you. She even wanted to go to California to see Uncle Francis."

"Well, that all sounds pretty ambitious for a woman her age, doesn't it? But then Mom was always that."

Lisa detects a note of something in Phoebe's voice, a deeper feeling or thought behind the words. Aware that she would never stray into these waters had it not been for all that has happened on the train, she asks as gently as she can, "Aunt Phoebe, how do feel about Nan?"

"Feel about her? What do you mean?" Phoebe, startled, looks over at Lisa, but before she can answer the waiter approaches. Phoebe orders their meal and then decides on a bottle of wine, Chianti. She whispers across the table to Lisa, "Maybe we're going to need two bottles of wine for this."

"It's not going to be that bad." Lisa laughs at Phoebe's face, her eyes rolled to the side in mock desperation. "It's just that Nan was telling me about her life during the trip, and some of the things she said… Well, some of it made sense, some of it gave me an insight into the whole dynamics of our family."

"Okay, now I'm intrigued. What did she say?" Phoebe leans

back while the waiter sets down their glasses, pours the wine, and smiles at the women.

"Well, there was a lot.. I mean, it was a long trip!" Lisa laughs. "And she is quite a character."

"That's the truth! She has a big personality. She's full of life, full of adventure, and she's great in company, always on stage. You know what she believed about the stage?" Phoebe asks. Smiling at the memory, she continues without waiting for Lisa to reply, "When you're on the stage, take it!" Swinging her arms in the air for emphasis, Phoebe laughs, short and loud, a sound that leaves a heavy echo in the heart.

Moving into the silence Phoebe has left, Lisa begins, hesitantly, to tip-toe into the deep water, wondering what could possibly be compelling her. "I suppose one of the things she said that struck me was that she thought she was afraid of you. Did you ever feel that, that she was afraid of you?"

"No, I never thought that," Phoebe answers, staring into the candle and continuing after a moment. "Sometimes I wondered.... I mean, I am her daughter and I know she loves me, but I wondered sometimes if she ever really liked me? For years, I felt she didn't actually like me." She shakes her head again. "But no, I never thought she was afraid of me. The only thing that makes me think of is that when she was younger, she had great feminine power, and she knew how to use it. Was she afraid of other women? Of me? Was I competition? None of us, Francis or your dad or I, pursued the arts in any way; that was our mother's realm, and I guess we instinctively knew that. But I never thought she might be afraid of me. It's an interesting insight." She pauses. "Ruby Grace was a force to be reckoned with, a star in her own right, a singer, an actor, and I think a bit of a narcissist, too busy being loved to really love."

"Do you actually think that, Phoebe?"

"Sometimes. We—her children, especially Francis and me—we were afterthoughts, casualties. I think that's why neither of us have had successful relationships. I think we have to come to terms with that. Your dad was different; he was the youngest, the baby, and Leland adored him."

"Nan talks about Leland James a lot. I think she still misses him."

"Yes, that was a love match, but again maybe it was more about Leland loving her." Phoebe reaches across the table and smiles into Lisa's troubled face. "Don't look so downcast, honey. I might be way off base here. I'm just trying to come to terms with a childhood that sometimes left me feeling lost more than anything. If you grow up like I did, you end up wondering why, and then you spend the best part of your life trying to figure it out and come to terms with it.

"But yes, Leland James and Ruby Grace were a love match. I have never had that, never experienced what it was that they had ... a devotional love. I think your mom and dad have some of that, Lisa. Gary and Bernadette. I wonder if they know how lucky they are?"

"I think they do."

"Good. How's your mom doing, anyway? I haven't seen Bernadette since Christmas."

"She's great. She's a principal now and I think she's enjoying the new challenges. Dad's always teasing her about wanting her to give him detention." Lisa smiles at the memory of her parents, flirting and joking in the kitchen before she left for Chicago. *Was it really only yesterday?*

"And you and Jacklyn have been spending time together, as usual." Phoebe smiles at the thought of the two cousins as young girls, always together. She always thought they were more like sisters than cousins.

"Jacklyn must have told you—she was trying to come with us, but with the kids it's hard to get away."

"Yes, she told me she was trying to get things organized to come, but she just didn't have enough time. Jacklyn has her hands full right now. It's a busy time for her."

Their meals arrive, the same smiling waiter placing the

dishes before them with a flourish. The heavy fragrance of rosemary and garlic floods the table, and Lisa's mouth salivates in anticipation. They eat in silence, savouring the food, enjoying the wine, although Phoebe notices that Lisa is hardly touching hers.

"I want to tell you something, Lisa. I haven't even told Jacklyn, but it looks like I'll be moving back to Ontario."

"Wow, that's great, Aunt Phoebe! Jacklyn will be so happy."

"Yes, I'll be happy to be back too. I'm missing Jacklyn and the kids, and I feel like I'm too far away from everything living in Vancouver. I've enjoyed my years out there, but I'm ready to move back. I applied for a transfer a few months ago, and I just found out yesterday that it was granted." Phoebe smiles, lifting her glass in a salute.

"This is wonderful! Dad will be pleased about this. And Mom. Well, everyone will be." Lisa's voice rises with enthusiasm.

"Yes, I'm looking forward to coming home. And now with your grandmother and everything that has happened, I think the timing couldn't be better."

"Would you ladies like to order dessert?" the waiter asks, holding out a thin white menu like a trophy.

Phoebe looks across at Lisa and raises her eyebrows questioningly.

"Not tonight, as tempting as it is. I'm just too tired," Lisa answers, stifling a yawn as if for emphasis.

"Just the cheque then, thank you," Phoebe says, speaking to the waiter but laughing at Lisa.

The cab ride to the hotel doesn't take long, but it is all Lisa can do to not fall asleep. Phoebe is quiet; she recognizes Lisa's fatigue, and she's anxious to get her comfortably situated in her room.

"Here we are," Phoebe says, pulling the plastic card from its slot and opening the door to the hotel room. "I'll get you a night dress if you want to use the bathroom and wash up or something. You can use any of my stuff in there. There's night cream and makeup remover, although at your age you probably don't need the night cream."

By the time they are in bed, it is after midnight. Turning out the side lamp, the darkness almost complete, Phoebe relaxes for the first time that day.

"Thanks for the dinner tonight, Aunt Phoebe," Lisa says into the darkness. "And for being there."

"You're welcome." Phoebe laughs. "It was my pleasure. What else is family for?"

Lisa smiles at the sound of her aunt's voice, familiar and re-assuring across the few feet of darkness separating them. The pull toward sleep is overwhelming; Lisa can feel her eyelids closing, but her mind is still active, alive with the thoughts and feelings of the day. "Phoebe?"

"Yes?"

"You said that Leland adored my dad. Do you know why?"

There is silence for a moment before Phoebe answers. Her voice low and tired, she speaks into a darkness that contains them both. "He was the baby. He was only about four when Leland and Mom married. I suppose he just fell in love with Gary, and Gary with him. It's hard to resist a baby—they open up a world in you that you never thought possible."

Lisa, no longer able to hold onto her conscious self, mumbles into the darkness, "Thanks, Aunt Phoebe."

"Good night, honey."

THE LIGHT IN RUBY'S EYES is painful as she turns her head away from the window. Mostly she has been floating in a place without edges, without physicality and with only mild interruptions from the forms who move around her in hur-ried, frustrating ways. Things blur, energy merges, and images flow into one another like fluid, suspending her until she can hardly tell if she is asleep or awake. There are moments of staggering clarity during which she can grasp a thought, a word, an emotion, anchoring her to something outside her own moment of being—for she is aware of her being, aware of this moment, this floating beautiful moment, with no past and no future tethering her to continuity. She could stay here forever, but there is always something pulling at her, sounds that jar her reverie, sounds that are too loud, too confusing to attend to. Turning her face away, she avoids the intrusion until suddenly recognition dawns, and for an instant she knows there is something beyond where she finds herself. There it is again, a voice within a dream, an impression, forcing itself into her being.

"Mom. Mom, can you hear me? It's Gary. I'm here with Francis and Phoebe. Mom?" His voice is gentle, a caress, and for a moment he sees clarity in Ruby's eyes, a struggle for connection.

"*Mom. What does 'Mom' mean?*" Ruby tries to ask, but her voice is broken and laboured, her words indistinguishable, the effort ultimately too great.

"Your mother has suffered an Ischemic blood clot in the left hemisphere. Her ability to understand language has been affected." A tall dark-haired young man enters the room. He addresses them all, but he looks specifically at Gary, who is still holding his mother's hand in his own. Extending his hand, the young man continues, "I'm Dr. Phil Drummon, from the neurology department."

"I'm Ruby Grace's son, Gary." He accepts the doctor's handshake. "This is my brother Francis, my sister Phoebe, and my daughter Lisa."

"Nice to meet you. It's good that you are all here for support. I realize you have travelled from Canada."

"Yes, we are Canadian," Francis nods, "but I live and work in California at the university, and our mother is originally from Chicago."

"Well, it's unfortunate that she's returned under such cir-cumstances."

"She was determined to make the trip. My sister was attending a conference here, and Mom insisted on visiting her, and the city of her birth—that's how she always refers to Chicago." Gary smiles weakly, catching Lisa's eye.

"Well, hopefully that determination will help in her recovery." The doctor moves toward Ruby and speaks directly to her. "I hear you were quite an accomplished singer and an actor, Ruby Grace."

"Yes, she was," Francis answers, moving to the head of the bed opposite the doctor. "I've just recently finished writing a book on her life as a singer. It's just for the family, but she was a great talent in her time. She sang opera and jazz."

"That's quite the combination." Smiling, the doctor turns to Francis. "You might want to bring in some music for her to listen to while she's here." Removing a small pen light from his pocket and moving it from Ruby's left eye to her right, he continues, "Quiet stimulation is good. It's hard to tell what information will be processed and how, but stimulation is always good."

Light passes before her eyes, and for a moment Ruby realizes she is something separate from the energy around her. The pain has subsided, opening up a window to the present, unexpectedly pulling her back into consciousness with a crease of recognition. There is sound washing up onto the shore of understanding, a voice she knows...

"How long will she have to be here, Doctor?" Phoebe asks.

"I think she recognizes your voice, Phoebs." Gary comments. "Speak to her again."

Moving to take her mother's hand, Phoebe speaks above a whisper. "Mom, it's me Phoebe, your daughter. Can you hear me?"

What is 'daughter'? Ruby wonders. The tangle of knowledge runs just beyond her grasp, her attention held by the sound of a voice she can recognize as familiar.

"This is good." Dr. Drummon stands, smiling at Ruby and then looking around at the concerned faces in the room. "The first couple of days are the most critical. We have stopped the bleeding, and she is recognizing things around her. Good work, Mrs. Grace." He pats her hand and pulls her attention to his face.

Turning, Ruby focuses on his mouth as it forms words, elusive as summer fire flies and just as mesmerizing. Then her lids, heavy with the need to obliterate the present, close over her eyes, and she sinks into the beauty of oblivion.

SOUNDS, FLOATING like dandelion seeds in the breeze, whirl around, some deep and distant, others lighter and clear, all of them beautifully suspended in and around her. There is meaning to this, a sound ... music, Ruby thinks, as she is pulled into focus. Music is playing, the kind of music that she sings in the smoky night clubs of Toronto. Smiling, Ruby floats into the past, memories running through her mind with a clarity so sharp it is startling. The piano and the bass, are behind her on the stage, their notes blending and turning, and her voice is running just ahead, sometimes behind, in and around the notes like a fish in a stream. Leland is somewhere in the crowd, and she sings for him. But the crowd is noisy tonight, their conversations too loud to sing above, infringing on the music, on her concentration and her enjoyment. The light is too bright, breaking the atmosphere, ruining the verisimilitude. And there's something else, an odour in the air making her feel physically sick, the cloying, heavy smell of flowers—roses. She squints into the light and turns her head from the smell, looking and listening for Leland. He must be out there; there's his voice in the crowd—she can hear it. Yes, it is Leland.

"Lisa, who brought the flowers into the room?" Gary asks, walking into the room with Francis. "They're agitating your nan. Let's get them out of here."

"A nurse brought them in while you and Uncle Frank were gone for coffee." Lisa picks up the offensive flower arrangement and heads for the door.

"Sorry, Gary, I forgot about mom's aversion to flowers," Phoebe says, taking up her mother's hand. "They were sent by some colleagues at the conference. They didn't know, and I didn't realize she was reacting to them." Speaking to Ruby, Phoebe continues, "Is that better, Mom? We got rid of those offensive flowers."

It's really only the roses that I can't abide, Ruby thinks, her eyes adjusting to the light in the room. She's starting to recognize those around her; their energy swirls like light particles, but they are slowly becoming more familiar, more distinct. And there is something else she recognizes—*voices, yes, that's it, voices*. The concentration it takes to focus on these things is tedious, the pull too oblivion too seductive. But there is a reason to hold on. There is something I must do, Ruby thinks as again she is lost in the pulse of light, of sound, of being.

"Funny how she's never liked the smell of flowers," Phoebe muses.

"I don't think it's flowers that bother her just roses," Francis answers as he leans up against the large windowsill in their mother's semi-private room Ruby has been moved to. "We could never have them in the house. Don't you remember what she said about them?"

"Yes, she said they smelled liked blood." Phoebe looks from Francis to Ruby. "I never got that. They can be overpowering, but I like the smell of roses."

"Well, she's always been pretty particular about things, too much of a perfectionist if you ask me." Francis stands in the window, a silhouette in the late afternoon light.

"Yes, she's always been that." Phoebe pauses. "They say that perfectionists are trying to make up for the lack of control they feel in their lives."

"I don't know about that." Gary laughs "Then we'd all be perfectionists, since control is only an illusion."

"Wow, Dad, when did you become an existentialist?" Lisa asks, coming back into the room.

"Maybe I've always been one," Gary says, smiling at his daughter. "I just didn't realize it."

"I think Mom just always wanted to feel in control," Francis says, his eyes drawn to his mother's. "I think she had great potential, great talent, but life for a woman in those days dictated a certain amount of conformity. I don't think she ever really felt in control of her own life."

"And I think we have all suffered for that," Phoebe says, looking at her brother, her eyes sharp with memory.

"Maybe," Francis answers.

"No, not maybe, Francis. We have. You're right when you say that Mom felt like she had to conform, felt like she was caught." Phoebe looks from Francis to Gary and then back to Ruby. "It's not that she didn't love us, it's just that at a different time, given the choice, she may never have wanted to have children."

"Really, Phoebe? You think that?" Gary asks.

"Don't you?"

"I don't know. I haven't really thought about it."

"Well, maybe you should think about it. It has affected all of us. I mean, look at me and look at Francis." Phoebe smiles at her older brother. "No offence, Francis, but have you been able to stay in a stable relationship? And why have you never had children? And it's not just you. I'm separated from a second husband; I have struggled in every relationship I have ever had. I have only one child; and Gary only has one child too. We aren't exactly big on family."

"Bernadette couldn't have any more children after Lisa. We would have liked more."

"Well, Gary, you're a little different. You're the baby of the family, and things were easier for you." Phoebe smiles again, her voice level and devoid of judgment.

Gary shrugs, turning to Francis for confirmation.

"Yeah, it's true," Francis answers, nodding. "Things were easier for you. You had us."

"I didn't think it was that bad for you guys." Gary looks from Francis to Phoebe.

"We're not saying it was bad. It was just ... different for us," Phoebe says.

"Mom and Dad were off and on for years, and Phoebe and I were left alone a lot of the time because Mom was still trying to make it in the music business. Dad was always travelling. I don't know for sure, but that could have been a big part of the problem." Francis shrugs, an effort to push the past behind. "Anyway, it was years ago. And as they say, that which does not kill us makes us stronger. We are who we are because of who we were. Don't you think so, Phoebe?"

Phoebe laughs at Francis. He looks a little like an old sage, sitting in the light and staring down at her, the look on his face daring her to defy him. "Yes, oh great one," she answers, bowing to him. "We are who we are."

Who we are, Ruby thinks. The words fall like stones in a pool, images and insight rippling from them in growing measure. *Who we are,* the words sounding in her head feel heavy and concrete, holding meaning that she can almost grasp. But the effort is too consuming, the thread too convoluted to understand.

"We are who we are," Lisa says, watching her grandmother but aware of the others in the room. "And ultimately, we are who we want to be. We create our own lives, our own meaning."

"Well," Gary laughs, extending his hand to take Lisa's, "who's the existentialist now?"

They look at each other for a long moment, Lisa squeezing her father's hand before letting it go.

"Speaking of who we are," Francis stands, breaking the silence that shimmered in the light moments ago, a smile still playing at the corner of his mouth, "how have you been feeling, Gary? I heard you were going for some tests."

"Well, nothing conclusive yet, just tests and more tests. I've been having pain in my stomach and back, and some enzyme is showing up in my blood. It's all pretty vague. There's nothing they can put their finger on yet."

"So they've ruled out any problem with your heart? Did you tell them about Dad's heart problems?" Phoebe asks, moving to take her mother's hand, the fingers still long and shapely, the nails neatly trimmed and polished. "That's something you don't want to fool around with, Gary."

"Yeah, they took a full history. I told them about Dad's heart attack, so that was the first thing they checked. Everything seems pretty good there." Gary shrugs.

"You can never be too careful." Phoebe's voice is heavy with concern as she looks over and catches Gary's eye.

"How old was Dad when he died? Sixty? I can't remember." Francis shakes his head.

No! John was only fifty-eight when he died, Ruby thinks, present for a moment. The image of John Grace is sharp in her mind, and she holds onto it for a moment, remembering their relationship, a lifetime of emotions. And then the image is gone, leaving only a vague impression in its wake, like a wave retreating from the sand.

"I think so. That's what I told my doctor—fifty-nine or sixty."

"It seems too young," Phoebe answers.

"Yeah it does seem young, now. But Dad always seemed older somehow."

"That was just because we didn't see very much of him. Sometimes weeks and months would go by before we saw him. Then when we did see him it was all a hurried blur." Francis's voice is heavy with regret.

"Well, at least we have longevity on Mom's side of the family." Phoebe jokingly breaks the silence in the room.

"Yes, that's true; her parents both had a good run for their money. I always remember their summer house in Maine. Whatever happened to it?" Gary asks, watching Phoebe as she pushes Ruby's hair from her forehead, her fingers lingering against the smooth, white skin.

"I'm not sure." Francis shakes his head. "It never stayed in the family. Maybe Gran sold it after Grandpa died."

"There are a lot of mysteries to that family, don't you think?" Phoebe draws her eyes from Ruby to Francis. "I mean, why did Grandpa Kenny leave Chicago? Mom always says he left 'suddenly in '24.'" Phoebe's impersonation of Ruby is excellent. Gary coughs out a laugh. "Who knows? We've been speculating about that for years though, haven't we?"

"What about Leland's family?" Lisa asks, her eyes steady on her father's.

"He had a couple of brothers. They were around a bit when we were young. But his family was from out east, so I don't know much about them." Gary looks to Francis.

"Yeah, Leland's brothers were good guys." Francis smiles, remembering. "They were younger than Leland, funny and a bit wild. They stayed with us in Toronto for a while before they headed out west. I was fourteen at the time, and I used to swipe their cigarettes." Laughing, Francis continues, "I think they knew and left them out for me. Mom would have killed them."

"And you, if she knew." Phoebe smiles. "She was ahead of her time on that one. At a time when everyone smoked and thought nothing of it, Mom never liked it."

"I think it had something to do with all the night clubs she sang in. I remember the smell of smoke from her gowns mingling with the smell of her perfume." Gary answers.

"Chanel No. 5," they all say, laughing at the knowledge that connects them, the shared memories of their childhood.

"The world's most legendary fragrance," Phoebe says, affecting Ruby's voice and attitude as she repeats their mother's famous line. She used to say it every time she applied the perfume.

Lisa, laughing along with her aunt and uncle and father, is struck by their camaraderie. She looks from one to the other: Francis, his scalp showing through his thinning hair in the fading light; Phoebe, face drawn with stress and fatigue; and

Gary, the lines around his eyes pronounced with the weight he has lost. As she looks, somehow all of this dissolves, and they become the children they once were.

"So, big brother, you were stealing cigarettes when you were a kid. I never knew." Gary shakes his head with fake disapproval at Francis, who shrugs and smiles.

"Well, you can't talk, Gary. When Francis was swiping their cigarettes, you were swiping their change," Phoebe admonishes, laughing at the look of shock on her brother's face.

"I didn't do that!" Gary answers, a little louder than he had intended.

"Yeah, Gary, you did. You were only a little guy, but you used to steal the change they left on the dresser in the back bedroom." Francis laughs.

"No, I didn't steal their money! I was probably only playing with it." Gary is only half serious. "If I did take anything—and I am saying *if*—I was probably going to give it back."

"Well, little brother, that's your story. We remember it differently." Phoebe leans over and pats Gary on the side of the cheek, then turns to Lisa. "He was quite the going concern, your father."

"Oh, I have no doubt."

"Don't believe anything they say, Lisa. They were always ganging up on me."

"You mean we were always left taking care of you!" Francis corrects.

"It's like Francis said, Mom was always rushing off to something or other, and we had to take care of baby Gary."

"What about Leland?" Lisa asks, feeling protective of her father even though the teasing is in fun. "Wasn't he around to take care of Dad?"

"Leland was around," Francis answers. "Mom married Leland when I was ten, Phoebe was six, and your dad was around four, but Leland and Mom were always together. If she was singing, he'd be there. They were inseparable."

"I think they had quite the love story," Phoebe says, looking at Ruby. "Didn't you, Mom? You and Leland—remember how he'd dance with you in the kitchen, always asking you to sing?"

"What was the song he always wanted her to sing, Phoebs?" Francis asks, his voice lost in nostalgia.

"'I'll Be Seeing You.'"

"We have it here on one of the CDs." Lisa flips through the small stack of cases lying beside the CD player in the corner. Busy looking for the song, Lisa continues, her attention divided but anxious to know the answer to her next question. "Did you guys love Leland? Like a father?" Lisa keeps her head down, her eyes still on the list of songs.

"Yes, I think we did. Didn't we?" Francis answers, looking from Phoebe to Gary for confirmation.

"I loved him." Gary nods. "I remember him more clearly sometimes than I remember Dad. And he loved us."

"Yes, Leland loved us," Phoebe answers, her eyes focused on the past.

Lisa, looking from one to the other, breaks the silence that has settled around the room like water. "What did Leland die of?"

"What is it with you and all these questions about Leland James, honey?" Gary asks, shaking his head in bemused frustration.

"I, I don't know..." Lisa stammers. "Nan was talking about him, and it kind of piqued my interest, I guess."

"Did you find the song yet, Lisa?" Francis asks. "The doctor said that the stimulation will be good for her."

"Okay, here it is." Lisa lines up the track and pushes the button.

The music fills the room like liquid honey, the first few lines thin and almost tinny as Lisa adjusts the tone. *I'll be seeing you in all the old familiar places/ that this heart of mine embraces/ all day through...*

"Phoebe, are you crying?" Francis asks, moving to the windowsill and grabbing the box of Kleenex to hand to his sister.

"Yeah, silly me," Phoebe answers, her voice hoarse with emotion.

"I think Mom recognizes the song," Gary says with excitement. He walks over to Ruby and looks searchingly into her eyes.

Struggling up, as if from the depths of the ocean, Ruby's mind clears. Her awareness sharpens with understanding, and suddenly she can identify who she is, where she is, and what is happening. The knowledge excites her. Words form as clearly as the music she hears, but they can go no further than her mind. Unable to articulate her thoughts, she lies back in frustration.

"Yes, Mom, that's your song. Yours and Leland's. Do you remember?" Phoebe says, her voice soothing, sensing her mother's recognition and frustration.

My song and Leland's, Ruby thinks, and my children. *Yes, my children. I must tell you something.* Ruby tries to force the words from her mind and into her mouth, but she cannot push them forward, cannot make the correct shapes or the right sound. Her efforts result only in a garbled, frightening croak of guttural noise.

"It's okay, Mom. We're here. It's okay," Francis says from beside Phoebe, his hand on Ruby's arm in an attempt to calm her.

Francis. Ruby finds the word floating to the surface as she looks at her son. Then she turns to her daughter. *Phoebe.* There is more, more, she thinks, sensing the presence of others in the room. Turning her head and forcing her mind to concentrate, she finds Gary. *Gary, I must tell you—you and your brother and sister.*

"I think she recognizes you, Dad," Lisa says above a whisper. Moving in beside Gary, she takes Ruby's hand. "Nan, it's me Lisa. Can you hear me? Do you understand what I'm saying?"

Lisa, Lisa. Tell Gary, tell Gary....

"I think she wants to tell you something, Lisa." Gary watches his mother's efforts and touches Lisa's shoulder as Ruby stares at her granddaughter, willing her thoughts forward, forcing the sounds in her mouth to fall into recognizable words. The effort is overwhelming, and tears of frustration slip from her eyes, adding to her confusion and to the tension in the room.

"What is it, Lisa? What do you think she wants to tell you?" Gary asks, the anxiety in his voice spilling across the room as Ruby's efforts disintegrate into nonsensical sounds, flailing motions.

"Lisa, honey?" Gary asks again. "What is she trying to tell you?"

Lisa turns to her father and smiles, a look of understanding and resignation on her face. Turning back to Ruby, Lisa lifts her grandmother's hand again. "I don't think she wants to tell me anything, Dad. I think she wants me to tell you something."

"Tell me something? Tell me what?"

Lisa looks from her grandmother to her father and then to Francis and Phoebe, only steps away across the bed, their faces pinched with tension. "I think she wants me to tell all of you."

"Tell us what?" Phoebe asks, her voice fearful.

"Well, I ... we were talking all the way here. Nan was telling me stories from her life, you know, and I ... I don't know how to say this. This is her story. I don't even know if it's true.... I mean, maybe she was confused. The paramedic and the doctor asked me if she seemed confused and I said no, but maybe she was.... Maybe it's not true. I'm just not sure...."

"What did she say, Lisa?" Gary asks, his voice level.

Lisa, quickly glancing at Ruby, turns to face her father, forcing her eyes to meet his intent and serious gaze. "She said that you, Dad, are Leland's son, not Grandpa Grace's."

Unsure if her father has heard her, Lisa waits, afraid to repeat herself, but more afraid of the silence that has opened up between them, leaving only the slow, sad sound of the music bleating from the corner.

"Dad." Reaching out to Gary, Lisa continues. "Dad, she was confused."

Gary, feeling his daughter's hand on his arm, its pressure pulling him back to the room, turns to Lisa and exhales a short, forced breath. Then he smiles from the corner of his mouth and turns to look at Ruby, whose frustration of moments ago has dissipated like mist in the morning, leaving her limp and lifeless, her eyes closed with fatigue.

"She was confused, Dad," Lisa says again, leaning her body toward him, longing to ease the pain and confusion she recognizes in his subtle smile, a boy's smile, lost and confused.

"No, Lisa. She wasn't confused," Gary says, moving to the closest chair and sitting.

"I don't know, Dad. She told me this just before the stroke. I think she was confusing everything—you know how she gets sometimes. She was even confusing me with Aunt Phoebe."

"No, Lisa. She wasn't confused."

"But how can you be so sure. You don't know for sure, do you?" Lisa asks, her voice loud with the distress she feels.

"It's true, honey." Gary glances at his brother and sister, and then looks back at Lisa. "Sometimes you're told something," he shrugs, then blinks rapidly, "and as soon as you hear it, you know it for what it is: the truth. Maybe I always knew it. Deep down, maybe I always knew it."

"Gary?" Phoebe asks, breaking the silence that hangs in the air. Her eyes search her brother's face. "Gary?"

When their eyes finally meet, Phoebe continues, her voice soft with understanding. "Leland died of cancer."

12.

"GARY, THIS DOESN'T CHANGE ANYTHING, you know. Well, except that maybe the doctors might have a better idea of what they're looking for now." Phoebe, struggling to decipher the emotions behind Gary's gaze, looks up at Francis for support.

Francis, unsure what Phoebe wants him to say, or what Gary needs to hear, clears his throat. "Phoebe's right, Gary. This doesn't change anything. Except for the better."

"Did you know?" Gary asks, looking at Francis.

"No."

"But you believe it?"

"Yes," Francis answers evenly. "But does it matter?"

"I don't know." Gary shrugs. "I mean, it's all in the past."

"And the present is the past unrolled for understanding," Francis quips.

"And that's all it is," Phoebe says, "an understanding."

"You look like Leland, Gary." Francis smiles, assessing his brother as if for the first time. "And you have his mannerisms."

"So, why didn't we know before now that he was my father?" Gary asks, his voice still distant. "I guess it's true—the mind only sees what it wants to see." He answers his own question.

"I wonder if he knew, if Leland knew?" Phoebe asks, looking at her brothers. "Did your nan say anything about that?" She turns to Lisa.

"Nan said that she never told him, but that she thought Le-

land must have known, just ... as you all must have known,"
Lisa answers, faltering, her eyes seeking out her father's.

"I guess now we'll never know for sure what she did or didn't
say." Phoebe looks around and shrugs slightly. "And does it
really even matter?"

"No, it doesn't," Gary answers, shaking his head slightly at
the rhetorical question.

The milky blue afternoon light has bleached the room of
colour, making contours and corners sharper and more distinct
by contrast. Only Ruby—with her white hair and skin, the
white sheet pulled around her—looks like she belongs, floating
in suspended animation, above reproach.

"So, what do we do now?" Phoebe asks, leaning over her
mother and pushing the hair from her forehead. "We are going
to have to make some arrangement to get Mom home."

Ruby tries to force out her words, her eyes focused on her
daughter. She knows the meaning of the word *home*. She has
been able to find pictures in her mind and to connect them
to herself, to an emotion that feels like warmth, but language
is beyond her. Her confusion and frustration bring about uncontrolled movements, and she shakes her head, her hands,
her body.

"I know, Mom," Phoebe says soothingly. "You want to go
home." She takes Ruby's hand, her voice soft and gentle. "We'll
take you home as soon as we can. Don't worry."

Phoebe's gentle manner calms Ruby, and although she cannot follow all the words, she understands that this woman is
connected to her, will take care of her.

"We should find the doctor and discuss what our options
are," Francis says, placing his hand on Phoebe's shoulder and
watching Ruby, her eyes closing in sleep.

"I'll come with you." Gary nods, standing and looking at
Francis before turning to Phoebe. "You should come with us.
We have to decide together what our next steps will be."

"Maybe I should just stay with Mom."

"No, Aunt Phoebe, go with Dad and Uncle Francis. I'll stay with Nan; she'll be fine," Lisa says, moving into the chair Gary has just vacated, her attitude one of serious vigilance.

"Okay." Phoebe laughs. "I guess she will be fine with you."

Music begins to play, soft and low, and Gary smiles, turning from the CD player. "That will keep you two company."

The music is familiar and comforting, and Lisa relaxes into the chair, the thought of catching a few minutes of sleep a prospect she can't pass up. Her fatigue feels bone deep. The room is warm, and although the chair is uncomfortable, Lisa begins to drift off.

"Lisa."

"Dad!" She is startled. "Sorry, I must have dozed off for a bit. Where are Phoebe and Francis?"

"They've gone for lunch. We made arrangements with the hospital for Nan's transfer, and everything is set up. They'll move her tomorrow morning as long as her condition stays stable."

"Well, that's good news!" Lisa sits up and stretches out her arms, thinking about home, her apartment, Stephen.

"Francis and Phoebe went for lunch. I told them I'd stay with you. When they get back, we can go. We all need a break from this place."

"That's for sure," Lisa says, smiling. Then after a moment, she asks, "How are you doing, Dad?"

"I'm fine, honey." He takes Lisa's outstretched hand in his and winks at her.

"Dad, I'm sorry it had to be me to tell you about Leland. Nan said she was going to tell you and Phoebe and Francis; it was the last thing she said to me. I just wish she had been able to. It's her story to tell."

"Well, now it's told." Gary laughs half-heartedly.

"How do you feel about it, Dad? Is it bothering you? I imagine it must be," Lisa says hesitantly.

"I'm not sure how I feel about it. It's funny. Part of me feels shocked and somehow cheated, while another part of me feels at peace." Looking from Lisa to Ruby, his thoughts tumble through the years, through moments, impressions, searching for something—he's not sure what—but something, some meaning. "I suppose we all experience life so differently, so separately. Every life is its own unique story, affected by other unique stories. But they're stories that we can never really know, never really share. Words are just too inaccurate, too limited and feeble, and memory is too selective. So all we have are relationships, family stories that we all share, each one a piece of a kaleidoscope. When they all twist together, they reveal a picture. These are the stories that connect us, consciously or unconsciously. We can fight with each other and aggravate each other and never understand each other, but still we're connected. I guess that means something, is worth something.

"I guess that's life. Family."

"We are all family. We always have been. Grampa Grace, Leland James, Ruby Grace, Francis, Phoebe, me. You and Jaclyn and her boys."

"I've always liked the name Leland James," Lisa muses, her voice shimmering in the early afternoon light, the music in the background playing out like a soundtrack to a movie. Gary, Lisa, and Ruby, each of them listens in their own way, connects to the music in their own way—Ruby enriched by her musical background, her experiences, her father, her memories of performing some of these same songs; Gary through Ruby; and now Lisa, through them all.

"Dad?"

"Yes?" Gary answers, the tone of his daughter's voice causing him to look at her curiously.

"I have some good news to tell you. Well, I think it's good news, I hope you do too."

Gary gives Lisa his full attention, nodding for her to continue.

"Dad, I'm pregnant. I'm almost ten weeks pregnant, and

I want to have the baby." Lisa looks at her father, his dark eyes paling in the light. She rushes on. "You're going to be a grandfather."

"Wow." Gary smiles slowly. "Does your mother know?"

"No, nobody knows. I haven't even told Stephen. I was waiting to be sure, and now I am."

"Wow."

"Dad?"

"It's great news, Lisa. Really, it is but I'm just a little overwhelmed."

"Yeah, you must be. First, you find out that you're father isn't the man you always thought, and now you find out you're going to be a grandfather, all in the same day.

"Yes, it's a lot to get my head around."

"But you're okay with it all, aren't you, Dad?"

"It's life I suppose, my life and your life and your Nan's life, and now a new life," Gary says, looking from Ruby to Lisa. "And I think I'm okay with it all. I'll have seven months or so to get used to your news and the rest of my life to settle into the other news. Leland was a good man and the only father I knew. And really, what does it change?"

"Well, it might change some of your answers on your medical questionnaire."

"Yes, there's that," Gary says, nodding. "It might help fill in a few things."

"And you're really okay with being a grandfather?"

"I think it's good news, Lisa and we deserve to hear some good news around here." He turns to Ruby. "Did you hear that, Mom? I'm going to be a grandfather. Isn't that's great?" Gary laughs, pulling Lisa up from the chair and spinning her around.

"What's going on you two?" Phoebe asks, coming through the door, a coffee in both hands, Francis following with two more.

"I just heard some great news," Gary answers, the smile on his face pulling at the corners of his eyes. Draping his arm around Lisa's shoulders, who nods and smiles, he continues, "I'm going to be a grandfather."

Both Francis and Phoebe look from Gary to Lisa. "Congratulations, Lisa," Francis says, placing the coffee down and pulling Lisa into a hug.

"Okay, okay, my turn!" Phoebe pushes them apart. "Congratulations, honey. That's wonderful news!" Laughing, she hugs Lisa again.

Gary stands beside Ruby, beaming with a grandfather's pride. When he speaks, his voice is raw with emotion. "Hear that, Mom? Lisa is going to have a baby and I'm going to be a grandfather."

"And I think that's just what the world needs, don't you?" Phoebe says, moving beside Gary and looking at Ruby. "A little more Grace."

Acknowledgements

I would like to thank Angie Littlefield, without whom this book would not be, thank you for your tenaciousness and your ever present belief in me. Thank you, Brenda Whiteman for your hours of interviews and insights in the house across from the theater. To Jill McArthur's grandmother, Margaret Jean Irwin, ninety-two years young when I interviewed you, thank you for your time and perspective.

Like people, books sometimes fall into your hands when you need them the most, books like, *The Lessons of History* by Will and Ariel Durant; *My Stroke of Insight* by Jill Bolte Taylor; and *Rum Running and the Roaring Twenties* by Philip P. Mason.

I would also like to thank Luciana Ricciutelli, Editor-in-Chief, for her editing and guidance, and all those at Inanna Publications for their dedication and support.

Thank you also to, RC, who listened to each chapter I wrote.

Kate Kelly is an educator, singer/song writer, poet, and now a novelist. A mother of three, she lives and works in Peterborough. Kate is also a spoken-word artist and has competed nationally in Toronto and Montreal. She can be found on Youtube, performing spoken word, and a sample of some of her writings are posted on her blog: https://thesoulfulside.com. *A Harsh and Private Beauty* is her debut novel.